ITERATIONS

Novels by Robert J. Sawyer

Golden Fleece
Far-Seer
Fossil Hunter
Foreigner
End of an Era
The Terminal Experiment
Starplex
Frameshift
Illegal Alien
Factoring Humanity
Flashforward
Calculating God
Hominids
Humans
Hybrids

Short-Story Collection

Iterations

Anthologies

Tesseracts 6 (with Carolyn Clink)
Crossing the Line (with David Skene-Melvin)
Over the Edge (with Peter Sellers)

ITERATIONS

Robert J. Sawyer

Introduction by James Alan Gardner

Red Deer PRESS

Published by Red Deer Press
A Fitzhenry & Whiteside Company
1512, 1800–4 Street S.W.
Calgary, Alberta, Canada t2s 2s5
www.reddeerpress.com

Cover design by Karen Petherick Thomas
Cover image courtesy NASA/JPL – Caltech/NOAO
Text design by Susan Hannah
Printed and bound in Canada by Friesens for Red Deer Press

Financial support provided by the Canada Council, and the Government of Canada through the Book Publishing Industry Development Program (BPIDP).

Canada Council   Conseil des Arts
for the Arts   du Canada

Library and Archives Canada Cataloguing in Publication
Sawyer, Robert J
[Iterations]
        Iterations and other stories / Robert J. Sawyer ; introduction by James
Alan Gardner.
Previously published under title: Iterations.
ISBN 978-0-88995-416-8
        I. Title.   II. Title: Iterations.
PS8587.A389835I84 2008   C813'.54   C2008-900365-9

United States Cataloguing-in-Publication Data
Sawyer, Robert J.
        Iterations / Robert J. Sawyer ; introduction by James Alan Gardner.
Originally published: Kingston : Quarry Press, 2002.
[240] p. : cm.
ISBN-13: 9780889954168 (pbk.)
1. Canadian short stories – 20th century. I. Gardner, James Alan. II. Title.
813.54 dc22   PR9199.3.S2533It 2008

Dedication

For

Andrew Weiner

*friend and mentor throughout my
first career as a nonfiction writer
and my second one as a fiction writer*

with thanks

Acknowledgments

Sincere thanks to the editors who originally published these stories, especially Martin H. Greenberg (who bought seven of them—every year, Marty is one of my nominees for the Best Editor Hugo Award; he is the driving force behind short-fiction publishing today, and richly deserves the honor), Edward E. Kramer (who bought four of them), and Mike Resnick (who bought three), plus Isaac Asimov, Cathrin Bradbury, Terry Carr, Lesley Choyce, John Robert Colombo, Peter Crowther, Julie E. Czerneda, Keith R. A. DeCandido, Marcel Gagné, Dr. Henry Gee, Ed Greenwood, John Helfers, Brad Linaweaver, Sally McBride, Shawna McCarthy, the *On Spec* editorial collective, Patrick Lucien Price, Victoria Schochet, Larry Segriff, Robert Sheckley, Josepha Sherman, Dale Sproule, Sally Tomasevic, and Edo van Belkom.

Thanks doubled to Edo van Belkom, who brought this book to Quarry Press; to Quarry publisher Bob Hilderley; to Susan Hannah, also of Quarry; to David G. Hartwell of Tor Books; to my agent Ralph Vicinanza; to James Alan Gardner for the wonderful introduction; and to those who were always there for me when these stories were being written, especially Ted Bleaney, David Livingstone Clink, Terence M. Green, Andrew Weiner, and, most of all, my lovely wife, Carolyn Clink.

Contents

Introduction

First things first:

If you're browsing through this book in a bookstore, rush to the checkout immediately and BUY THE BOOK.

If you've already bought the book, don't just leave it on the coffee table to impress your friends—SIT DOWN AND READ EVERY STORY.

There: I've fulfilled my obligations as an introduction writer. Now I can relax and just generally burble on about the glories of Robert J. Sawyer.

Also known as the Rob-Man.

Or the Robster.

Or R.J.

Or the Dean of Canadian Science Fiction.

Or the Man Who Really Deserves A Cool Nickname But No One Has Quite Found Anything That Clicks. It's hard to come up with a short snappy sobriquet that combines talented writer, inspired visionary, and good friend all in one tight verbal package.

I've known Rob for more than a decade, and I'm honored to be the person who gets to gush up front about Rob's first collection of short stories. It's my chance to repay him for all the support and advice he's given me over the years, not to mention the pleasure of reading his work.

Of course, Rob is best known in science-fiction circles for his novels: from his earliest book, *Golden Fleece* (told mostly from the viewpoint of a serial-killing computer), through his Quintaglio trilogy (featuring dinosaur versions of Galileo, Darwin, and Freud), to the space opera of *Starplex* and on into his near-future pieces (*The Terminal Experiment, Frameshift, Factoring Humanity, Calculating God, et al.*), which are balanced mixes of thriller-adventure stories, well-researched speculation, and philosophical musings. You owe it to yourself to get your hands on those books, too . . . but in the meantime, the book you're holding now is an admirable microcosm of Rob Sawyer's interests and concerns.

You'll see, for example, Rob's ongoing fascination with What Might Have Been, often embodied in multiple realities showing alternative ways in which one person's life might have unfolded: what would have happened if you made a different decision at some crucial moment, if you turned left instead of right? There's also the theme of simulated life, found in several of his novels—human intelligence copied into a computer, usually as a way of cheating death, but sometimes as a technique for understanding who a man or woman truly is. Several of the pieces in this book also reveal a covert inclination toward fantasy; Rob will probably deny it, but hey, there are three stories featuring the devil, one with vampires, and another that literally sends someone to hell. (And he keeps claiming to be a "hard science fiction" writer!)

Last and most enduringly, this book shows Rob's love of Earth's distant past: dinosaurs, early hominids, and paleontologists pop up over and over again, sometimes as protagonists, sometimes in disguise as aliens, sometimes in even more surprising forms . . . but always depicted with affection and a detailed attention to scientific accuracy. These are not trendy stage props thrown in for their current Coolness Factor—they *matter* to Rob, and he makes them matter to us.

Enough preamble. I could go on to enthuse about what a

fine human being Rob is, or what important contributions he's made to Canadian science fiction and to the science-fiction community as a whole; perhaps I could come up with a few telling anecdotes about the guy (or at least some juicy embarrassing ones); I could even rustle up praise and testimonials from dozens of other writers who are glad to have Rob Sawyer as their friend; but if you have any sense, you aren't interested in blather, you just want to read some good stories.

Lucky you. This book is full of them. Enjoy!

—James Alan Gardner

James Alan Gardner is a Nebula and Hugo Award finalist whose short stories have appeared in *Asimov's Science Fiction Magazine* and *The Magazine of Fantasy & Science Fiction*. His novels include *Expendable*, *Vigilant*, *Hunted*, and *Ascending*.

The Hand You're Dealt

Finalist for the Hugo Award
for Best Short Story of the Year

Winner of the *Science Fiction Chronicle* Reader Award
for Best Short Story of the Year

Author's Introduction

Edward E. Kramer is one of my favorite editors; he always asks me for something challenging. But when he approached me to contribute to a libertarian science-fiction anthology he was co-editing with Brad Linaweaver, I said, Ed, baby, I'm a Canadian—I don't think it's technically possible to be both a Canadian and a libertarian. As he always does, Ed said a few magic words: "Well, you could write a story that shows potential problems with libertarianism—we're looking for a balanced book." And, lo and behold, "The Hand You're Dealt" was created.

The Hand You're Dealt

And ye shall know the truth, and the truth shall make you free.
—John 8:32

"Got a new case for you," said my boss, Raymond Chen. "Homicide."

My heart started pounding. Mendelia habitat is supposed to be a utopia. Murder is almost unheard of here.

Chen was fat—never exercised, loved rich foods. He knew his lifestyle would take decades off his life, but, hey, that was his choice. "Somebody offed a soothsayer, over in Wheel Four," he said, wheezing slightly. "Baranski's on the scene now."

My eyebrows went up. A dead soothsayer? This could be very interesting indeed.

I took my pocket forensic scanner and exited The Cop Shop. That was its real name—no taxes in Mendelia, after all. You needed a cop, you hired one. In this case, Chen had said, we were being paid by the Soothsayers' Guild. That meant we could run up as big a bill as necessary—the SG was stinking rich. One of the few laws in Mendelia was that everyone had to use soothsayers.

Mendelia consisted of five modules, each looking like a wagon wheel with spokes leading in to a central hub. The hubs were all joined together by a long axle, and separate travel tubes connected the outer edges of the wheels. The whole thing spun to simulate gravity out at the rims, and the travel tubes saved you having to go down to the zero-g of the axle to move from one wheel to the next.

The Cop Shop was in Wheel Two. All the wheel rims were hollow, with buildings growing up toward the axle from the outer interior wall. Plenty of open spaces in Mendelia—it wouldn't be much of a utopia without those. But our sky was a hologram, projected on the convex inner wall of the rim, above our heads. The Cop Shop's entrance was right by Wheel Two's transit loop, a series of maglev tracks along which robocabs ran. I hailed one, flashed my debit card at an unblinking eye, and the cab headed out. The Carling family, who owned the taxi concession, was one of the oldest and richest families in Mendelia.

The ride took fifteen minutes. Suzanne Baranski was waiting outside for me. She was a good cop, but too green to handle a homicide alone. Still, she'd get a big cut of the fee for being the original responding officer—after all, the cop who responds to a call never knows who, if anyone, is going to pick up the tab. When there *is* money to be had, first-responders get a disproportionate share.

I'd worked with Suze a couple of times before, and had even gone to see her play cello with the symphony once. Perfect example of what Mendelia's all about, that. Suze Baranski had blue-collar parents. They'd worked as welders on the building of Wheel Five; not the kind who'd normally send a daughter for music lessons. But just after she'd been born, their soothsayer had said that Suze had musical talent. Not enough to make a living at it—that's why she's a cop by day—but still sufficient that it would be a shame not to let her develop it.

"Hi, Toby," Suze said to me. She had short red hair and big green eyes, and, of course, was in plain clothes—you wanted a uniformed cop, you called our competitors, Spitpolish, Inc.

"Howdy, Suze," I said, walking toward her. She led me over to the door, which had been locked off in the open position. A holographic sign next to it proclaimed:

Skye Hissock
Soothsayer
Let Me Reveal Your Future!
Fully Qualified for Infant and Adult Readings

We stepped into a well-appointed lobby. The art was unusual for such an office—it was all original pen-and-ink political cartoons. There was Republic CEO Da Silva, her big nose exaggerated out of all proportion, and next to it, Axel Durmont, Earth's current president, half buried in legislation printouts and tape that doubtless would have been red had this been a color rendering. The artist's signature caught my eye, the name Skye with curving lines behind it that I realized were meant to represent clouds. Just like Suze, our decedent had had varied talents.

"The body is in the inner private office," said Suze, leading the way. That door, too, was already open. She stepped in first, and I followed.

Skye Hissock's body sat in a chair behind his desk. His head had been blown clean off. A great carnation bloom of blood covered most of the wall behind him, and chunks of brain were plastered to the wall and the credenza behind the desk.

"Christ," I said. Some utopia.

Suze nodded. "Blaster, obviously," she said, sounding much more experienced in such matters than she really was. "Probably a gigawatt charge."

I began looking around the room. It was opulent; old Skye had obviously done well for himself. Suze was poking around, too. "Hey," she said, after a moment. I turned to look at her. She was climbing up on the credenza. The blast had knocked a small piece of sculpture off the wall—it lay in two pieces on the floor—and she was examining where it had affixed.

"Thought that's what it was," she said, nodding. "There's a hidden camera here."

My heart skipped a beat. "You don't suppose he got the whole thing on disk, do you?" I said, moving over to where she was. I gave her a hand getting down off the credenza, and we opened it up—a slightly difficult task; crusted blood had sealed its sliding doors. Inside was a dusty recorder unit. I turned to Skye's desk, and pushed the release switch to pop up his monitor plate. Suze pushed the recorder's playback button. As we'd suspected, the unit was designed to feed into the desk monitor.

The picture showed the reverse angle from behind Skye's desk. The door to the private office opened and in came a young man. He looked to be eighteen, meaning he was just the right age for the mandatory adult soothsaying. He had shoulder length dirty-blond hair, and was wearing a t-shirt imprinted with the logo of a popular meed. I shook my head. There hadn't been a good multimedia band since The Cassies, if you ask me.

"Hello, Dale," said what must have been Skye's voice. He spoke with deep, slightly nasal tones. "Thank you for coming in."

Okay, we had the guy's picture, and his first name, and the name of his favorite meed. Even if Dale's last name didn't turn up in Skye's appointment computer, we should have no trouble tracking him down.

"As you know," said Skye's recorded voice, "the law requires two soothsayings in each person's life. The first is done just after you're born, with one or both of your parents in attendance. At that time, the soothsayer only tells them things they'll need to know to get you through childhood. But when you turn eighteen, you, not your parents, become legally responsible for all your actions, and so it's time you heard everything. Now, do you want the good news or the bad news first?"

Here it comes, I thought. He told Dale something he didn't want to hear, the guy flipped, pulled out a blaster, and blew him away.

Dale swallowed. "The—the good, I guess."

"All right," said Skye. "First, you're a bright young man—not a genius, you understand, but brighter than average. Your IQ should run between 126 and 132. You are gifted musically—did your parents tell you that? Good. I hope they encouraged you."

"They did," said Dale, nodding. "I've had piano lessons since I was four."

"Good, good. A crime to waste such raw talent. You also have a particular aptitude for mathematics. That's often paired with musical ability, of course, so no surprises there. Your visual memory is slightly better than average, although your ability to do rote memorization is slightly worse. You would make a good long-distance runner, but..."

I motioned for Suze to hit the fast-forward button; it seemed like a typical soothsaying, although I'd review it in depth later, if need be. Poor Dale fidgeted up and down in quadruple speed for a time, then Suze released the button.

"Now," said Skye's voice, "the bad news." I made an impressed face at Suze; she'd stopped speeding along at precisely the right moment. "I'm afraid there's a lot of it. Nothing devastating, but still lots of little things. You will begin to lose your hair around your twenty-seventh birthday, and it will begin to gray by the time you're thirty-two. By the age of forty, you will be almost completely bald, and what's left at that point will be half brown and half gray.

"On a less frivolous note, you'll also be prone to gaining weight, starting at about age thirty-three—and you'll put on half a kilo a year for each of the following thirty years if you're not careful; by the time you're in your mid-fifties, that will pose a significant health hazard. You're also highly likely to develop adult-onset diabetes. Now, yes, that can be cured, but the cure is expensive, and you'll have to pay for it—so either keep your weight down, which will help stave off its onset, or start saving now for the operation..."

I shrugged. Nothing worth killing a man over. Suze fast-forwarded the tape some more.

"—and that's it," concluded Skye. "You now know everything significant that's coded into your DNA. Use this information wisely, and you should have a long, happy, healthy life."

Dale thanked Skye, took a printout of the information he'd just heard, and left. The recording stopped. It *had* been too much to hope for. Whoever killed Skye Hissock had come in after young Dale had departed. He was still our obvious first suspect, but unless there was something awful in the parts of the genetic reading we'd fast-forwarded over, there didn't seem to be any motive for him to kill his soothsayer. And besides, this Dale had a high IQ, Skye had said. Only an idiot would think there was any sense in shooting the messenger.

After we'd finished watching the recording, I did an analysis of the actual blaster burn. No fun, that: standing over the open top of Skye's torso. Most of the blood vessels had been cauterized by the charge. Still, blasters were only manufactured in two places I knew of—Tokyo, on Earth, and New Monty. If the one used here had been made on New Monty, we'd be out of luck, but one of Earth's countless laws required all blasters to leave a characteristic EM signature, so they could be traced to their registered owners, and—

Good: it *was* an Earth-made blaster. I recorded the signature, then used my compad to relay it to The Cop Shop. If Raymond Chen could find some time between stuffing his face, he'd send an FTL message to Earth and check the pattern—assuming, of course, that the Jeffies don't scramble the message just for kicks. Meanwhile, I told Suze to go over Hissock's client list, while I started checking out his family—fact is, even though it doesn't make much genetic sense, most people are killed by their own relatives.

Skye Hissock had been fifty-one. He'd been a soothsayer for twenty-three years, ever since finishing his Ph.D. in genetics. He was unmarried, and both his parents were long dead. But he did have a brother named Rodger. Rodger was married to Rebecca

Connolly, and they had two children, Glen, who, like Dale in Skye's recording, had just turned eighteen, and Billy, who was eight.

There are no inheritance taxes in Mendelia, of course, so barring a will to the contrary, Hissock's estate would pass immediately to his brother. Normally, that'd be a good motive for murder, but Rodger Hissock and Rebecca Connolly were already quite rich: they owned a controlling interest in the company that operated Mendelia's atmosphere-recycling plant.

I decided to start my interviews with Rodger. Not only had brothers been killing each other since Cain wasted Abel, but the DNA-scanning lock on Skye's private inner office was programmed to recognize only four people—Skye himself; his office cleaner, who Suze was going to talk to; another soothsayer named Jennifer Halasz, who sometimes took Skye's patients for him when he was on vacation (and who had called in the murder, having stopped by apparently to meet Skye for coffee); and dear brother Rodger. Rodger lived in Wheel Four, and worked in One.

I took a cab over to his office. Unlike Skye, Rodger had a real flesh-and-blood receptionist. Most companies that did have human receptionists used middle-aged, businesslike people of either sex. Some guys got so rich that they didn't care what people thought; they hired beautiful blonde women whose busts had been surgically altered far beyond what any phenotype might provide. But Rodger's choice was different. His receptionist was a delicate young man with refined, almost feminine features. He was probably older than he looked; he looked fourteen.

"Detective Toby Korsakov," I said, flashing my ID. I didn't offer to shake hands—the boy looked like his would shatter if any pressure were applied. "I'd like to see Rodger Hissock."

"Do you have an appointment?" His voice was high, and there was just a trace of a lisp.

"No. But I'm sure Mr. Hissock will want to see me. It's important."

The boy looked very dubious, but he spoke into an intercom. "There's a cop here, Rodger. Says it's important."

There was a pause. "Send him in," said a loud voice. The boy nodded at me, and I walked through the heavy wooden door—mahogany, no doubt imported all the way from Earth.

I had thought Skye Hissock's office was well-appointed, but his brother's put it to shame. *Objets d'art* from a dozen worlds were tastefully displayed on crystal stands. The carpet was so thick I was sure my shoes would sink out of sight. I walked toward the desk. Rodger rose to greet me. He was a muscular man, thick-necked, with lots of black hair and pale gray eyes. We shook hands; his grip was a show of macho strength. "Hello," he said. He boomed out the word, clearly a man used to commanding everyone's attention. "What can I do for you?"

"Please sit down," I said. "My name is Toby Korsakov. I'm from The Cop Shop, working under a contract to the Soothsayer's Guild."

"My God," said Rodger. "Has something happened to Skye?"

Although it was an unpleasant duty, there was nothing more useful in a murder investigation than being there to tell a suspect about the death and seeing his reaction. Most guilty parties played dumb far too long, so the fact that Rodger had quickly made the obvious connection between the SG and his brother made me suspect him less, not more. Still . . . "I'm sorry to be the bearer of bad news," I said, "but I'm afraid your brother is dead."

Rodger's eyes went wide. "What happened?"

"He was murdered."

"Murdered," repeated Rodger, as if he'd never heard the word before.

"That's right. I was wondering if you knew of anyone who'd want him dead?"

"How was he killed?" asked Rodger. I was irritated that this wasn't an answer to my question, and even more irritated that I'd have to explain it so soon. More than a few homicides had been solved by a suspect mentioning the nature of the crime in advance of him or her supposedly having learned the details. "He was shot at close range by a blaster."

"Oh," said Rodger. He slumped in his chair. "Skye dead." His head shook back and forth a little. When he looked up, his gray eyes were moist. Whether he was faking or not, I couldn't tell.

"I'm sorry," I said.

"Do you know who did it?"

"Not yet. We're tracing the blaster's EM signature. But there were no signs of forcible entry, and, well ..."

"Yes?"

"Well, there are only four people whose DNA would open the door to Skye's inner office."

Rodger nodded. "Me and Skye. Who else?"

"His cleaner, and another soothsayer."

"You're checking them out?"

"My associate is. She's also checking all the people Skye had appointments with recently—people he might have let in of his own volition." A pause. "Can I ask where you were this morning between ten and eleven?"

"Here."

"In your office?"

"That's right."

"Your receptionist can vouch for that?"

"Well . . . no. No, he can't. He was out all morning. His sooth says he's got a facility for languages. I give him a half-day off every Wednesday to take French lessons."

"Did anyone call you while he was gone?"

Rodger spread his thick arms. "Oh, probably. But I never answer my own compad. Truth to tell, I like that half-day where I can't be reached. It lets me get an enormous amount of work done without being interrupted."

"So no one can verify your presence here?"

"Well, no . . . no, I guess they can't. But, Crissakes, Detective, Skye was my *brother* . . ."

"I'm not accusing you, Mr. Hissock—"

"Besides, if I'd taken a robocab over, there'd be a debit charge against my account."

"Unless you paid cash. Or unless you walked." You can walk down the travel tubes, although most people don't bother.

"You don't seriously believe—"

"I don't believe anything yet, Mr. Hissock." It was time to change the subject; he would be no use to me if he got too defensive. "Was your brother a good soothsayer?"

"Best there is. Hell, he read my own sooth when I turned eighteen." He saw my eyebrows go up. "Skye is nine years older than me; I figured, why not use him? He needed the business; he was just starting his practice at that point."

"Did Skye do the readings for your children, too?"

An odd hesitation. "Well, yeah, yeah, Skye did their infant readings, but Glen—that's my oldest; just turned 18—he decided to go somewhere else for his adult reading. Waste of money, if you ask me. Skye would've given him a discount."

My compad bleeped while I was in a cab. I turned it on.

"Yo, Toby." Raymond Chen's fat face appeared on the screen. "We got the registration information on that blaster signature."

"Yeah?"

Ray smiled. "Do the words 'open-and-shut case' mean anything to you? The blaster belongs to one Rodger Hissock. He bought it about eleven years ago."

I nodded and signed off. Since the lock accepted his DNA, rich little brother would have no trouble waltzing right into big brother's inner office, and exploding his head. Rodger had method and he had opportunity. Now all I needed was to find his motive—and for that, continuing to interview the family members might prove useful.

Eighteen-year-old Glen Hissock was studying engineering at Francis Crick University in Wheel Three. He was a dead ringer for his old man: built like a wrestler, with black hair and quick-silver eyes. But whereas father Rodger had a coarse, outgoing way about him—the crusher handshake, the loud voice—young Glen was withdrawn, soft-spoken, and nervous.

"I'm sorry about your uncle," I said, knowing that Rodger had already broken the news to his son.

Glen looked at the floor. "Me too."

"Did you like him?"

"He was okay."

"Just okay."

"Yeah."

"Where were you between ten and eleven this morning?"

"At home."

"Was anyone else there?"

"Nah. Mom and Dad were at work, and Billy—that's my little brother—was in school." He met my eyes for the first time. "Am I a suspect?"

He wasn't really. All the evidence seemed to point to his father. I shook my head in response to his question, then said, "I hear you had your sooth read recently."

"Yeah."

"But you didn't use your uncle."

"Nah."

"How come?"

A shrug. "Just felt funny, that's all. I picked a guy at random from the online directory."

"Any surprises in your sooth?"

The boy looked at me. "Sooth's private, man. I don't have to tell you that."

I nodded. "Sorry."

Two hundred years ago, in 2029, the Palo Alto Nanosystems Laboratory developed a molecular computer. You doubtless read about it in history class: during the Snow War, the U.S. used it to disassemble Bogatá atom by atom.

Sometimes, though, you *can* put the genie back in the bottle. Remember Hamasaki and DeJong, the two researchers at

PANL who were shocked to see their work corrupted that way? They created and released the nano-Gorts—self-replicating microscopic machines that seek out and destroy molecular computers, so that nothing like Bogatá could ever happen again. We've got PANL nano-Gorts here, of course. They're everywhere in Free Space. But we've got another kind of molecular guardian, too—inevitably, they were dubbed helix-Gorts. It's rumored the SG was responsible for them, but after a huge investigation, no indictments were ever brought. Helix-Gorts circumvent any attempt at artificial gene therapy. We can tell you everything that's written in your DNA, but we can't do a damned thing about it. Here, in Mendelia, you play the hand you're dealt.

My compad bleeped again. I switched it on. "Korsakov here."

Suze's face appeared on the screen. "Hi, Toby. I took a sample of Skye's DNA off to Rundstedt"—a soothsayer who did forensic work for us. "She's finished the reading."

"And?" I said.

Suze's green eyes blinked. "Nothing stood out. Skye wouldn't have been a compulsive gambler, or an addict, or inclined to steal another person's spouse—which eliminates several possible motives for his murder. In fact, Rundstedt says Skye would have had a severe aversion to confrontation." She sighed. "Just doesn't seem to be the kind of guy who'd end up in a situation where someone would want him dead."

I nodded. "Thanks, Suze. Any luck with Skye's clients?"

"I've gone through almost all the ones who'd had appointments in the last three days. So far, they all have solid alibis."

"Keep checking. I'm off to see Skye's sister-in-law, Rebecca Connolly. Talk to you later."

"Bye."

Sometimes I wonder if I'm in the right line of work. I know, I know—what a crazy thing to be thinking. I mean, my parents knew from my infant reading that I'd grow up to have an aptitude for puzzle-solving, plus superior powers of observation. They made sure I had every opportunity to fulfill my potentials, and when I had my sooth read for myself at eighteen, it was obvious that this would be a perfect job for me to pursue. And yet, still, I have my doubts. I just don't feel like a cop sometimes.

But a soothsaying can't be wrong: almost every human trait has a genetic basis—gullibility, mean-spiritedness, a goofy sense of humor, the urge to collect things, talents for various sports, every specific sexual predilection (according to my own sooth, my tastes ran to group sex with Asian women—so far, I'd yet to find an opportunity to test that empirically).

Of course, when Mendelia started up, we didn't yet know what each gene and gene combo did. Even today, the SG is still adding new interpretations to the list. Still, I sometimes wonder how people in other parts of Free Space get along without soothsayers—stumbling through life, looking for the right job; sometimes completely unaware of talents they possess; failing to know what specific things they should do to take care of their health. Oh, sure, you can get a genetic reading anywhere—even down on Earth. But they're only mandatory here.

And my mandatory readings said I'd make a good cop. But, I have to admit, sometimes I'm not so sure . . .

Rebecca Connolly was at home when I got there. On Earth, a family with the kind of money the Hissock-Connolly union had would own a mansion. Space is at a premium aboard a habitat, but their living room *was* big enough that its floor showed a hint of curvature. The art on the walls included originals by both Grant Wood and Bob Eggleton. There was no doubt they were loaded—making it all the harder to believe they'd done in Uncle Skye for his money.

Rebecca Connolly was a gorgeous woman. According to the press reports I'd read, she was forty-four, but she looked twenty years younger. Gene therapy might be impossible here, but anyone who could afford it could have plastic surgery. Her hair was copper-colored, and her eyes an unnatural violet. "Hello, Detective Korsakov," she said. "My husband told me you were likely to stop by." She shook her head. "Poor Skye. Such a darling man."

I tilted my head. She was the first of Skye's relations to actually say something nice about him as a person—which, after all, could just be a clumsy attempt to deflect suspicion from her. "You knew Skye well?"

"No—to be honest, no. He and Rodger weren't that close. Funny thing, that. Skye used to come by the house frequently when we first got married—he was Rodger's best man, did he tell you that? But when Glen was born, well, he stopped coming around as much. I dunno—maybe he didn't like kids; he never had any of his own. Anyway, he really hasn't been a big part of our lives for, oh, eighteen years now."

"But Rodger's DNA was accepted by Skye's lock."

"Oh, yes. Rodger owns the unit Skye has his current offices in."

"I hate to ask you this, but—"

"I'm on the Board of Directors of TenthGen Computing, Detective. We were having a shareholders' meeting this morning. Something like eight hundred people saw me there."

I asked more questions, but didn't get any closer to identifying Rodger Hissock's motive. And so I decided to cheat—as I said, sometimes I *do* wonder if I'm in the right kind of job. "Thanks for your help, Ms. Connolly. I don't want to take up any more of your time, but can I use your bathroom before I go?"

She smiled. "Of course. There's one down the hall, and one upstairs."

The upstairs one sounded more promising for my purposes. I went up to it, and the door closed behind me. I really did need to go, but first I pulled out my forensic scanner and started looking for specimens. Razors and combs were excellent places to find DNA samples; so were towels, if the user rubbed vigorously enough. Best of all, though, were toothbrushes. I scanned everything, but something was amiss. According to the scanner, there was DNA present from one woman—the XX chromosome pair made the gender clear. And there was DNA from one man. But *three* males lived in this house: father Rodger, elder son Glen, and younger son Billy.

Perhaps this bathroom was used only by the parents, in which case I'd blown it—I'd hardly get a chance to check out the other bathroom. But no—there were four sets of towels, four toothbrushes, and there, on the edge of the tub, a toy aquashuttle . . . precisely the kind an eight-year-old boy would play with.

Curious. Four people obviously used this john, but only two had left any genetic traces. And that made no sense—I mean, sure, I hardly ever washed when I was eight like Billy, but no one can use a washroom day in and day out without leaving some DNA behind.

I relieved myself, the toilet autoflushed, and I went downstairs, thanked Ms. Connolly again, and left.

Like I said, I was cheating—making me wonder again whether I really was cut out for a career in law enforcement. Even though it was a violation of civil rights, I took the male DNA sample I'd found in the Hissock-Connolly bathroom to Dana Rundstedt, who read its sooth for me.

I was amazed by the results. If I hadn't cheated, I might never have figured it out—it was a damn-near perfect crime.

But it all fit, after seeing what was in the male DNA.

The fact that of the surviving Hissocks, only Rodger apparently had free access to Skye's inner office.

The fact that Rodger's blaster was the murder weapon.

The fact that there were apparently only two people using the bathroom.

The fact that Skye hated confrontation.

The fact that the Hissock-Connolly family had a lot of money they wanted to pass on to the next generation.

The fact that young Glen looked just like his dad, but was subdued and reserved.

The fact that Glen had gone to a different soothsayer.

The fact that Rodger's taste in receptionists was . . . unusual.

The pieces all fit—that part of my sooth, at least, must have been read correctly; I *was* good at puzzling things out. But I was still amazed by how elegant it was.

Ray Chen would sort out the legalities; he was an expert at that kind of thing. He'd find a way to smooth over my unauthorized soothsaying before we brought this to trial.

I got in a cab and headed off to Wheel Three to confront the killer.

"Hold it right there," I said, coming down the long, gently curving corridor at Francis Crick. "You're under arrest."

Glen Hissock stopped dead in his tracks. "What for?"

I looked around, then drew Glen into an empty classroom. "For the murder of your uncle, Skye Hissock. Or should I say, for the murder of your brother? The semantics are a bit tricky."

"I don't know what you're talking about," said Glen, in that subdued, nervous voice of his.

I shook my head. Soothsayer Skye *had* deserved punishment, and his brother Rodger *was* guilty of a heinous crime—in fact, a crime Mendelian society considered every bit as bad as murder. But I couldn't let Glen get away with it. "I'm sorry for what happened to you," I said. The mental scars no doubt explained his sullen, withdrawn manner.

He glared at me. "Like that makes it better."

"When did it start?"

He was quiet for a time, then gave a little shrug, as if realizing there was no point in pretending any longer. "When I was twelve— as soon as I entered puberty. Not every night, you understand. But often enough." He paused, then: "How'd you figure it out?"

I decided to tell him the truth. "There are only two different sets of DNA in your house—one female, as you'd expect, and just one male."

Glen said nothing.

"I had the male DNA read. I was looking for a trait that might have provided a motive for your father. You know what I found."

Glen was still silent.

"When your dad's sooth was read just after birth, maybe his parents were told that he was sterile. Certainly the proof is there, in his DNA: an inability to produce viable sperm." I paused, remembering the details Rundstedt had explained to me. "But the soothsayer back then couldn't have known the effect of having the variant form of gene ABL-419d, with over a hundred T-A-T repeats. That variation's function hadn't been identified that long ago. But it *was* known by the time Rodger turned eighteen, by the time he went to see his big brother Skye, by the time Skye gave him his adult soothsaying." I paused. "But Uncle Skye hated confrontation, didn't he?"

Glen was motionless, a statue.

"And so Skye lied to your dad. Oh, he told him about his sterility, all right, but he figured there was no point in getting into an argument about what that variant gene meant."

Glen looked at the ground. When at last he did speak, his voice was bitter. "I had thought Dad knew. I confronted him— Christ sakes, Dad, if you knew you had a gene for incestuous pedophilia, why the hell didn't you seek counseling? Why the hell did you have kids?"

"But your father didn't know, did he?"

Glen shook his head. "That bastard Uncle Skye hadn't told him."

"In fairness," I said, "Skye probably figured that since your father couldn't have kids, the problem would never come up. But your dad made a lot of money, and wanted it to pass to an heir. And since he couldn't have an heir the normal way . . ."

Glen's voice was full of disgust. "Since he couldn't have an heir the normal way, he had one made."

I looked the boy up and down. I'd never met a clone before. Glen really was the spitting image of the old man—a chip off the old block. But like any dynasty, the Hissock-Connolly clan wanted not just an heir, but an heir and a spare. Little Billy, ten years younger than Glen, was likewise an exact genetic duplicate of

Rodger Hissock, produced from Rodger's DNA placed into one of Rebecca's eggs. All three Hissock males had indeed left DNA in that bathroom—exactly identical DNA.

"Have you always known you were a clone?" I asked.

Glen shook his head. "I only just found out. Before I went for my adult soothsaying, I wanted to see the report my parents had gotten when I was born. But none existed—my dad had decided to save some money. He didn't need a new report done, he figured; my sooth would be identical to his, after all. When I went to get my sooth read and found that *I* was sterile, well, it all fell into place in my mind."

"And so you took your father's blaster, and, since your DNA is the same as his . . ."

Glen nodded slowly. His voice was low and bitter. "Dad never knew in advance what was wrong with him—never had a chance to get help. Uncle Skye never told him. Even after Dad had himself cloned, Skye never spoke up." He looked at me, fury in his cold gray eyes. "It doesn't work, dammit—our whole way of life doesn't work if a soothsayer doesn't tell the truth. You can't play the hand you're dealt if you don't know what cards you've got. Skye deserved to die."

"And you framed your dad for it. You wanted to punish him, too."

Glen shook his head. "You don't understand, man. You can't understand."

"Try me."

"I didn't want to punish Dad—I wanted to protect Billy. Dad can afford the best damn lawyer in Mendelia. Oh, he'll be found guilty, sure, but he won't get life. His lawyer will cut it down to the minimum mandatory sentence for murder, which is—"

"Ten years," I said, realization dawning. "In ten years, Billy will be an adult—and out of danger from Rodger."

Glen nodded once.

"But Rodger could have told the truth at any time—revealed that you were a clone of him. If he'd done that, he would have gotten off, and suspicion would have fallen on you. How did you know he wasn't going to speak up?"

Glen sounded a lot older than his eighteen years. "If Dad exposed me, I'd expose him—and the penalty for child molestation is also a minimum ten years, so he'd be doing the time anyway." He looked directly at me. "Except being a murderer gets you left alone in jail, and being a pedophile gets you wrecked up."

I nodded, led him outside, and hailed a robocab.

Mendelia *is* a great place to live, honest.

And, hell, I did solve the crime, didn't I? Meaning I *am* a good detective. So I guess *my* soothsayer didn't lie to me.

At least—at least I hope not . . .

I had a sudden cold feeling that the SG would stop footing the bill long before this case could come to public trial.

Peking Man

Winner of the Aurora Award
for Best Short Story of the Year

Author's Introduction

Ed Kramer wanted to do an anthology in honor of the one hundredth anniversary of a particular literary character. That character wasn't one I was fascinated with, but I did have a lifelong interest in paleoanthropology, although at this point, I'd never written any fiction on that theme (later, I went on to write a trilogy about Neanderthals). But having recently looked at a picture of a Chinese *Homo erectus* skull, and having thought, gee, those perfect, square teeth *must* be fake, an idea occurred to me that I thought might be right for Ed's book.

To my delight, Ed used this story as the lead piece in his anthology (editors usually put what they consider to be the best stories in the first and last slots). I occasionally think about expanding the premise of this story into a novel; perhaps someday I will.

Peking Man

The lid was attached to the wooden crate with eighteen nails. The return address, in blue ink on the blond wood, said, "Sender: Dept. of Anatomy, P.U.M.C., Peking, China." The destination address, in larger letters, was:

Dr. Roy Chapman Andrews
The American Museum of Natural History
Central Park West at 79th Street
New York, N.Y. U.S.A.

The case was marked "Fragile!" and "REGISTERED" and *"Par Avion."* A brand had burned the words "Via Hongkong and by U.S. Air Service" into the wood.

Andrews had waited anxiously for this arrival. Between 1922 and 1930, he himself had led the now-famous Gobi Desert expeditions, searching for the Asian cradle of humanity. Although he'd brought back untold scientific riches—including the first-ever dinosaur eggs—Andrews had failed to discover a single ancient human remain.

But now a German scientist, Franz Weidenreich, had shipped to him a treasure trove from the Orient: the complete fossil remains of *Sinanthropus pekinensis.* In this very crate were the bones of Peking Man.

Andrews was actually salivating as he used a crowbar to pry off the lid. He'd waited so long for these, terrified that they wouldn't survive the journey, desperate to see what humanity's forefathers had looked like, anxious—

The lid came off. The contents were carefully packed in smaller cardboard boxes. He picked one up and moved over to his cluttered desk. He swept the books and papers to the floor, laid down the box, and opened it. Inside was a ball of rice paper, wrapped around a large object. Andrews carefully unwrapped the sheets, and—

White.

White?

No—no, it couldn't be.

But it was. It was a skull, certainly—but *not* a fossil skull. The material was bright white.

And it didn't weigh nearly enough.

A plaster cast. Not the original at all.

Andrews opened every box inside the wooden crate, his heart sinking as each new one yielded its contents. In total, there were fourteen skulls and eleven jawbones. The skulls were subhuman, with low foreheads, prominent brow ridges, flat faces, and the most unlikely looking perfect square teeth. Amazingly, each of the skull casts also showed clear artificial damage to the foramen magnum.

Oh, some work could indeed be done on these casts, no doubt. But where were the original fossils? With the Japanese having invaded China, surely they were too precious to be left in the Far East. What was Weidenreich up to?

Fire.

It was like a piece of the sun, brought down to earth. It kept the tribe warm at night, kept the saber-toothed cats away—and it did something wonderful to meat, making it softer and easier to chew, while at the same time restoring the warmth the flesh had had when still part of the prey.

Fire was the most precious thing the tribe owned. They'd had it for eleven summers now, ever since Bok the brave had brought out a burning stick from the burning forest. The glowing coals were always fanned, always kept alive.

And then, one night, the Stranger came—tall, thin, pale, with red-rimmed eyes that somehow seemed to glow from beneath his brow ridge.

The Stranger did the unthinkable, the unforgivable.

He doused the flames, throwing a gourd full of water on to the fire. The logs hissed, and steam rose up into the blackness. The children of the tribe began to cry; the adults quaked with fury. The Stranger turned and walked into the darkness. Two of the strongest hunters ran after him, but his long legs had apparently carried him quickly away.

The sounds of the forest grew closer—the chirps of insects, the rustling of small animals in the vegetation, and—

A flapping sound.

The Stranger was gone.

And the silhouette of a bat fluttered briefly in front of the waning moon.

Franz Weidenreich had been born in Germany in 1873. A completely bald, thickset man, he had made a name for himself as an expert in hematology and osteology. He was currently Visiting Professor at the University of Chicago, but that was coming to an end, and now he was faced with the uncomfortable prospect of having to return to Nazi Germany—something, as a Jew, he desperately wanted to avoid.

And then word came of the sudden death of the Canadian paleontologist Davidson Black. Black had been at the Peking Union Medical College, studying the fragmentary remains of early man being recovered from the limestone quarry at Chou Kou Tien. Weidenreich, who once made a study of Neanderthal bones found in Germany, had read Black's papers in *Nature* and *Science* describing *Sinanthropus*.

But now, at fifty, Black was as dead as his fossil charges—an unexpected heart attack. And, to Weidenreich's delight, the China Medical Board of the Rockefeller Foundation wanted him to fill Black's post. China was a strange, foreboding place—and tensions between the Chinese and the Japanese were high—but it beat all hell out of returning to Hitler's Germany . . .

At night, most of the tribe huddled under the rocky overhang or crawled into the damp, smelly recesses of the limestone cave. Without the fire to keep animals away, someone had to stand watch each night, armed with a large branch and a pile of rocks for throwing. Last night, it had been Kart's turn. Everyone had slept well, for Kart was the strongest member of the tribe. They knew they were safe from whatever lurked in the darkness.

When daybreak came, the members of the tribe were astounded. Kart had fallen asleep. They found him lying in the dirt, next to the cold, black pit where their fire had once been. And on Kart's neck there were two small red-rimmed holes, staring up at them like the eyes of the Stranger . . .

During his work on hematology, Weidenreich had met a remarkable man named Brancusi—gaunt, pale, with disconcertingly sharp canine teeth. Brancusi suffered from a peculiar anemia, which Weidenreich had been unable to cure, and an almost pathological photophobia. Still, the gentleman was cultured and widely read, and Weidenreich had ever since maintained a correspondence with him.

When Weidenreich arrived in Peking, work was still continuing at the quarry. So far, only teeth and fragments of skull had been found. Davidson Black had done a good job of cataloging and describing some of the material, but as Weidenreich went through the specimens he was surprised to discover a small collection of sharp, pointed fossil teeth.

Black had evidently assumed they weren't part of the *Sinanthropus* material, as he hadn't included them in his descriptions. And, at first glance, Black's assessment seemed correct—

they were far longer than normal human canines, and much more sharply pointed. But, to Weidenreich's eye, the root pattern was possibly hominid. He dropped a letter to his friend Brancusi, half-joking that he'd found Brancusi's great-to-the-nth grandfather in China.

To Weidenreich's infinite surprise, within weeks Brancusi had arrived in Peking.

Each night, another member of the tribe stood watch—and each morning, that member was found unconscious, with a pair of tiny wounds to his neck.

The tribe members were terrified. Soon multiple guards were posted each night, and, for a time, the happenings ceased.

But then something even more unusual happened . . .

They were hunting deer. It would not be the same, not without fire to cook the meat, but, still, the tribe needed to eat. Four men, Kart included, led the assault. They moved stealthily amongst the tall grasses, tracking a large buck with a giant rack of antlers. The hunters communicated by sign language, carefully coordinating their movements, closing in on the animal from both sides.

Kart raised his right arm, preparing to signal the final attack, when—

—a streak of light brown, slicing through the grass—

—fangs flashing, the roar of the giant cat, the stag bolting away, and then—

—Kart's own scream as the saber-tooth grabbed hold of his thigh and shook him viciously.

The other three hunters ran as fast as they could, desperate to get away. They didn't stop to look back, even when the cat let out the strangest yelp . . .

That night, the tribe huddled together and sang songs urging Kart's soul a safe trip to heaven.

One of the Chinese laborers found the first skull. Weidenreich was summoned at once. Brancusi still suffered from his photophobia, and apparently had never adjusted to the shift in time zones—he slept during the day. Weidenreich thought about waking him to see this great discovery, but decided against it.

The skull was still partially encased in the limestone muck at the bottom of the cave. It had a thick cranial wall and a beetle brow—definitely a more primitive creature than Neanderthal, probably akin to Solo Man or Java Man ...

It took careful work to remove the skull from the ground, but, when it did come free, two astonishing things became apparent.

The loose teeth Davidson Black had set aside had indeed come from the hominids here: this skull still had all its upper teeth intact, and the canines were long and pointed.

Second, and even more astonishing, was the foramen magnum—the large opening in the base of the skull through which the spinal cord passes. It was clear from its chipped, frayed margin that this individual's foramen magnum had been artificially widened—

—meaning he'd been decapitated, and then had something shoved up into his brain through the bottom of his skull.

Five hunters stood guard that night. The moon had set, and the great sky river arched high over head. The Stranger returned—but this time, he was not alone. The tribesmen couldn't believe their eyes. In the darkness, it looked like—

It was. Kart.

But—but Kart was dead. They'd seen the saber-tooth take him.

The Stranger came closer. One of the men lifted a rock, as if to throw it at him, but soon he let the rock drop from his hand. It fell to the ground with a dull thud.

The Stranger continued to approach, and so did Kart.

And then Kart opened his mouth, and in the faint light they saw his teeth—long and pointed, like the Stranger's.

The men were unable to run, unable to move. They seemed transfixed, either by the Stranger's gaze, or by Kart's, both of whom continued to approach.

And soon, in the dark, chill night, the Stranger's fangs fell upon one of the guard's necks, and Kart's fell upon another...

Eventually, thirteen more skulls were found, all of which had the strange elongated canine teeth, and all of which had their foramen magnums artificially widened. Also found were some mandibles and skull fragments from other individuals—but there was almost no post-cranial material. Someone in dim prehistory had discarded here the decapitated heads of a group of protohumans.

Brancusi sat in Weidenreich's lab late at night, looking at the skulls. He ran his tongue over his own sharp teeth, contemplating. These subhumans doubtless had no concept of mathematics beyond perhaps adding and subtracting on their fingers. How would they possibly know of the problem that plagued the Family, the problem that every one of the Kindred knew to avoid?

If all those who feel the bite of the vampire themselves become vampires when they die, and all of those new vampires also turn those they feed from into vampires, soon, unless care is exercised, the whole population will be undead. A simple geometric progression.

Brancusi had long wondered how far back the Family went. It wasn't like tracing a normal family tree—oh, yes, the lines were bloodlines, but not as passed on from father to son. He knew his own lineage—a servant at Castle Dracula before the Count had taken to living all alone, a servant whose loyalty to his master extended even to letting him drink from his neck.

Brancusi himself had succumbed to pneumonia, not an uncommon ailment in the dank Carpathians. He had no family, and no one mourned his passing.

But soon he rose again—and now he did have Family.

An Englishman and an American had killed the Count, removing his head with a kukri knife and driving a bowie knife through his heart. When news of this reached Brancusi from the gypsies, he traveled back to Transylvania. Dracula's attackers had simply abandoned the coffin, with its native soil and the dust that the Count's body had crumbled into. Brancusi dug a grave on the desolate, wind-swept grounds of the Castle, and placed the Count's coffin within.

Eventually, over a long period, the entire tribe had felt the Stranger's bite directly or indirectly.

A few of the tribefolk lost their lives to ravenous bloodthirst, drained dry. Others succumbed to disease or giant cats or falls from cliffs. One even died of old age. But all of them rose again.

And so it came to pass, just as it had for the Stranger all those years before, that the tribe had to look elsewhere to slake its thirst.

But they had not counted on the Others.

Weidenreich and Brancusi sat in Weidenreich's lab late at night. Things had been getting very tense—the Japanese occupation was becoming intolerable. "I'm going to return to the States," said Weidenreich. "Andrews at the American Museum is offering me space to continue work on the fossils."

"No," said Brancusi. "No, you can't take the fossils."

Weidenreich's bushy eyebrows climbed up toward his bald pate. "But we can't let them fall into Japanese hands."

"That is true," said Brancusi.

"They belong somewhere safe. Somewhere where they can be studied."

"No," said Brancusi. His red-rimmed gaze fell on Weidenreich in a way it never had before. "No—no one may see these fossils."

"But Andrews is expecting them. He's dying to see them. I've been deliberately vague in my letters to him—I want to be there to see his face when he sees the dentition."

"No one can know about the teeth," said Brancusi.

"But he's expecting the fossils. And I have to publish descriptions of them."

"The teeth must be filed flat."

Weidenreich's eyes went wide. "I can't do that."

"You can, and you will."

"But—"

"You can and you will."

"I—I can, but—"

"No buts."

"No, no, there *is* a but. Andrews will never be fooled by filed teeth; the structure of teeth varies as you go into them. Andrews will realize at once that the teeth have been reduced from their original size." Weidenreich looked at Brancusi. "I'm sorry, but there's no way to hide the truth."

The Others lived in the next valley. They proved tough and resourceful—and they could make fire whenever they needed it. When the tribefolk arrived it became apparent that there was never a time of darkness for the Others. Large fires were constantly burning.

The tribe had to feed, but the Others defended themselves, trying to kill them with rock knives.

But that didn't work. The tribefolk were undeterred.

They tried to kill them with spears.

But that did not work, either. The tribefolk came back.

They tried strangling the attackers with pieces of animal hide.

But that failed, too. The tribefolk returned again.

And finally the Others decided to try everything they could think of simultaneously.

They drove wooden spears into the hearts of the tribefolk.

The used stone knives to carve off the heads of the tribefolk.

And then they jammed spears up into the severed heads, forcing the shafts up through the holes at the bases of the skulls.

The hunters marched far away from their camp, each carrying a spear thrust vertically toward the summer sun, each one crowned by a severed, pointed-toothed head. When, at last, they found a suitable hole in the ground, they dumped the heads in, far, far away from their bodies.

The Others waited for the tribefolk to return.

But they never did.

"Do not send the originals," said Brancusi.

"But—"

"The originals are mine, do you understand? I will ensure their safe passage out of China."

It looked for a moment like Weidenreich's will was going to reassert itself, but then his expression grew blank again. "All right."

"I've seen you make casts of bones before."

"With plaster of Paris, yes."

"Make casts of these skulls—and then file the teeth on the casts."

"But—"

"You said Andrews and others would be able to tell if the original fossils were altered. But there's no way they could tell that the casts had been modified, correct?"

"Not if it's done skillfully, I suppose, but—"

"Do it."

"What about the foramen magnums?"

"What would you conclude if you saw fossils with such widened openings?"

"I don't know—possibly that ritual cannibalism had been practiced."

"Ritual?"

"Well, if the only purpose was to get at the brain, so you could eat it, it's easier just to smash the cranium, and—"

"Good. Good. Leave the damage to the skull bases intact. Let your Andrews have that puzzle to keep him occupied."

The casts were crated up and sent to the States first. Then Weidenreich himself headed for New York, leaving, he said, instructions for the actual fossils to be shipped aboard the S.S. *President Harrison*. But the fossils never arrived in America, and Weidenreich, the one man who might have clues to their whereabouts, died shortly thereafter.

Despite the raging war, Brancusi returned to Europe, returned to Transylvania, returned to Castle Dracula.

It took him a while in the darkness of night to find the right spot—the scar left by his earlier digging was just one of many on the desolate landscape. But at last he located it. He prepared a series of smaller holes in the ground, and into each of them he laid one of the grinning skulls. He then covered the holes over with dark soil.

Brancusi hoped never to fall himself, but, if he did, he hoped one of his own converts would do the same thing for him, bringing his remains home to the Family plot.

Iterations

Author's Introduction

In 1999, the Canadian SF magazine *TransVersions*, which had previously published my story "Lost in the Mail" (elsewhere in this collection) changed hands. The new editors were good friends of mine: the husband-and-wife team of Marcel Gagné and Sally Tomasevic. They asked me for a story to help them relaunch the magazine.

A nonfiction book that had a huge impact on the SF field was *The Physics of Immortality* by Frank Tipler (1994). Tipler's theory suggested the core of this short story, as well as that of many SF novels of the last few years, including my friend Robert Charles Wilson's terrific *Darwinia*. Indeed, when I told Bob that I'd done a story for *TransVersions*, he asked me what it was about. I said it was a riff on Tipler. Bob smiled and replied, "I love being part of a community in which a phrase like 'a riff on Tipler' actually means something."

So do I.

Iterations

"I'm going to have to kill you," I said to myself, matter-of-factly.

The face looking back at me across the desktop was my own, of course, but not the way I was used to seeing it; it wasn't flopped left-to-right like it is in a mirror. The other me reacted with an appropriate mixture of surprise and disbelief. The shaggy eyebrows went up—God, why don't I trim those things?—the brown eyes widened, and the mouth opened to utter a protest.

"You can't kill me," he—I—said. "I'm you."

I frowned, disappointed that he didn't understand. "You're a me that never should have existed."

He spread his arms a bit. "Who's to say which of us should have existed?"

One of the interesting things about working in the publishing industry in Canada is this: it's full of Americans who came here during Vietnam. And, even if they didn't want to go to war, some of them *do* know how to get guns. "Who's to say which of us should have existed?" I repeated. I took the Glock 9 mm that Jack Spalding had procured for me out of my pocket and pulled the trigger. "I am."

I was at home with Mary, my wife and, until everything had fallen apart, my business partner. We were in our bedroom, and I was trying to get through to her. "Don't you see?" I said, sitting on the edge of the bed. "None of this is real—it can't be."

She sat down next to me and began brushing her hair. "What are you talking about?"

"You. Me. This bed. This house. This *planet*. It's all faked. It's all a computer-based simulation."

Mary shook her head slightly. She hated it when I talked like this.

"It's true," I said. "It's true—and I can prove it."

She pressed her lips tightly together, and blew air out of her nose. She didn't say "How?" She didn't say anything.

I wished there were a more obvious way. I wished I could grab hold of—of that wall there, say, and pull it aside, revealing the machinery beyond, but, of course, I couldn't. The wall was simulated perfectly; the rest of Toronto was simulated perfectly, too. So was all of Canada, of North America, the entire planet. There was no place I could take her where she would see that corners had been cut, see scaffolding propping up a false front to a non-existent building. This Earth—at least all of its surface, and its atmosphere thinning out to almost nothing a few hundred kilometers up, and its rocky crust, and maybe even some portion of its mantle—were flawlessly reproduced.

But even *they* had limits. Yes, they could reproduce Earth, or as much of it as humans could ever access, but—

"Look," I said. "Imagine a space probe that could travel at one-tenth the speed of light."

She was staring at me as though I wasn't even speaking English anymore.

I pressed on. "Imagine that space probe, taking decades to get to the next star. And imagine it finding raw materials there to build ten duplicates of itself, and then sending those duplicates, at the same speed, to ten other nearby stars. Even if it took fifty years to find the raw materials and make the duplicates, and fifty more years for those duplicates to travel to their target stars, if the process continued, how long do you think it would take for such probes to colonize the entire galaxy?"

"What are you talking about?" said Mary again.

"Sixty thousand years," I said, triumphantly. "Give or take. One single probe, launched into space by any civilization anywhere in the Milky Way, could colonize this whole giant galaxy in just sixty thousand years."

Our little publishing company had been called CanScience Books; I'd been editorial director. Mary didn't know much about science, but she was a wiz at accounting. "So?"

"So," I said, "the universe is maybe twelve billion years old." I grabbed her shoulders. "Don't you see? Someone somewhere *must* have launched self-replicating probes like the ones I described. This planet should have been visited by them . . . but it hasn't."

"Maybe there aren't any other civilizations."

"Of *course* there are. There must be." It drove me nuts that she never read the books we'd published. "Everything we know about physics and chemistry and biology says the universe should be overrun with life. But none of it has come here." I shifted my weight; maybe I shook her slightly. I so much wanted her to *see.* "And what about SETI? The search for extraterrestrial intelligence? We've been listening for half a century now and haven't picked up a thing. We shouldn't need to do anything more than point a radio dish up at the night sky to pick up thousands—millions—of alien signals. But there's nothing.

"And think about the moon. Do you know how many people have gone to the moon? Twelve! That's all, in the total history of our race—twelve people have stood on its surface. And no one has gone back; no one even has *plans* to go back. And what about Mars? We should have landed on it within a few years of going to the moon, but no one's made it there—and, again, no one is planning to go. And the space probes we send there keep failing. The Mars Climate Orbiter, the Mars Polar Lander—complete write-offs! I mean, let's be real: an important mission to Mars junked because some engineer couldn't convert between imperial and metric measurements? It's unbelievable."

"I still don't see—" began Mary.

"Let me spell it out, then: it's one thing to simulate the Earth. That's a big computing problem, sure, but it's doable."

"Not on any computer I've ever seen," said Mary.

"Well, no, of course it's not doable *yet*. But it will be. Eventually, the Earth and everyone who ever lived on it *will* be simulateable on sufficiently advanced computers."

"When?" said Mary.

"Who knows? A million years from now? A billion? Ten billion? Or maybe—Frank Tipler wrote about this—maybe at the very end of time, as the universe is collapsing back down in a big crunch. Eventually there *will* be sufficient computing power to simulate the entire planet and everyone who ever lived on it."

"How would they know anything about us?" asked Mary. "How could they possibly simulate you and me without records of what we were like?"

"They won't *need* any records." Why couldn't she see this? "A human being consists of about thirty thousand active genes. That means that there are about three-to-the-millionth-power possible genetically distinct humans. And there are about 2-to-the-10th-to-the-17th power possible human memories. Multiply it all out, and you'll find that you could reproduce all possible versions of our world—including every possible combination of human beings, with every possible set of memories—in 10-to-the-10th-to-the-123rd bits."

"Ten to the tenth to ..."

"To the 123rd, yes," I said. "And that amount will surely eventually be computable. Meaning that you could—well, Tipler used the word 'resurrect,' and that's as good as any—you could resurrect everyone who ever lived as computer simulations, without knowing anything specific about them."

Mary looked at me. "And you think that's what we are? Resurrected versions of people who died billions of years ago?"

"We *have* to be. It's the only thing that explains the absence of extraterrestrial probes here, or of radio signals from other civilizations. To simulate Von Neumann probes—that's what those self-replicating robots are called—and the chatter of alien races would mean simulating the rest of the universe, with its billions of different lifeforms. But they don't have enough computer memory—or, if they do, they consider it wasteful. So, yes, this world *seems* real to us, but it's fake. It has to be."

"Oh, Erik," said Mary, shaking her head, then letting out a sigh. "Go to sleep."

She kissed me and lay down.

I lay down too, but it was hours before I fell asleep.

If I'm a computer simulation, created millions or billions of years in the future of what I think of as the present, and if I was created simply as one possible human being with one possible set of memories, do other versions of me exist?

Did the simulators—whoever they are—pick one state of humanity at random for their experiment? Maybe. But Tipler said they would actually simulate *all* the possible states.

And if they did—

If there are other versions of me—

All the horrid things I'd ever thought about doing: the stealing, the cheating, and, yes, the murders. In other parts of this vast computer simulation, there must exist other Erik Hansens who had done those things. Some, of course, will have been arrested for their crimes, and will be paying their debts to their simulated societies.

But others ...

I once heard a statistic that ninety percent of men would commit rape if they felt sure they could get away with it. I'd never believed that figure; rarely did I meet an attractive woman that I didn't have at least a passing thought about having sex with, but never would it occur to me to force myself upon her.

Well, almost never ...

If they had simulated this me, they could have simulated *that* me, too—indeed, all the other possible mes: a me who had raped Connie Hughes in high school, when she hadn't wanted to go as far as I'd wanted to; a me who had stolen a thousand dollars from Gideon Dillings; a me who ...

Mary and I hated to even mention his name: my *bête noire*, the bane of my existence. Roscoe Harada, that goddamned son of a bitch ...

Yes, the version of me who had done what I had fantasized about doing. The version of me who had caved in Harada's brow-ridged cranium with an aluminum baseball bat ...

And the version of me who had shot him in the face, watching his skull open up like time-lapse film of a rose blooming ...

And the version of me who had pushed him off the Bloor Street viaduct, letting him fall to the Don Valley Parkway, his body going *splat*, and then being run over by car after car after car ...

They were *all* conceivable memory states. And if they *were* possible, then perhaps they did exist in other iterations of this simulation.

And that was intolerable.

It took a while to work it out, but I could now slip between worlds. I rather suspect the designers of the simulation didn't know I was doing it. Sure, murders were occurring as I eliminated other versions of myself—versions whose existence I couldn't countenance. But murders happen all the time. And if there were billions of versions of reality, well, on any given day, the same person would be snuffed out in millions of them anyway.

As I'd guessed, the simulators apparently had constraints on how much memory they could use, and so had decided to reconstruct Earth but none of the rest of the universe—at least not in any detail. And since there *were* memory constraints, some sort of data compression was being employed. Whenever the operating system saw that there were two or more identical versions of any given object, rather than code them both twice, it apparently would code only one version and simply put a pointer to it in the other iterations of the simulation.

I've always had an eidetic memory and a vivid imagination—I dream in color, unlike Mary. By fully and completely imagining myself to be as I would have been in one of the alternative realities, by essentially convincing myself that I *had* killed Roscoe Harada, even for an instant, the operating system saw this me and the other version of me as identical. And then—don't ask me how I did this; I can't explain it any more than I can explain how I walk—I manage somehow to access the pointer registry, and slip into the version of the simulation in which that other me, the one I was imagining, does exist.

Granted, not everything I could imagine is possible. I could imagine—indeed, relish—an image of a world in which Harada had fallen down some stairs and broken his back and then, later, in which he and I had ended up in a knockdown, drag-out fist-fight in which I pounded him into a bloody pulp. But, of course, if he were paralyzed, the subsequent brawl wouldn't have been possible. No, there was no pointer to *that* world.

But to other possibilities, the pointers did exist.

And I traveled to them, world after world, iteration after iteration, putting an end to the unconscionable versions of me.

"I'm sorry, Erik," I said, "but I've got to kill you."

Of course, the other me wasn't in my office at CanScience—he couldn't be. In any iteration in which I still had that office, cramped though it had been, Harada would still be alive. Instead, I was confronting him in the basement of our house; it was 10:00 a.m. on a weekday, but I guess his shift didn't start until later today.

The voice of the other me was edged with panic. "Why would you want to kill me?"

"Because you murdered Roscoe Harada."

The brown eyes darted left and right. There was only one way out of the basement—up the wooden staircase—and I was blocking that. "You can't prove that."

"I don't have to prove it to anyone but me. I'm here—in this version of the simulation—because I imagined a world in which we'd killed Harada with a knife to the left kidney. If that *wasn't* what really happened here, I wouldn't have been able to transfer to this iteration."

The other me hesitated, as if unsure what to say. Then he frowned. "So what if I did do it? You must have wanted to do it, too. After what he did to us—"

"I don't dispute that he should be dead. But what makes us better than Harada is that we never did anything awful to him to get even. And I can't live with the knowledge that a version of reality exists in which we did."

"But if you kill me, then you'll be a murderer, too."

"Is it murder? Or is it suicide?" My turn to frown. "Perhaps it's neither. Perhaps it's just me setting things straight."

"This won't bring Harada back to life in this iteration."

"No. But it will serve as a fitting punishment for his death, allowing me to enjoy my existence without guilt."

"But, look, the many-worlds interpretation of quantum mechanics says that—"

I cut him off. "It says that even in the real, non-simulated world that must have existed at one time, whenever an action can go two ways, it *does* go both ways, but in separate universes, spinning off new timelines for each possible version of reality."

The other me nodded vigorously. "Exactly. So this vast multiplexed computer simulation is no different from that."

"Except that John Cramer's transactional interpretation solves all the quandaries of quantum physics without recourse to parallel universes. If this were the real world, I could believe that Cramer was right and Hugh Everett was wrong, and there was only one timeline. But here I know—*know!*—that there are versions of the simulation in which all the base things I've ever thought of doing actually happened. And if I'm going to have peace—"

"If you're going to have peace," said the other me, with resignation, "you're going to have to put an end to me."

I squeezed the trigger and said "Exactly," but the bark of the Glock drowned out the word.

What did Roscoe Harada do to me, you might ask? CanScience was a small publishing company, and he was the buyer for a large bookstore chain. We solicited pre-pub orders for a book called *Y2canucK: A Canadian Guide to Preparing for the Year 2000.* For us, a thousand copies was a normal print run. Chapters had taken four hundred copies; Indigo, a hundred and seventy-five. And then Harada's order came in for his company: 25,000 copies, by far the biggest order we'd ever had.

We printed the books and delivered them: five hundred and twenty cartons, all shipped at our expense to Harada's warehouse in Oshawa.

And Harada had his people sit on them, never even putting them out into the stores.

And then, in January 2000, he returned them all. Every single copy. They were in the same cartons we'd shipped them out in; they'd never even been opened.

Y2K didn't turn out to be a disaster—so said all the newspapers.

But it was a disaster for Mary and me.

Books are fully returnable, and Harada's chain had used its buying clout to get not just CanScience but all publishers to offer them extended payment terms. The books came back before his company had ever paid a single dime on the original invoice.

And, of course, there was no longer any market anywhere for that title.

I couldn't pay even a fraction of the printer's bill, and the printer sued, forcing Mary and me into bankruptcy.

We lost our company.

We came within inches of losing our home.

Why had Harada done it? Because I'd spoken harshly about his company's bullying practices in an interview in *Quill & Quire*, the Canadian publishing trade journal.

Why had he done it?

Because he could.

Of course maybe neither he nor I had ever really existed. We were merely possible combinations of genes, recalling possible permutations of memory. Maybe all these iterations of him and me have no basis in reality.

In which case, killing him wouldn't be so awful. After all, maybe he never was meant to exist. Maybe I was never meant to exist, either.

No, no, when you came right down to it, killing him would not be that bad. And it would be a way for me to regain mental peace, wouldn't it? I didn't like arguing with Mary; I didn't like laying awake at night, haunted by what had happened.

If I killed Harada, if I made him pay for what he'd done to us, then maybe I could relax. Mary and I wouldn't get our publishing company back, but at least I'd have the comfort that came with knowing he hadn't gotten away with it.

And—let's face it—there must be trillions of iterations of the simulation, if all theoretically possible humans have been generated. I'd made a start, to be sure, but I couldn't possibly track down all the versions of me that have already gotten rid of Harada.

But if I killed him, too, in *this* reality—

Well, then, I wouldn't be so tortured by the existence of other versions of me who *had* killed him, and—

No.

No, dammit, no.

Be honest with yourself, Erik.

I'm not tortured by them.

I'm *jealous* of them—jealous that they get to live in worlds without Roscoe Harada, and I do not.

But if I joined them . . .

If I joined them, I'd at last be free.

The smorgasbord of possibilities made me giddy. Stabbing? Gun shot? Electrocution? Drowning? Poison? Dismemberment? Running him over with my car? Hacking away at him with an ax . . .

I savored the options, but finally came back down to Earth. It didn't have to be anything dramatic; indeed, I didn't have to do it myself. In fact, I probably *shouldn't* do it myself. When I need wiring done I call an electrician, because I'd just mess things up if I tried to handle it on my own.

So why not call a professional this time?

The phone call came a week later. Just two words, in a lilting Québecois accent: "It's done." I didn't tell Mary, of course, but it was the lead story on the *CityPulse News at Six*: "Book company executive found shot to death."

Mary and I made love that night like we hadn't for years, like we were the only people in the universe.

I was free. At last, I was free of Harada.

Mary left for work in the morning—she, at least had a marketable skill; she'd found work at a midsize accounting firm. But I decided to call in sick—I worked as a clerk at the Chapters superstore in Bayview Village now, making not much more than minimum wage. But at least I was still in the book business—although nobody from the trades ever called to ask me for a quote anymore.

No, today was a day to kick back and, for the first time in years, it seemed, to relax.

I didn't think much of it when I heard sounds coming from downstairs a few minutes after Mary had left; she often forgot her purse or gloves and had to come back to fetch them.

Still, I decided to head down. Maybe I could entice her to stay home, too. We could spend the day drinking wine and making love, and—

I should have seen it coming, of course.

Downstairs, in my living room, was another version of me, holding a gun. He looked into my eyes, and I looked into his.

"I can't live knowing that what you've done is going to go unpunished," he said.

"He deserved to die," I said. "You know that."

The gun was pointed at my chest, unwavering. The other me said nothing.

"You want him out of our lives—out of every version of our lives—as much as I do," I said.

"But I can't countenance what you did," said the me with the gun. "It's not right."

"But it's what we wanted."

"But to live, knowing that you've done this and will likely get away with it . . ," he said. "I'm sorry, but there *has* to be a version of us that is at peace."

And, as the gun fired, I realized, there was—or, at least, there was about to be.

And it was me.

Gator

Author's Introduction

Josepha Sherman—one of my favorite people in the SF world—
asked me to contribute to an anthology she was editing with
Keith R. A. DeCandido of stories based on urban legends, like
those described in the nonfiction books of Jan Howard
Brunvand, such as *The Vanishing Hitchhiker.* Although this was
to be a dark-fantasy anthology, I decided to do a science-fictiony
take on the rumored alligators in the sewers beneath New York.

Jo and Keith loved the story, and used it as the lead piece in
their anthology; the story also garnered an honorable mention in
The Year's Best Fantasy and Horror.

Gator

Something scampered by in the dark, its footfalls making tiny splashing sounds. Ludlam didn't even bother to look. It was a rat, no doubt—the sewers were crawling with them, and, well, if Ludlam could get used to the incredible stench, he could certainly get used to the filthy rodents, too.

This was his seventy-fourth night skulking about the sewers beneath New York. He was dressed in a yellow raincoat and rubber boots, and he carried a powerful flashlight—the kind with a giant brick battery hanging from the handle.

In most places, the ceiling was only inches above his head; at many points, he had to stoop to get by. Liquid dripped continuously on the raincoat's hood. The walls, sporadically illuminated by his flashlight beam, were slick with condensation or slime. He could hear the rumble of traffic up above—even late at night it never abated. Sometimes he could hear the metal-on-metal squeal of subway trains banking into a turn on the other side of the sewer wall. There was also the constant background sound of running water; here, the water was only a few inches deep, but elsewhere it ran in a torrent, especially after it had rained.

Ludlam continued to walk along. Progress was always slow: the stone floor was slippery, and Ludlam didn't want to end up yet again falling face forward into the filth.

He paused after a time, and strained to listen. Rats continued to chatter nearby, and there was the sound of a siren, audible through a grate in the sewer roof. But, as always, he failed to hear what he wanted to hear.

It seemed as though the beast would never return.

The double doors to Emergency Admitting swung inward, and ambulance attendants hustled the gurney inside. A blast of ice-cold air, like the ghostly exhaling of a long-dead dragon, followed them into the room from the November night.

Dennis Jacobs, the surgeon on duty, hurried over to the gurney. The injured man's face was bone-white—he had suffered severe blood loss and was deep in shock. One of the attendants pulled back the sheet, exposing the man's left leg. Jacobs carefully removed the mounds of gauze covering the injury site.

A great tract of flesh—perhaps five pounds of meat—had been scooped out of his thigh. If the injury had been another inch or two to the right, the femoral artery would have been clipped, and the man would have bled to death before help could have arrived.

"Who is he?" asked Jacobs.

"Paul Kowalski," said the same attendant who had exposed the leg. "A sewer worker. He'd just gone down a manhole. Something came at him, and got hold of his leg. He hightailed it up the ladder, back onto the street. A passerby found him bleeding all over the sidewalk, and called 9-1-1."

Jacobs snapped his fingers at a nurse. "O.R. 3," he said.

On the gurney, Kowalski's eyes fluttered open. His hand reached up and grabbed Jacobs's forearm. "Always heard the stories," said Kowalski, his voice weak. "But never believed they were really there."

"What?" said Jacobs. "What's really there?"

Kowalski's grip tightened. He must have been in excruciating pain. "Gators," he said at last through clenched teeth. "Gators in the sewers."

Around 2:00 a.m., Ludlam decided to call it a night. He began retracing his steps, heading back to where he'd come down. The sewer was cold, and mist swirled in the beam from his flashlight. Something brushed against his foot, swimming through the fetid water. So far, he'd been lucky—nothing had bit him yet.

It was crazy to be down here—Ludlam knew that. But he couldn't give up. Hell, he'd patiently sifted through sand and gravel for years. Was this really that different?

The smell hit him again. Funny how he could ignore it for hours at a time, then suddenly be overpowered by it. He reached up with his left hand, pinched his nostrils shut, and began breathing through his mouth.

Ludlam walked on, keeping his flashlight trained on the ground just a few feet in front of him. As he got closer to his starting point, he tilted the beam up and scanned the area ahead.

His heart skipped a beat.

A dark figure was blocking his way.

Paul Kowalski was in surgery for six hours. Dr. Jacobs and his team repaired tendons, sealed off blood vessels, and more. But the most interesting discovery was made almost at once, as one of Jacobs's assistants was prepping the wound for surgery.

A white, fluted, gently curving cone about four inches long was partially embedded in Kowalski's femur.

A tooth.

"What the hell are you doing down here?" said the man blocking Ludlam's way. He was wearing a stained Sanitation Department jacket.

"I'm Dr. David Ludlam," said Ludlam. "I've got permission." He reached into his raincoat's pocket and pulled out the letter he always carried with him.

The sanitation worker took it and used his own flashlight to read it over. "'Garbologist,'" he said with a snort. "Never heard of it."

"They give a course in it at Columbia," said Ludlam. That much was true, but Ludlam wasn't a garbologist. When he'd first approached the City government, he'd used a fake business card—amazing what you could do these days with a laser printer.

"Well, be careful," said the man. "The sewers are dangerous. A guy I know got a hunk taken out of him by an alligator."

"Oh, come on," said Ludlam, perfectly serious. "There aren't any gators down here."

"Thank you for agreeing to see me, Professor Chong," said Jacobs. Chong's tiny office at the American Museum of Natural History was packed floor to ceiling with papers, computer printouts, and books in metal shelving units. Hanging from staggered coat hooks on the wall behind Chong was a stuffed anaconda some ten feet long.

"I treated a man two days ago who said he was bit by an alligator," said Jacobs.

"Had he been down south?" asked Chong.

"No, no. He said it happened here, in New York. He's a sewer worker, and—"

Chong laughed. "And he said he was bitten by an alligator down in the sewers, right?"

Jacobs felt his eyebrows lifting. "Exactly."

Chong shook his head. "Guy's trying to file a false insurance claim, betcha anything. There aren't any alligators in our sewers."

"I saw the wound," said Jacobs. "Something took a massive bite out of him."

"This alligators-in-the-sewers nonsense has been floating around for years," said Chong. "The story is that kids bring home baby gators as pets from vacations in Florida, but when they grow tired of them, they flush 'em down the toilet, and the things end up living in the sewers."

"Well," said Jacobs, "that sounds reasonable."

"It's crap," said Chong. "We get calls here at the Herpetology Department about that myth from time to time—but that's all it is: a myth. You know how cold it is out there today?"

"A little below freezing."

"Exactly. Oh, I don't doubt that some alligators have been flushed over the years—people flush all kinds of stuff. But even assuming gators could survive swimming in sewage, the winter temperatures here would kill them. Alligators are cold-blooded, Dr. Jacobs."

Jacobs reached into his jacket pocket and pulled out the tooth. "We extracted this from the man's thigh," he said, placing it on Chong's cluttered desk.

Chong picked it up. "Seriously?"

"Yes."

The herpetologist shook his head. "Well, it's not a gator tooth—the root is completely wrong. But reptiles do shed their teeth throughout their lives—it's not unusual for one or more to pop loose during a meal." He ran his thumb lightly over the edge of the tooth. "The margin is serrated," he said. "Fascinating. I've never seen anything quite like it."

Ludlam went down into the sewers again the next night. He wasn't getting enough sleep—it was hard putting in a full day at the museum and then doing this after dark. But if he was right about what was happening . . .

Homeless people sometimes came into the sewers, too. They mostly left Ludlam alone. Some, of course, were schizophrenics—one of them shouted obscenities at Ludlam as he passed him in the dark tunnel that night.

The water flowing past Ludlam's feet was clumpy. He tried not to think about it.

If his theory was right, the best place to look would be near the biggest skyscrapers. As he often did, Ludlam was exploring the subterranean world in the area of the World Trade Center. There, the stresses would be the greatest.

Ludlam exhaled noisily. He thumbed off his flashlight, and waited for his eyes to adjust to the near-total darkness.

After about two minutes, he saw a flash of pale green light about ten feet in front of him.

Jacobs left Chong's office, but decided not to depart the museum just yet. It'd been years since he'd been here—the last time had been when his sister and her kids had come to visit from Iowa. He spent some time looking at various exhibits, and finally made his way into the dinosaur gallery. It had been fully renovated since the last time he'd seen it, and—

Christ.

Jesus Christ.

It wasn't identical, but it was close. Damn close.

The tooth that had been removed from Kowalski's leg looked very much like one of those on the museum's pride and joy—its Tyrannosaurus rex.

Chong had said there couldn't be alligators in New York's sewers.

Alligators were cold-blooded.

But dinosaurs—

His nephew had told him that last time they were here—he'd been six back then, and could rattle off endless facts and figures about the great beasts—

Dinosaurs had been warm-blooded.

It was crazy.

Crazy.

And yet—

He had the tooth. He had it right here, in his hand. Serrated, conical, white—

White. Not the brown of a fossilized tooth. White and fresh and modern.

Dinosaurs in the sewers of New York.

It didn't make any sense. But something had taken a huge bite out of Kowalski, and—

Jacobs ran out of the dinosaur gallery and hurried to the lobby. There were more dinosaurs there: the museum's rotunda was dominated by a giant Barosaurus, rearing up on its hind legs to defend its baby from two marauding allosaurs. Jacobs rushed to the information desk. "I need to see a paleontologist," he panted, gripping *the sides of the desk with both arms.*

"Sir," said the young woman sitting behind the desk, "if you'll just calm down, I'll—"

Jacobs fumbled for his hospital ID and dropped it on the desktop. "I'm a doctor," he said. "It's—it's a medical emergency. Please hurry. I need to talk to a dinosaur specialist."

A security guard had moved closer to the desk, but the young woman held him at bay with her eyes. She picked up a black telephone handset and dialed an extension.

Piezoelectricity.

It had to be the answer, thought Ludlam, as he watched the pale green light pulsate in front of him.

Piezoelectricity was the generation of electricity in crystals that have been subjected to stress. He'd read a geological paper about it once—the skyscrapers in New York are the biggest in the world, and there are more of them here than anywhere else. They weigh tens of thousands of tons, and all of that weight is taken by girders sunk into the ground, transferring the stress to the rocks beneath. The piezoelectric discharges caused the flashes of light—

—and maybe, just maybe, caused a whole lot more.

"Son of a gun," said David Ludlam, the paleontologist who agreed to speak to Dr. Jacobs. "Son of a gun."

"It's a dinosaur tooth, isn't it?" asked the surgeon.

Ludlam was quiet for a moment, turning the tooth over and over while he stared at it. "Definitely a theropod tooth, yes—but it's not exactly a tyrannosaur, or anything else I've ever seen. Where on Earth did you get it?"

"Out of a man's leg. He'd been bitten."

Ludlam considered this. "The bite—was it a great scooping out, like this?" He gestured with a cupped hand.

"Yes—yes, that's it exactly."

"That's how a tyrannosaur kills, all right. We figure they just did one massive bite, scooping out a huge hunk of flesh, then waited

patiently for the prey animal to bleed to death. But—but—"

"Yes?"

"Well, the last tyrannosaur died sixty-five million years ago."

"The asteroid impact, I know—"

"Oh, the asteroid had nothing to do with it. That's just a popular myth; you won't find many paleontologists who endorse it. But all the dinosaurs have been dead since the end of the Cretaceous."

"But this tooth looks fresh to me," said Jacobs.

Ludlam nodded slowly. "It does seem to be, yes." He looked at Jacobs. "I'd like to meet your patient."

Ludlam ran toward the green light.

His feet went out from under him.

He fell down with a great splash, brown water going everywhere. The terminals on his flashlight's giant battery hissed as water rained down on them.

Ludlam scrambled to his feet.

The light was still there.

He hurled himself toward it.

The light flickered and disappeared.

And Ludlam slammed hard against the slimy concrete wall of the sewer.

"Hello, Paul," said Dr. Jacobs. "This is David Ludlam. He's a paleontologist."

"A what?" said Paul Kowalski. He was seated in a wheelchair. His leg was still bandaged, and a brace made sure he couldn't move his knee while the tendons were still healing.

"A dinosaur specialist," said Ludlam. He was sitting in one of the two chairs in Jacobs's office. "I'm with the American Museum of Natural History."

"Oh, yeah. You got great sewers there."

"Umm, thanks. Look, I want to ask you about the animal that attacked you."

"It was a gator," said Kowalski.

"Why do you say that?"

Kowalski spread his hands. "'Cause it was big and, well, not scaly, exactly, but covered with those little plates you see on gators at the zoo."

"You could see it clearly?"

"Well, not that *clearly. I was underground, after all. But I had my flashlight."*

"Was there anything unusual about the creature?"

"Yeah—it was some sort of cripple."

"Cripple?"

"It had no arms."

Ludlam looked at Jacobs, then back at the injured man. Jacobs lifted his hands, palms up, in a this-is-news-to-me gesture. *"No arms at all?"*

"None," said Kowalski. "It had kind of reared up on its legs, and was holding its body like this." He held an arm straight out, parallel to the floor.

"Did you see its eyes?"

"Christ, yes. I'll never forget 'em."

"What did they look like?"

"They were yellow, and—"

"No, no. The pupils. What shape were they?"

"Round. Round and black."

Ludlam leaned back in his chair.

"What's significant about that?" asked Jacobs.

"Alligators have vertical pupils; so do most snakes. But not theropod dinosaurs."

"How do you possibly know that?" said Jacobs. "I thought soft tissues don't fossilize."

"They don't. But dinosaurs had tiny bones inside their eyes; you can tell from them what shape their pupils had been."

"And?"

"Round. But it's something most people don't know."

"You think I'm lying?" said Kowalski, growing angry. "Is that what you think?"

"On the contrary," said Ludlam, his voice full of wonder. "I

think you're telling the truth."

"'Course I am," said Kowalski. "I been with the City for eighteen years, and I never took a sick day—you can check on that. I'm a hard worker, and I didn't just imagine this bite." He gestured dramatically at his bandaged leg. But then he paused, as if everything had finally sunk in. He looked from one man to the other. "You guys saying I was attacked by a dinosaur?"

Ludlam lifted his shoulders. "Well, all dinosaurs had four limbs. As you say, the one you saw must have been injured. Was there scarring where its forearms should have been?"

"No. None. Its chest was pretty smooth. I think maybe it was a birth defect—living down in the sewer, and all."

Ludlam exhaled noisily. "There's no way dinosaurs could have survived for sixty-five million years in North America without us knowing it. But . . ." He trailed off.

"Yes?" said Jacobs.

"Well, the lack of arms. You saw the T. rex *skeleton we've got at the AMNH. What did you notice about its arms?"*

The surgeon frowned. "They were tiny, almost useless."

"That's right," said Ludlam. "Tyrannosaur arms had been growing smaller and smaller as time went by—more-ancient theropods had much bigger arms, and, of course, the distant ancestors of T. rex *had walked around on all fours. If they hadn't gone extinct, it's quite conceivable that tyrannosaurs would have eventually lost their arms altogether."*

"But they did *go extinct," said Jacobs.*

Ludlam locked eyes with the surgeon. "I've got to go down there," he said.

Ludlam kept searching, night after night, week after week.

And finally, on a rainy April night a little after 1:00 a.m., he encountered another piezoelectric phenomenon.

The green light shimmered before his eyes.

It grew brighter.

And then—and then—an outline started to appear.

Something big.

Reptilian.

Three meters long, with a horizontally held back, and a stiff tail sticking out to the rear.

Ludlam could see through it—see right through it to the slick wall beyond.

Growing more solid now . . .

The chest was smooth. The thing lacked arms, just as Kowalski had said. But that wasn't what startled Ludlam most.

The head was definitely tyrannosaurid—loaf-shaped, with ridges of bone above the eyes. But the top of the head rose up in a high dome.

Tyrannosaurs hadn't just lost their arms over tens of millions of years of additional evolution. They'd apparently also become more intelligent. The domed skull could have housed a sizable brain.

The creature looked at Ludlam with round pupils. Ludlam's flashlight was shaking violently in his hand, causing mad shadows to dance behind the dinosaur.

The dinosaur had *faded* in.

What if the dinosaurs hadn't become extinct? It was a question Ludlam had pondered for years. Yes, in this reality, they had succumbed to—to something, no one knew exactly what. But in another reality—in another *timeline*—perhaps they hadn't.

And here, in the sewers of New York, piezoelectric discharges were causing the timelines to merge.

The creature began moving. It was clearly solid now, clearly *here*. Its footfalls sent up great splashes of water.

Ludlam froze. His head wanted to move forward, to approach the creature. His heart wanted to run as fast as he possibly could in the other direction.

His head won.

The dinosaur's mouth hung open, showing white conical teeth. There were some gaps—this might indeed have been the same individual that attacked Kowalski. But Kowalski had been a fool—doubtless he'd tried to run, or to ward off the approaching beast.

Ludlam walked slowly toward the dinosaur. The creature tilted its head to one side, as if puzzled. It could have decapitated Ludlam with a single bite, but for the moment it seemed merely curious. Ludlam reached up gently, placing his flat palm softly against the beast's rough, warm hide.

The dinosaur's chest puffed out, and it let loose a great roar. The sound started long and loud, but soon it was attenuating, growing fainter—

—as was the beast itself.

Ludlam felt a tingling over his entire body, and then pain shooting up into his brain, and then a shiver that ran down his spine as though a cold hand were touching each vertebra in turn, and then he was completely blind, and then there was a flash of absolutely pure, white light, and then—

—and then, he was there.

On the other side.

In the other timeline.

Ludlam had been in physical contact with the dinosaur as it had returned home, and he'd been swept back to the other side with it.

It had been nighttime in New York, and, of course, it was nighttime here. But the sky was crystal clear, with, just as it had been back in the other timeline, the moon perfectly full. Ludlam saw stars twinkling overhead—in precisely the patterns he was used to seeing whenever he got away from the city's lights.

This was the present day, and it was Manhattan Island—but devoid of skyscrapers, devoid of streets. They were at the bank of a river—a river long ago buried in the other timeline as part of New York's sanitation system.

The tyrannosaur was standing next to Ludlam. It looked disoriented, and was rocking back and forth on its two legs, its stiff tail almost touching the ground at the end of each arc.

The creature eyed Ludlam.

It had no arms; therefore, it had no technology. But Ludlam

felt sure there must be a large brain beneath that domed skull. Surely it would recognize that Ludlam meant it no harm—and that his scrawny frame would hardly constitute a decent meal.

The dinosaur stood motionless. Ludlam opened his mouth in a wide, toothy grin—

—and the great beast did the same thing—

—and Ludlam realized his mistake—

A territorial challenge.

He ran as fast as he could.

Thank God for arms. He managed to clamber up a tree, out of reach of the tyrannosaur's snapping jaws.

He looked up. A pterosaur with giant furry wings moved across the face of the moon. Glorious.

He *would* have to be careful here.

But he couldn't imagine any place he'd rather be.

Sixty-five million years of additional evolution! And not the boring, base evolution of mice and moles and monkeys. No, this was *dinosaurian* evolution. The ruling reptiles, the terrible lizards—the greatest creatures the Earth had ever known, their tenure uninterrupted. The way the story of life was really meant to unfold. Ludlam's heart was pounding, but with excitement, not fear, as he looked down from his branch at the tyrannosaur-like being, its lean, muscled form stark in the moonlight.

He'd wait till morning, and then he'd try again to make friends with the dinosaur.

But—hot damn!—he was so pleased to be here, it *was* going to be a real struggle to keep from grinning.

The Blue Planet

Author's Introduction

On December 3, 1999, the *Mars Polar Lander* disappeared as it descended toward the red planet. Five days later, an editor with the wonderfully appropriate surname of Bradbury at *The Globe and Mail: Canada's National Newspaper* called to ask me if I could write a science-fiction story explaining the probe's disappearance. The only catch: they needed the finished story in just twenty-four hours. I said I couldn't contemplate such a tight deadline for less than a dollar a word, the editor said fine (much to my surprise), and—*voilà!*—a story was born.

Newspapers are notorious for changing writers' words, but the only thing *The Globe* changed was my title, from "The Blue Planet" to the rather histrionic "Mars Reacts!"

David G. Hartwell took this story for his fifth-annual *Year's Best SF* anthology, but he preferred my original title, and so the story was republished there—and now here—as "The Blue Planet."

The Blue Planet

The round door to the office in the underground city irised open. "Teltor! Teltor!"

The director of the space-sciences hive swung her eyestalks to look wearily at Dostan, her excitable assistant. "What is it?"

"Another space probe has been detected coming from the third planet."

"Again?" said Teltor, agitated. She spread her four exoskeletal arms. "But it's only been a hundred days or so since their last probe."

"Exactly. Which means this one must have been launched *before* we dealt with that one."

Teltor's eyestalks drooped as she relaxed. The presence of this new probe didn't mean the people on the blue planet had ignored the message. Still . . .

"Is this one a lander, or just another orbiter?"

"It has a streamlined component," said Dostan. "Presumably it plans to pass through the atmosphere and come to the surface."

"Where?"

"The south pole, it looks like."

"And you're sure there's no life on board?"

"I'm sure."

Teltor flexed her triple-fingered hands in resignation. "All right," she said. "Power up the neutralization projector; we'll shut this probe off, too."

That night, Teltor took her young daughter, Delp, up to the surface. The sky overhead was black—almost as black as the interior of the tunnels leading up from the buried city. Both tiny moons were out, but their wan glow did little to obscure the countless stars.

Teltor held one of her daughter's four hands. No one could come to the surface during the day; the ultraviolet radiation from the sun was deadly. But Teltor was an astronomer—and that was a hard job to do if you always stayed underground.

Young Delp's eyestalks swung left and right, trying to take in all the magnificence overhead. But, after a few moments, both stalks converged on the bright blue star near the horizon.

"What's that, Mama?" she asked.

"A lot of people call it the evening star," said Teltor, "but it's really another planet. We're the fourth planet from the sun, and that one's the third."

"A whole other planet?" said Delp, her mandible clicking in incredulity.

"That's right, dear."

"Are there any people there?"

"Yes, indeed."

"How do you know?"

"They've been sending space probes here for years."

"But they haven't come here in person?"

Teltor moved her lower arms in negation. "No," she said sadly, "they haven't."

"Well, then, why don't we go see them?"

"We can't, dear. The third planet has a surface gravity almost three times as strong as ours. Our exoskeletons would crack open there." Teltor looked at the blue beacon. "No, I'm afraid the only way we'll ever meet is if they come to us."

"Dr. Goldin! Dr. Goldin!"

The NASA administrator stopped on the way to his car. Another journalist, no doubt. "Yes?" he said guardedly.

"Dr. Goldin, this is the latest in a series of failed missions to Mars. Doesn't that prove that your so-called 'faster, better, cheaper' approach to space exploration isn't working?"

Goldin bristled. "I wouldn't say that."

"But surely if we had human beings on the scene, they could deal with the unexpected, no?"

Teltor still thought of Delp as her baby, but she was growing up fast; indeed, she'd already shed her carapace twice.

Fortunately, though, Delp still shared her mother's fascination with the glories of the night sky. And so, as often as she could, Teltor would take Delp up to the surface. Delp could name many of the constellations now—the zigzag, the giant scoop, the square—and was good at picking out planets, including the glaringly bright fifth one.

But her favorite, always, was planet three.

"Mom," said Delp—she no longer called her "Mama"— "there's intelligent life here, and there's also intelligent life on our nearest neighbor, the blue planet, right?"

Teltor moved her eyestalks in affirmation.

Delp spread her four arms, as if trying to encompass all of the heavens. "Well, if there's life on two planets so close together, doesn't that mean the universe must be teeming with other civilizations?"

Teltor dilated her spiracles in gentle laughter. "There's no native life on the third planet."

"But you said they'd been sending probes here—"

"Yes, they have. But the life there couldn't have originated on that world."

"Why?"

"Do you know why the third planet is blue?"

"It's mostly covered with liquid water, isn't it?"

"That's right," said Teltor. "And it's probably been that way since shortly after the solar system formed."

"So? Our world used to have water on its surface, too."

"Yes, but the bodies of water here never had any great depth. Studies suggest, though, that the water on the third planet is, and always has been, many biltads deep."

"So?"

Teltor loved her daughter's curiosity. "So early in our solar system's history, both the blue planet and our world would have been constantly pelted by large meteors and comets—the debris left over from the solar system's formation. And if a meteor hits land or a shallow body of water, heat from the impact might raise temperatures for a short time. But if it hits deep water, the heat would be retained, raising the planet's temperature for dozens or even grosses of years. A stable environment suitable for the origin of life would have existed here eons before it would have on the third planet. I'm sure life only arose once in this solar system—and that it happened here."

"But—but how would life get from here to the blue planet?"

"That world has prodigious gravity, remember? Calculations show that a respectable fraction of all the material that has ever been knocked off our world by impacts would eventually get swept up by the blue planet, falling as meteors there. And, of course, many forms of microbes can survive the long periods of freezing that would occur during a voyage through space."

Delp regarded the blue point of light, her eyestalks quavering with wonder. "So the third planet is really a colony of this world?"

"That's right. All those who live there now are the children of this planet."

Rosalind Lee was giving her first press conference since being named the new administrator of NASA. "It's been five years since we lost the Mars Climate Orbiter and the Mars Polar Lander," she said. "And, even more significantly, it's been thirty-five years—over a third of a century!—since Neil Armstrong set foot on the moon. We should follow that giant leap with an even higher jump. For whatever reason, many of the unmanned probes we've sent to Mars have failed. It's time some people went there to find out why."

The door to Teltor's office irised open. "Teltor!"

"Yes, Dostan?"

"Another ship has been detected coming from the blue planet—and it's huge!"

Teltor's eyestalks flexed in surprise. It had been years since the last one. Still, if the inhabitants of planet three had understood the message—had understood that we didn't want them dumping mechanical junk on our world, didn't want them sending robot probes, but rather would only welcome them in person—it would indeed have taken years to prepare for the journey. "Are there signs of life aboard?"

"Yes! Yes, indeed!"

"Track its approach carefully," said Teltor. "I want to be there when it lands."

The *Bradbury* had touched down beside Olympus Mons during the middle of the Martian day. The seven members of the international crew planted flags in the red sand and explored on foot until the sun set.

The astronauts were about to go to sleep; Earth had set, too, so no messages could be sent to Mission Control until it rose again. But, incredibly, one of the crew spotted something moving out on the planet's surface.

It was—

No. No, it couldn't be. It couldn't.

But it was. A spindly, insectoid figure, perhaps a meter high, coming toward the lander.

A Martian.

The figure stood by one of the *Bradbury*'s articulated metal legs, next to the access ladder. It gestured repeatedly with four segmented arms, seemingly asking for someone to come out.

And, at last, the *Bradbury*'s captain did.

It would be months before the humans learned to understand the Martian language, but everything the exoskeletal being said into the thin air was recorded, of course. *"Gitanda hatabk,"* were the first words spoken to the travelers from Earth.

At the time, no human knew what Teltor meant, but nonetheless the words were absolutely appropriate. "Welcome home," the Martian had said.

Wiping Out

Author's Introduction

The commission for this story came with a deadline only eight weeks away. I was swamped with other projects, including cohosting a two-hour TV documentary for Discovery Channel Canada, but I agreed to the assignment anyway.

The editors wanted space opera, a subgenre of SF with clear-cut heroes and villains, and lots of shoot-'em-up action; *Star Wars* is space opera. I dislike the way that subgenre so often glorifies war, and found it difficult to come up with an idea.

Then, on January 2, 2000—just one week before the deadline for this story—the documentary I'd been working on aired, and I had a few friends over to watch it on TV with my wife and me. The program was called *Inventing the Future: 2000 Years of Discovery*, half of it was devoted to my predictions for the next millennium, and the other half was a retrospective of the seminal inventions of the last one thousand years, including the atomic bomb. Afterwards, one of my friends, Sally Tomasevic, noted that, "You can't put the genie back in the bottle." That comment inspired me, and I dived into writing this story the next morning.

Wiping Out

They say flashbacks are normal. Five hundred years ago, soldiers who'd come home from Vietnam experienced them for the rest of their lives. Gulf War vets, Colombian War vets, Utopia Planitia vets—they all relived their battle experiences, over and over again.

And now I was reliving mine, too.

But this would be different, thank God. Oh, I would indeed relive it all, in precise detail, but it would only happen just this once.

And for that, I was grateful.

In war, you're always taught to hate the enemy—and we had been at war my whole life. As a boy, I'd played with action figures. My favorite was Rod Roderick, Trisystems Interstellar Guard. He was the perfect twenty-fifth-century male specimen: tall, muscular, with coffee-colored skin; brown, almond-shaped eyes; and straight brown hair cropped short. Now that I was a Star Guard myself, I don't think I looked quite so dashing, but I was still proud to wear the teal-and-black uniform.

I'd had an Altairian action figure, too: dark green, naked— like the animal it was—with horns on its head, spikes down its back, and teeth that stuck out even when its great gash of a mouth was sealed. Back then, I'd thought it was a male—I'd always referred to is as "he"—but now, of course, I knew that there were three Altairian sexes, and none of them corresponded precisely to our two.

But, regardless of the appropriate pronoun, I hated that toy Altairian—just as I hated every member of its evil species.

The Altairian action figure could explode, its six limbs and forked tail flying out of its body (little sensors in the toy making sure they never headed toward my eyes, of course). My Rod Roderick action figure frequently blew up the Altairian, aiming his blaster right at the center of the thing's torso, at that hideous concavity where its heart should have been, and opening fire.

And now I was going to open fire on real Altairians. Not with a blaster sidearm—there was no one-on-one combat in a real interstellar war—but with something far more devastating.

I still had my Rod Roderick action figure; it sat on the dresser in my cabin here, aboard the *Pteranodon*. But the Altairian figure was long gone—when I was fifteen, I'd decided to really blow it up, using explosives I'd concocted with a chemistry set. I'd watched in giddy wonder as it burst into a thousand plastic shards.

The *Pteranodon* was one of a trio of Star Guard vessels now approaching Altair III: the others were the *Quetzalcoatlus* and the *Rhamphorhynchus*. Each had a bridge shaped like an arrowhead, with the captain—me in the *Pteranodon*'s case—at the center of the wide base, and two rows of consoles converging at a point in front. But, of course, you couldn't see the walls; the consoles floated freely in an all-encompassing exterior hologram.

"We're about to cross the orbit of their innermost moon," said Kalsi, my navigator. "The Alties should detect us soon."

I steepled my fingers in front of my face and stared at the planet, which was showing a gibbous phase. The harsh white light from its sun reflected off the wide oceans. The planet was more like Earth than any I'd ever seen; even Tau Ceti IV looks less similar. Of course, TC4 had had no intelligent life when we got to it; only dumb brutes. But Altair III did indeed have intelligent lifeforms: it was perhaps unfortunate that first contact, light-years from here, had gone so badly, all those decades ago. We never knew who had fired first—our survey ship, the *Harmony*, or their vessel, whatever it had been named. But, regardless, both ships were wrecked in the encounter, both crews killed, bloated bodies tumbling against the night—human ones and Altairians, too. When the rescue ships arrived, those emerald-dark corpses were our first glimpse of the toothy face of the enemy.

When we encountered Altairians again, they said we'd started it. And, of course, we said they'd started it. Attempts had been made by both sides to halt the conflict, but it had continued to escalate. And now—

Now, victory was at hand. That was the only thing I could think about today.

The captains of the *Rhamphorhynchus* and *Quetzalcoatlus* were both good soldiers, too, but only one of our names would be immortalized by history—the one of us who actually got through the defenses surrounding the Altairian homeworld, and—

And that one was going to be me, Ambrose Donner, Star Guard. A thousand years from now, nay, ten thousand years hence, humans would know who their savior had been. They would—

"Incoming ships," said Kalsi. "Three—no, four—*Nidichar*-class attack cruisers."

I didn't have to look where Kalsi was pointing; the holographic sphere instantly changed orientation, the ships appearing directly in front of me. "Force screens to maximum," I said.

"Done," said Nguyen, my tactical officer.

In addition to my six bridge officers, I could see two other faces: small holograms floating in front of me. One was Heidi Davinski, captain of the *Quetzalcoatlus*; the other, Peter Chin, captain of the *Rhamphorhynchus*. "I'll take the nearest ship," Heidi said.

Peter looked like he was going to object; his ship was closer to the nearest *Nidichar* than Heidi's was. But then he seemed to realize the same thing I did: there would be plenty to go around. Heidi had lost her husband Craig in an Altairian attack on Epsilon Indi II; she was itching for a kill.

The *Quetzalcoatlus* surged ahead. All three of our ships had the same design: a lens-shaped central hull with three spherical engine pods spaced evenly around the perimeter. But the holoprojector colorized the visual display for each one to make it easy for us to tell them apart: Heidi's ship appeared bright red.

"The *Q* is powering up its TPC," said Nguyen. I smiled, remembering the day I blew up my Altairian toy. Normally, a tachyon-pulse cannon was only used during hyperspace battles; it would be overkill in orbital maneuvering. Our Heidi *really* wanted to make her point.

Seconds later, a black circle appeared directly in front of me: the explosion of the first *Nidichar* had been so bright, the scanners had censored the information rather than blind my crew.

Like Peter Chin, I had been content to let Heidi have the first kill; that was no big deal. But it was time the *Pteranodon* got in the game.

"I'll take the ship at 124 by 17," I said to the other two captains. "Peter, why don't—"

Suddenly my ship rocked. I pitched forward slightly in my chair, the restraining straps holding me in place.

"Direct hit amidships—minimal damage," said Champlain, my ship-status officer, turning to face me. "Apparently they can now shield their torpedoes against our sensors."

Peter Chin aboard the *Rhamphorhynchus* smiled. "I guess we're not the only ones with some new technology."

I ignored him and spoke to Nguyen. "Make them pay for it."

The closer ship was presumably the one that had fired the torpedo. Nguyen let loose a blast from our main laser; it took a tenth of a second to reach the alien ship, but when it did, that ship cracked in two under the onslaught, a cloud of expelled atmosphere spilling out into space. A lucky shot; it shouldn't have been that easy. Still: "Two down," I said, "two to go."

"'Afraid not, Ambrose," said the Heidi hologram. "We've picked up a flotilla of additional Altairian singleships leaving the outer moon and heading this way. We're reading a hundred and twelve distinct sublight-thruster signatures."

I nodded at my colleagues. "Let's teach them what it means to mess with the Trisystems Interstellar Guard."

The *Rhamphorhynchus* and the *Quetzalcoatlus* headed off to meet the incoming flotilla. Meanwhile, I had the *Pteranodon* fly directly toward the two remaining *Nidichars*, much bigger than the singleships the others were going up against. The nearer of the *Nidichars* grew bigger and bigger in our holographic display. I smiled as the details resolved themselves. *Nidichar*-class vessels were a common Altairian type, consisting of three tubular bodies, parallel to each other, linked by connecting struts. Two of the tubes were engine pods; the third was the habitat module. On the *Nidichars* I'd seen before, it was easy to distinguish the living quarters from the other two. But this one had the habitat disguised to look just like another propulsion unit. Earlier in the war, the Star Guard had made a habit of shooting out the engine pods, humanely leaving the crew compartment intact. I guess with this latest subterfuge, the Alties thought we'd be reluctant to disable their ships at all.

They were wrong.

I didn't want to use our tachyon-pulse cannon; it depleted the hyperdrive and I wanted to keep that in full reserve for later. "Shove some photons down their throats," I said.

Nguyen nodded, and our lasers—thoughtfully animated in the holo display so we could see them—lanced out toward first one and then the other Altairian cruiser.

They responded in kind. Our force screens shimmered with auroral colors as they deflected the onslaught.

We jousted back and forth for several seconds, then my ship rocked again. Another stealth torpedo had made its way past our sensors.

"That one did some damage," said Champlain. "Emergency bulkheads are in place on decks seven and eight. Casualty reports are coming in."

The Altairians weren't the only ones with a few tricks at their disposal. "Vent our reserve air tanks," I said. "It'll form a fog around us, and—"

"And we'll see the disturbance created by an incoming torpedo," said Nguyen. "Brilliant."

"That's why they pay me the colossal credits," I said. "Meanwhile, aim for the struts joining the parts of their ships together; let's see if we can perform some amputations."

More animated laserfire crisscrossed the holobubble. Ours was colored blue; the aliens', an appropriately sickly green.

"We've got the casualty reports from that last torpedo hit," said Champlain. "Eleven dead; twenty-two injured."

I couldn't take the time to ask who had died—but I'd be damned if any more of my crew were going to be lost during this battle.

The computer had numbered the two remaining *Nidichars* with big sans-serif digits. "Concentrate all our fire on number two," I said. The crisscrossing lasers, shooting from the eleven beam emitters deployed around the rim of our hull, all converged on the same spot on the same ship, severing one of the three connecting struts. As soon as it was cut, the beams converged on another strut, slicing through it, as well. One of the cylindrical modules fell away from the rest of the ship. Given the plasma streamers trailing from the stumps of the connecting struts, it must have been an engine pod. "Continue the surgery," I said to Nguyen. The beams settled on a third strut.

I took a moment to glance back at the *Rhamphorhynchus* and *Quetzalcoatlus*. The Altairian singleships were swarming around the *Rhamphorhynchus* (colored blue in the display). Peter Chin's lasers were sweeping through the swarm, and every few seconds I saw a singleship explode. But he was still overwhelmed.

Heidi, aboard the *Quetzalcoatlus*, was trying to draw the swarm's fire, but with little success. And if she fired into the cloud of ships, either her beams or debris from her kills might strike the *Rhamphorhynchus*.

I swung to look at the hologram of Peter's head. "Do you need help?" I asked.

"No, I'm okay. We'll just—"

The fireball must have roared through his bridge from stern to bow; the holocamera stayed online long enough to show me the wall of flame behind Pete, then the flesh burning off his skull, and then—

And then nothing; just an ovoid of static where Peter Chin's head had been. After a few seconds, even that disappeared.

I turned to the holo of Heidi, and I recognized her expression: it was the same one I myself was now forcing onto my face. She knew, as I did, that the eyes of her bridge crew were on her. She couldn't show revulsion. She especially couldn't show fear— not while we were still in battle. Instead, she was displaying steel-eyed determination. "Let's get them," she said quietly.

I nodded, and—

And then my ship reeled again. We'd all been too distracted by what had happened to the *Rhamphorhynchus* to notice the wake moving through the cloud of expelled gas around our ship. Another stealth torpedo had exploded against our hull.

"Casualty reports coming in—" began Champlain.

"Belay that," I said. The young man looked startled, but there was nothing I could do about the dead and injured now. "What's the status of our cargo?"

Champlain recovered his wits; he understood the priorities, too. "Green lights across the board," he said.

I nodded, and the computer issued an affirming *ding* so that those crew members who were no longer looking at me would know I'd acknowledged the report. "Leave the *Nidichars*; let's get rid of those singleships before they take out the *Quetzalcoatlus*."

The starfield wheeled around us as the *Pteranodon* changed direction.

"Fire at will," I said.

Our lasers lanced forward, taking out dozens of the single-ships. The *Quetzalcoatlus* was eliminating its share of them, too.

The two remaining *Nidichar*s were now barreling towards us. Kalsi used the ACS thrusters to spin us like a top, lasers shooting off in all directions.

Suddenly, a black circle appeared in front of my eyes again: there had been an explosion on the *Quetzalcoatlus*. A stealth torpedo had connected directly with one of the *Q*'s three engine spheres, and, as I saw once the censor disengaged, the explosion had utterly destroyed the sphere and taken a big, ragged chunk out of the lens-shaped main hull.

We'd cut the singleship swarm in half by now, according to the status displays. Heidi powered up her tachyon-pulse cannon again; it was risky, with her down to just two engines, but we needed to level the playing field. The discharge from her TCP destroyed one of the two remaining *Nidichar*s: there was now only one big Altairian ship to deal with, and forty-seven single-occupant craft.

I left Heidi to finish mopping up the singleships; we were going to take out the final *Nidichar*. I really didn't want to use our TCP—the energy drain was too great. But we couldn't risk being hit by another stealth torpedo; we'd left our cloud of expelled atmosphere far behind when we'd gone after the swarm, and—

And the *Pteranodon* rocked again. A structural member dropped from the ceiling, appearing as if by magic as it passed through the holobubble; it crashed to the deck next to my chair.

"Evasive maneuvers!" I shouted.

"Not possible, Captain," said Kalsi. "That came from the planet's surface; its rotation must have finally given a ground-based disruptor bank a line-of-sight at us."

"Cargo status?"

"Still green, according to the board," said Champlain.

"Send someone down there," I said. "I want an eyeball inspection."

Heidi had already moved the *Quetzalcoatlus* so that the remaining singleships were between her and the planet; the ground-based cannon couldn't get her without going through its own people.

The remaining *Nidichar* fired at us again, but—

Way to go, Nguyen!

A good, clean blast severed the habitat module from the two engines—a lucky guess about which was which had paid off. The habitat went pinwheeling away into the night, atmosphere puffing out of the connecting struts.

We swung around again, carving into the remaining singleships. Heidi was doing the same; there were only fifteen of them left.

"Incom—" shouted Kalsi, but he didn't get the whole word out before the disruptor beam from the planet's surface shook us again. An empty gray square appeared in the holobubble to my right; the cameras along the starboard side of the ship had been destroyed.

"We won't survive another blast from the planet's surface," Champlain said.

"It must take them a while to recharge that cannon, or they'd have blown both of us out of the sky by now," Heidi's hologram said. "It's probably a meteor deflector, never intended for battle."

While we talked, Nguyen took out four more singleships, and the *Quetzalcoatlus* blasted another five into oblivion.

"If it weren't for that ground-based cannon . . ." I said.

Heidi nodded once, decisively. "We all know what we came here to do—and that's more important than any of us." The holographic head swiveled; she was talking to her own bridge crew now. "Mr. Rabinovitch, take us down."

If there was a protest, I never heard it. But I doubt there was. I didn't know Rabinovitch—but he was a Star Guard, too.

Heidi turned back to me. "This is for Peter Chin," she said. And then, perhaps more for her own ears than my own, "And for Craig."

The *Quetzalcoatlus* dived toward Altair III, its sublight thrusters going full blast. Its force screens had no trouble getting it through the atmosphere, and apparently the ground-based cannon wasn't yet recharged: her ship crashed right into the facility housing it on the southern continent. We could see the shockwave moving across the planet's surface, a ridge of compressed air expanding outward from where the *Quetzalcoatlus* had hit.

Nguyen made short work of the remaining singleships, their explosions a series of pinpoint novas against the night.

And Altair III spun below us, defenseless.

Humanity had just barely survived five hundred years living with the nuclear bomb. It had been used eleven times on Earth and Mars, and over one hundred million had died—but the human race had gone on.

But our special cargo, the Annihilator, was more—much more. It was a planet killer, a destroyer of whole worlds. We'd said when Garo Alexanian invented the technology that we'd never, ever use it.

But, of course, we were going to. We were going to use it right now.

It could have gone either way. Humans certainly weren't more clever than Altairians; the technology we'd recovered from wrecked ships proved that. But sometimes you get a lucky break.

Our scientists were always working to develop new weapons; there was no reason to think that Altairian scientists weren't doing the same thing. Atomic nuclei are held together by the strong nuclear force; without it, the positively charged protons would repel each other, preventing atoms from forming. The Annihilator translates the strong nuclear force into electromagnetism for a fraction of a second, causing atoms to instantly fling apart.

It was a brilliant invention from a species that really wasn't all that good at inventing. With the countless isolated communities that had existed in Earth's past, you'd expect the same fundamental inventions to have been made repeatedly—but they weren't. Things we now consider intuitively obvious were invented only once: the water wheel, gears, the magnetic compass, the windmill, the printing press, the camera obscura, and the alphabet itself arose only a single time in all of human history; it was only trade that brought them to the rest of humanity. Even that seemingly most obvious of inventions, the wheel, was created just twice: first, near the Black Sea, nearly six thousand years ago, then again, much later, in Mexico. Out of the hundred billion human beings who have existed since the dawn of time, precisely two came up with the idea of the wheel. All the rest of us simply copied it from them.

So it was probably a fluke that Alexanian conceived of the Annihilator. If it hadn't occurred to him, it might never have occurred to anyone else in the Trisystems; certainly, it wouldn't have occurred to anybody any time soon. Five hundred years ago, they used to say that string theory was twenty-first-century science accidentally discovered in the twentieth century; the Annihilator was perhaps thirtieth-century science that we'd been lucky enough to stumble upon in the twenty-fifth.

And that luck could have just as easily befallen an Altairian physicist instead of a human one. In which case, it would be Earth and Tau Ceti IV and Epsilon Indi II that would have been about to feel its effects, instead of Altair III.

We released the Annihilator—a great cylindrical contraption, more than three hundred meters long—from our cargo bay; the *Quetzalcoatlus* and the *Rhamphorhynchus* had had Annihilators, too, each costing over a trillion credits. Only one was left.

But one was all it would take.

Of course, we'd have to engage our hyperdrive as soon as the annihilation field connected with Altair III. The explosion would be unbelievably powerful, releasing more joules than anyone could even count—but none of it would be superluminal. We would be able to outrun it, and, by the time the expanding shell reached Earth, sixteen years from now, planetary shielding would be in place.

The kill would go to the *Pteranodon*; the name history would remember would be mine.

They teach you to hate the enemy—they teach you that from childhood.

But when the enemy is gone, you finally have time to reflect. And I did a lot of that. We all did.

About three-quarters of Altair III was utterly destroyed by the annihilation field, and the rest of it, a misshapen chunk with its glowing iron core exposed, broke up rapidly.

The war was over.

But we were not at peace.

The sphere was an unusual sort of war memorial. It wasn't in Washington or Hiroshima or Dachau or Bogatá, sites of Earth's great monuments to the horrors of armed conflict. It wasn't at Elysium on Mars, or New Vancouver on Epsilon Indi II, or Pax City on Tau Ceti IV. Indeed it had no permanent home, and, once it faded from view, a short time from now, no human would ever see it again.

A waste of money? Not at all. We had to do *something*—people understood that. We had to commemorate, somehow, the race that we'd obliterated and the planet we'd destroyed, the fragment left of it turning into rubble, a spreading arc now, a full asteroid belt later, girdling Altair.

The memorial had been designed by Anwar Kanawatty, one of the greatest artists in the Trisystems: a sphere five meters across, made of transparent diamond. Representations of the continents and islands of the planet that had been Altair III (a world farther out from that star now had that designation) were laser-etched into the diamond surface, making it frostily opaque in those places. But at the gaps between—representing the four large oceans of that planet, and the thousands of lakes—the diamond was absolutely clear, and the rest of the sculpture was visible within. Floating in the center of the sphere were perfect renderings of three proud Altairian faces, one for each gender, a reminder of the race that had existed once but did no more.

Moments ago, the sphere had been launched into space, propelled for the start of its journey by invisible force beams. It was heading in the general direction of the Andromeda galaxy, never to be seen again. Kanawatty's plans had already been destroyed; not even a photograph or holoscan of the sphere was retained. Humans would never again look upon the memorial, but still, for billions of years, far out in space, it would exist.

No markings were put on it to indicate where it had come from, and, for the only time in his life, Kanawatty had not signed one of his works; if by some chance it was ever recovered, nothing could possibly connect it with humanity. But, of course, it probably would never be found by humans or anyone else. Rather, it would drift silently through the darkness, remembering for those who had to forget.

The flashback was necessary, they said. It was part of the process required to isolate the memories that were to be overwritten.

Memory revision will let us put the Annihilator genie back in the bottle. And, unlike so many soldiers of the past, unlike all those who had slaughtered in the name of king and country before me, I will never again have a flashback.

What if we need the Annihilator again?

What if we find ourselves in conflict with another race, as we had with the people of Altair? Isn't it a mistake to wipe out knowledge of such a powerful weapon?

I look at the war memorial one last time, as it drifts farther and farther out into space, a crystal ball against the velvet firmament. It's funny, of course: there's no air in space, and so it should appear rock-steady in my field of view. But it's blurring.

I blink my eyes.

And I have my answer.

The answer is no. It is not a mistake.

Uphill Climb

Author's Introduction

When I was fourteen, I discovered the work of SF writer Larry Niven, and began to read him voraciously. I was always particularly fond of his aliens, the most memorable of which are the puppeteers and the kzinti. Almost at once, I started putting together notes for my own alien race, the Quintaglios—descendants of Earth's dinosaurs, transplanted to another world millions of years ago. I eventually wrote a trilogy of novels about these beings—*Far-Seer* (published in 1992), *Fossil Hunter* (1993), and *Foreigner* (1994)— books which to this day generate the most fan mail of anything I've ever done.

The first print appearance of the Quintaglios, though, was in this little tale, which appeared in *Amazing Stories* in 1987 (and was my first sale to a major SF magazine).

Uphill Climb

"Service!" Livingstone Kivley lobbed his last tennis ball across the sagging net. At the sidelines, in the shade of the old brownstone office building, stood young Obno. She was thin for a Quintaglio, no more than 400 kilos, a dwarf tyrannosaur with nervous, darting eyes of polished obsidian. Kivley's opponent was a blue boxlike robot. The little machine swatted the ball with a nylon racquet. Kivley swung, missed, swore. Obno spoke to the robot, using the sub-language her people reserved for talking to beasts and gods. It rolled on rubber treads to the net, lifted it, slipped under, and dutifully collected the balls.

Kivley turned his face up at Obno in what he hoped the alien would read as mock despair. "Oh, the humiliation! I've been playing tennis for sixty years and your overgrown milk crate whips the pants off me." The blue box rolled up to Kivley and deposited three fuzzy spheres at his besneakered feet. Kivley saw the hurt look in the Quintaglio's eyes. "I'm kidding, Obno. You've done a fine job."

Obno didn't look much happier. "The robot is capable of many other complex tasks." She walked over to Kivley, lazy summer sun glinting off the scale vestiges embedded in her leathery hide. "It can work in manufacturing, run errands, look after infants, be a courier."

"Was it expensive to make?"

"This prototype? Yes. But the design is entirely solid-state, except for the treads and arms. We could sell them for walnuts."

"Peanuts," corrected Kivley. He reached a hand up to the alien's shoulder. "It's an excellent piece of work."

Obno slapped her tail against the asphalt. "Not excellent. Not even adequate. True, the robotic software is years beyond what your race has yet produced, but the treads cannot negotiate slopes greater than a rise of one meter in a run of twelve."

Kivley felt a twinge in his back as he went to his knees and inspected the endless belts of corded rubber under the robot. "That's what? Five degrees? Good! Entirely sufficient."

The Quintaglio's muzzle peeled back in a grimace, showing serrated teeth. "It's impractical. The machine cannot go up those stairs human architects are so fond of. You must allow me time to develop a more versatile locomotor system."

"No. Out of the question." He rose slowly to his feet. "We'll market them as is."

"As is?"

"Absolutely. The full energies of the Combinatorics Corporation shall be bent to the task." He wiped his hands on his tattered tennis shorts. "People will buy any good labor-saving device, no?" Kivley knew that Obno was going to remind him—again!—that the Quintaglios had bestowed a great trust upon him when they gave him the job of supervising the introduction of their technology to Earth. She did not disappoint him. He shrugged. "It's a living."

"But Combinatorics was to have been an altruistic undertaking."

"Altruistic this shall be."

"Yet I feel that—"

"That we should be providing something more important than electronic gophers?" Kivley hefted his racquet and headed towards the old office building.

"Precisely!" Obno scooped up the robot and tucked it under one rubbery arm. They walked around to the glass-fronted entrance. Obno was up the three stairs in one stride; for Kivley it took a trio of little hops. "So much we could do for humankind," said Obno.

"One step at a time, my friend. One step at a time."

Kivley trudged through the snow on his way in from the bus stop. He passed dozens of the little blue robots chugging to and fro on the sidewalk, tiny plows attached to their fronts. Kivley looked up at the sound of Obno *kaflumping* across the drifts towards him. "I had an idea last night that will improve the robots," Obno said, lashing her muff-wrapped tail violently to fight the cold. "If we install cleats on pistons, they could climb over small obstacles."

Kivley continued to walk. "We've sold many robots so far, no?"

Obno nodded, an acquired human gesture. "Thousands each month. The fabricators aboard the mothership are having trouble keeping up with the demand."

"Then let's leave well enough alone."

Obno's sigh was a massive white cloud in the cold air. "I know little of capitalism, but isn't it bad business to make customers install ramps at great expense?"

"It's a small price to pay. Our robots can save their owners thousands of dollars." He nodded. "You can get people to do almost anything if they think they're saving a buck."

Kivley stared out of his third-floor office window. Crocuses were blooming along the edge of the sidewalk. He heard a knock and swiveled to see Obno squeezing through the mahogany door frame. "Here!" She slapped a hardcopy sheet on his desk.

"What is it?" asked Kivley, rummaging through the clutter for his reading glasses.

"It's a letter from IBM. They want to purchase the right to manufacture robots like ours." Her voice took on an edge. "But with *legs*."

"You object to the machines requiring ramps, Obno." He tried to put a question mark at the end of the sentence, but it didn't quite make it past his lips.

"I am shamed by the inefficiency. Since we introduced them three years ago, nearly all public buildings in the industrial portions of this planet have had to be modified to accommodate the growing robot population."

"Very well," said Kivley, nodding as he gave the letter a quick looking over. "Sell the patent. Ask whatever seems fair."

Obno spluttered, a loud, sticky sound. "But you wouldn't let me—!"

Kivley swiveled around to look out at the street again. He gestured Obno to the window. A pretty woman rolled happily along the sidewalk in her wheelchair and up the gentle ramp into the building.

Obno smiled at last.

Last But Not Least

Author's Introduction

My friend Edo van Belkom is Canada's top horror-fiction writer.
He received a commission from Tundra Books, the young-adult
imprint of McClelland & Stewart, Canada's largest publisher, to
produce an anthology of horror stories, eventually entitled *Be
Afraid!* Edo wanted me to contribute to that book, and I wrote
the following, which, since it actually contains no supernatural ele-
ment, also qualifies as the first mainstream story I'd ever published.

Last But Not Least

Matt stood in the field on the bitter October morning. The wind's icy fingers reached right through Matt's skin to chill his bones. It was crazy that Mr. Donner made them wear their gym shorts on a day like today—but if Donner had any compassion in him, any humanity, any kindness at all, Matt had never seen it.

"*I'll take Spalding.*"

"*Gimme Chen.*"

Last week, Matt had tried to get out of phys. ed. class by pretending he'd lost his gym shorts; he'd put his own shorts in the school's lost and found. But Donner had an extra pair he lent him—and he said if Matt showed up without shorts again, he'd make him take the class in his underwear.

"*I pick Oxnard.*"

"*I'll take Modigliani.*"

Matt didn't mind being outdoors, and he didn't mind getting some exercise, but he hated phys. ed.—hated it as much as he hated it when his parents fought; when he had to go to the dentist; when that dog over on Parkhurst came chasing after him.

He knew he was scrawny, knew he was uncoordinated. But did he have to be humiliated because of it? Made to feel like a total loser?

"*Johnson.*"

"*Peelaktoak.*"

There were twenty-four boys in Matt's gym class. Today they were playing soccer. But it didn't matter what the sport was; it always worked the same way. Mr. Donner would pick two students to be captain.

And then the ritual would begin.

"Gimme Van Beek."

"Takahashi."

The captains would take turns picking from the other students to create the two teams.

Matt understood the sick, evil logic of it all: twenty-four kids wasn't a big group. If you just took the first dozen alphabetically and made them one team, and had the second dozen be the other team, you might end up with two unevenly matched sides.

But this way . . .

This humiliating, mortifying way . . .

This way supposedly ensured fairness, supposedly made sure the teams would be equal, made sure that the game would be exciting, that everyone would have a good time.

Everyone except those who were picked last, that is.

"Becquerel."

"Bergstrom."

Matt's big brother, Alf, was in law school. Alf said students fought hard for ranking in their classes. If you got the highest mark—if you finished first—you'd get a million-dollar contract from a huge law firm. If you finished last, well, Alf said maybe it would be time to think about another career. The stress on Alf was huge; Matt could see that every time his brother came home for a weekend. But Alf had *chosen* that stress, had chosen to be judged and ranked.

But phys. ed. wasn't something Matt had decided he wanted to take; he *had* to take it. Whether he liked it or not, he had to subject himself to this torture.

"Bonkowski."

Matt was the only one left now, and Cartwright, the other captain, didn't even bother to call out his name. Cartwright's rolled eyes said it all: he wasn't picking Matt Sinclair—he just happened to be the last guy left.

Matt blew out a heavy sigh. It was cold enough that he could see his breath form a frosty cloud.

Science class. The class Matt excelled in.

"And the process by which plants convert sunlight into food is called . . . ?" Mr. Pope looked out at the students, sitting in pairs behind black-topped lab desks.

Matt raised his hand.

"Yes, Matthew?"

"Photosynthesis," he said.

"That's right, Matthew. Very good. Now, although they both undergo photosynthesis, there are two very different types of trees. There are evergreens and the other kind, the kind that loses its leaves each fall. And that kind is called . . . ?"

Matt's hand shot into the air again.

"Anybody besides Matthew know?" asked Mr. Pope.

Blank faces all around. Matt smiled to himself. Why don't we arrange all the students in here, putting them in order by how intelligent they are? Take the smartest person first—which, well, gee, that would be Matt, of course—then the next smartest, then the one after that, right down to—oh, say, down to Johnson over there. Johnson was always an early pick in gym class, but if we made selections here in science class, he'd be the one left until the end every time.

"All right," said Mr. Pope, "since no one else seems to know, Matthew, why don't you enlighten your classmates?"

"Deciduous," Matt said, proudly.

"Browner," whispered the girl behind him. And "Brainiac" said Eddy Bergstrom, siting at the next desk.

It wasn't fair, thought Matt. They cheer when someone makes a goal. Why can't they cheer when someone gets an answer right?

This time, things would be different. This time, Mr. Donner had selected Paul Chandler, Matt's best friend, to be one of the team captains.

Matt felt himself relaxing. For once in his life, he wouldn't be last.

Paul called out his first pick. Esaki—a good choice. Esaki wasn't the strongest guy in the class, but he was one of the most agile.

The other captain, Oxnard, made his initial selection: Ehrlich. An obvious pick; Ehrlich towered half a head above everyone else.

Paul again: "Gimme Spalding."

Well, that made sense. Spalding was the biggest bully in school. Paul *had* to pick him early on, lest he risk being beaten up on the way home.

Oxnard's turn: "I'll take Modigliani."

Paul: "Ng."

Paul was playing it cool; that was good. It wouldn't do to take Matt *too* early—everyone would know that Paul was choosing him just because they were best friends.

"Let me have . . . Vanier," Oxnard said.

Paul made a show of surveying the remaining students. "Papadatos," he said.

Matt's heart was beginning to sink. Paul couldn't humiliate him the way the others had. Surely he would pick him in the next round.

"Herzberg."

"Peelaktoak."

Or the round after that . . .

"Becquerel"

"Johnson."

Or . . .

"Van Beek."

"Dowling."

But no—

No, it was going to be the same as always.

Paul—his friend—had left him for last, just as everyone else always did.

Matt felt his stomach churning.

At lunch, Paul sat down opposite Matt in the cafeteria. "Hey, Matt," he said.

Matt focussed all his attention on his sandwich—peanut butter and jelly on whole wheat, cut in half diagonally.

"Earth to Matt!" said Paul. "Helll-ooo!"

Matt looked up. He kept his voice low; he didn't want the others sitting nearby to hear. "Why didn't you pick me in gym class?"

"I *did* pick you," protested Paul.

"Yeah. Last."

Paul seemed to consider this, as if realizing for the first time that Matt might have taken his actions as a betrayal. "Hey, Matt-o, I'm sorry, man. But it was probably my only time getting to be a captain all year, you know? And I wanted a good team."

A miracle occurred.

Matt was picked—not for a team, not by one of his classmates. No, no—this was better. Much better. Matt had been picked by Mr. Donner to be one of the team captains. The game today was football; Matt didn't know much about it, except that some of the other boys had snickered when he'd once referred to a gain of ten meters, instead of ten yards. In theory, they would be playing touch football, but in reality—

In reality, he still had scabs on his knees from the last time they'd played this game, when Spalding had tackled Matt, driving him to the ground, his skin shredding on a broken piece of glass hidden in the grass.

And once, last year, Matt had actually managed to tag the runner going by him, the guy clutching the football. Matt *had* touched him—he was sure he had. A good, clean connection between his hand and the other guy's shoulder. But the other player had continued on, ignoring the touch—denying it, denying Matt, as if to be touched by him would be an unbearable humiliation. The guy had run on, into the endzone, doing the exaggerated victory dance he'd seen professional players do on TV. His teammates had demanded that Matt explain why he hadn't tagged the guy. He protested that he had, of course, but no one had believed him.

The boys were all lined up in a row. Matt moved out in front of them, as did Takahashi, the other person Mr. Donner had tapped to be a captain.

Donner looked at the two captains, then with a little shrug for the other boys, as if to convey that things were mismatched already, he said, "Matt, you choose first."

Matt surveyed the twenty-two remaining boys: different sizes and shapes, different colors of eyes and hair and skin, different temperaments, different aptitudes. None of them were foolish enough to say anything disparaging about Matt being chosen as a captain; they all wanted to be picked early on, and would do nothing to jeopardize that.

"Matt?" said Mr. Donner, prodding him to get on with it.

Matt continued to look at the faces in front of him. Either Esaki or Ehrlich would be a good choice, but—

No.

No, this was too good an opportunity to pass up. "Bonkowski," Matt called out.

There were some snickers. Little Leo Bonkowski, looking absolutely stunned at being chosen first, crossed over to stand next to Matt.

Takahashi wasted no time. "Ehrlich," he said. Kurt Ehrlich strutted over to stand next to Takahashi.

Matt's turn again. "Bergstrom," he said. Dillon Bergstrom was fat and clumsy. He moved over to stand with Matt.

"I'll take Esaki," said Takahashi.

The other obvious choice—Esaki was strong, and he studied martial arts in the evenings. He and Ehrlich were always the first two choices; Matt couldn't remember a time when they'd ended up on the same team.

Matt looked at the remaining boys. Sepp Van Beek was looking at the ground, oblivious to what was going on; Matt rather suspected he usually looked much the same way himself during the picking ritual. "Van Beek," he said.

Sepp didn't move; he hadn't been paying attention.

"Hey, Sepp!" Matt called out.

This time Van Beek did look up, astonished. He half ran across to join Matt's team, a silly grin splitting his features.

"Singh," said Takahashi, decisively. A burly fellow moved over to the other side.

"Modigliani," said Matt.

By now it was obvious to everyone what Matt was up to: he was taking the least physically adept boys, the ones who were puny, or overweight, or awkward, or just plain gentle.

Takahashi frowned; his expression conveyed that he felt the upcoming game was going to be like taking candy from a baby. "Gimme Ng," he said.

Matt surveyed the dwindling pool of boys. "Chen."

Takahashi snorted, then: "Cartwright."

"Take Vanier," Modigliani said to Matt, distancing himself from the obvious lunacy of what Matt was doing.

But Matt shook his head and said, "Oxnard."

"Vanier," said Takahashi.

It was Matt's turn again. Now things were getting difficult. There were no truly bad players left—only interchangeably mediocre ones. The next logical choice might have been Spalding, the bully, but Matt would have rather played a man short than have Spalding on his team. At last, he said, "Dowling."

Takahashi wasn't one to miss an opportunity. "Spalding," he said at once.

"Finkelstein," said Matt.

"Papadatos."

There were only six boys left: Herzberg, Johnson, Peelaktoak, Becquerel, Collins, and—

—and Paul Chandler.

Matt wondered whether he'd deliberately been avoiding choosing Paul, repayment for the indignity of last time. Perhaps. But the six remaining students were neither particularly good nor particularly bad. Maybe if Matt had paid more attention in gym class, he'd have some idea of how to rank them, but at this stage he really couldn't distinguish them on the basis of ability . . . or lack of it.

But he would not do to Paul what Paul had done to him.

"Chandler," Matt called out.

Paul came running over, an expression of gratitude on his freckled face; normally, of course, he'd have been taken long before this. Maybe he did now understand what it felt like without Matt having to actually put him through it.

"Collins," said Takahashi.

Matt tried not to shrug visibly. "Peelaktoak."

"Herzberg," said Takahashi.

"Becquerel."

And Takahashi took the final boy: "Johnson."

Matt looked at his team, then at the other side. The two groups could not have been more mismatched. For the first time since he'd started making choices, Matt glanced over at Mr. Donner. He'd hoped to see a small, understanding smile on the gym teacher's angular face—an acknowledgement that he got it, that he understood what Matt was trying to say. But Mr. Donner was frowning, and shaking his head slowly back and forth in disapproval.

"We're going to be slaughtered," said Bonkowski to Matt as the two teams moved out onto the field.

It was a day of multiple miracles. Not only had Matt been chosen to be captain, but he even caught the ball about a minute into the game. He realized in a panic that he had no idea which set of goal posts belonged to his team—the closer one, over by the road, or the farther one, by the fence that separated the schoolyard from the adjacent houses.

He had to pick one—had to make one more choice—and he needed to do it in a fraction of a second.

Matt chose the farther one. It would be a longer run, but there were fewer boys from either team deployed in that direction. He worked his legs as hard as he could, pumping them up and down like pistons. What a glorious victory it would be if the weaker team actually won the game! And if he—Matthew Sinclair!—got a . . . a *touchdown*, it was called—well, then, that would put an end to him being chosen last!

He ran and ran and ran, as fast as he could. His feet pounded into the sod, still damp from the morning dew. He thought, or imagined at least, that clods of dirt were flying up from his footfalls as he ate up meter after meter—no, no, no: *yard* after *yard*—coming closer and closer to the goal line. His lungs were aching from gulping in so much cold air, and his heart felt as though it would burst within his chest. But if he could only—

Ooof!

A hand had slammed into his back—he'd been touched!

No! It was unfair! He *deserved* this chance, this opportunity, but—

But the rules were clear: this was touch football, and Matt had to stop running now.

But he couldn't—for it had been more than a touch; it had been a good, firm shove, a push impelling him on.

He found himself pitching forward, the moist grass providing little traction. And the boy who had pushed him from behind was now slamming into him, as if he, too, were sliding on the slick turf. But Matt knew in an instant that that wasn't it; oh, it was supposed to look like an accident, but he was really being tackled.

Matt slammed into the ground, so hard that he thought the football, crushed beneath his chest, would actually pop open. The other boy—Spalding it was; he could see that now—slammed down on top of him. Almost at once, a third boy—Captain Takahashi himself—piled on top.

The sound of Mr. Donner's whistle split the air, but belatedly, as if he'd been reluctant to interrupt good theater, to bring an end to just punishment. But the whistle was ignored; Matt's crime of creating mismatched teams was too great. Somebody shouted out, "Pile on!" Another body slammed on top of them, and one more after that, and then—

Crrrackkk!

It was an incredible, heart-stopping sound, like a gunshot. If Matt hadn't been buried under so many bodies, he expected he would have heard it echo off the school's brick walls.

There was a moment of nothingness, of no sensation, while the other boys reacted to the sound.

And then—

And then pain, incredible pain, indescribable pain.

The agony coursed through Matt's body, starting in his leg, shooting up his spine, assaulting his brain.

The other boys, sensing something was deeply wrong, began to climb off. As their weight shifted on top of Matt, fresh, fiery pain sliced through him.

At last, Spalding got up. Matt looked up and saw an expression on the bully's face he'd never seen before: a look of fear, of horror. Spalding was staring at Matt's right leg.

Matt swung his head down to have a look himself, and—

For a moment, he thought he was going to vomit. The sight was horrifying, unnatural.

Matt's right thigh was *bent* in the middle, twisted in a hideous way. He reached down and hiked up his gym shorts as far as they would go, so he could see—

God, no.

His thighbone—his *femur*, as he'd gladly have told Mr. Pope—was clearly broken. The bone was pushed up toward the surface, pressing against the skin, as if any second now it would burst out, a skeletal eruption.

Matt stared at it a few seconds more, then looked up. Mr. Donner had arrived by now, panting slightly, and Matt saw him looming above. "Don't move, Matt," he said. "Don't move."

Matt enjoyed the look on the teacher's face—one of incredible unease; there would be an inquiry, of course. Donner would be in the hot seat. And the faces of the other boys were equally satisfying: eyes wide in fear or revulsion, mouths hanging loosely open. Matt opened his own mouth.

And a sound emerged—but not the sound the other boys might have expected. Not a scream, not a wail of pain, not the sound of crying.

No. As Matt looked down at his twisted leg again, he began to laugh, a throaty sound, starting as a bizarre chuckle and then growing louder and more raucous.

He looked back up at the other boys—his teammates, his tormentors—and he continued to laugh.

Some of the boys were backing slowly away now, their faces showing their confusion, their wariness. The damaged leg was bad enough, but this inappropriate laughter was just too darned *creepy*. They'd always known Sinclair was a little weird, but they'd never have said he was crazy . . .

They don't get it, thought Matt. They don't get it at all. He'd snapped his leg playing football! How cool was that! It was a badge of honor. People would talk about it for years: Matt Sinclair, the guy whose leg got broken on the—yes, he knew the word; it came to him—on the *gridiron*.

And there was more—wonderfully more. Matt's brother Alf had broken his leg once, falling off a ladder; Matt knew what was going to happen. He'd have to wear a cast for weeks, or even months. Yes, that would be uncomfortable; yes, it would be awkward. But he welcomed it, because it meant that, at least for a while, he would be excused from the horrors of phys. ed.

That reprieve would be great—but things would be fine after the cast was removed, too. For when he eventually came back to gym class, Matthew Sinclair, football hero, knew he would never be picked last again.

If I'm Here, Imagine Where They Sent My Luggage

Author's Introduction

In late 1980 and early 1981, *The Village Voice: The Weekly Newspaper of New York* sponsored a contest called "Sci-Fi Scenes." The rules were simple: write an SF story precisely 250 words in length—no more, no less (title words didn't count, a fact I took full advantage of). Ten weekly winners would be chosen by a trio of judges (Shawna McCarthy of *Isaac Asimov's Science Fiction Magazine*; Robert Sheckley, the fiction editor of *Omni*; and Victoria Schochet, the editor-in-chief of SF at Berkley Publishing). Each winner received a hardcover copy of the first edition of Peter Nicholls's *Science Fiction Encyclopedia*; my story won in the contest's fourth week.

For several years, I had this entire story—in tiny type—printed on the back of my business card, and in 1987 a Washington, D.C., outfit called Story Cards printed it as the text inside a *bon voyage* card.

If I'm Here, Imagine
Where They Sent My Luggage

One look at the eyes of that allosaur had been enough: fiery red with anger, darting with hunger, and a deeper glow of . . . cunning. Those sickle claws may be great for shredding prey, but he can't run worth a damn on mud.

Come on, Allo-baby, you may have the armament, but I took Paleo 250 with Professor Blackhart!

Damn the professor, anyway. If it weren't for his class, I'd be on Altair III now, not running for my life across a prehistoric mud flat.

Those idiots at Starport Toronto said teleportation was a safe way to travel. "Just concentrate on your destination and the Jump-Link belt will do the rest."

Hah! I *was* concentrating, but when I saw that fat broad, I couldn't help thinking of a brontosaur. So I let my mind wander for half a second: the JumpLink belt still shouldn't have dumped me here with the dinosaurs. There should be enough juice left for one more Jump, if I can get it to work.

Damn, it's hard fiddling with your belt buckle while doing a three-minute kilometer. Let's see: if I re-route those fiber optics through that picoprocessor . . .

The *thwock-thwock* of clawed feet sucking out of mud is getting closer. Got to hurry. *Thwock-thwock!*

There! The timer's voice counts down: "Four."

Concentrate on Starport Toronto. Concentrate. *Thwock-thwock!*

"Three."

Toronto. The Starport. Concentrate. *Thwock-thwock!*

"Two."

Concentrate hard. Starport Toronto. No stray thoughts. *Thwock- thwock!*

"One."

Boy, am I going to give them Hell—

Where the Heart Is

Author's Introduction

In the summer of 1982, I worked at Bakka, Toronto's venerable science-fiction specialty store. One Saturday in July, a man claiming to be a film producer came in looking for an SF story that he might adapt into a short film. I suggested I could write an original script instead (having just received a degree in Radio and Television Arts, breaking into scriptwriting was much on my mind). He agreed, I did so—and, as a new writer, I learned an important lesson: nothing ever comes of encounters like that one.

Years later, I converted the script into a short story. In 1991, Nova Scotia publisher Lesley Choyce bought it for *Ark of Ice*, an anthology of Canadian SF he was putting together. That began my relationship with Lesley's Pottersfield Press, which later issued two anthologies I co-edited (*Crossing the Line: Canadian Mysteries with a Fantastic Twist* with David Skene-Melvin in 1998, and *Over the Edge: The Crime Writers of Canada Anthology* with Peter Sellers in

2000).

What pleases me most about this piece is that even in the script version from 1982, I predicted a global network of computers, which I called "the TerraComp Web." That makes me one of the very few SF writers to foresee the World Wide Web (heck, I even came close to getting the name right . . .).

Where the Heart Is

It was not the sort of welcome I had expected. True, I'd been gone a long time—so long, in fact, that no one I knew personally could possibly still be alive to greet me. Not Mom or Dad, not my sisters . . . not Wendy. That was the damnable thing about relativity: it tended to separate you from your relatives.

But, dammit, I'm a hero. A starprober. I'd piloted the *Terry Fox* all the way to Zubenelgenubi. I'd—communed—with alien minds. And now I was home. To be greeted by the Prime Minister would have been nice. Or the mayor of Toronto. They could even have wheeled in a geriatric grand-nephew or grand-niece. But this, this would never do.

I cupped my hands against naked cheeks—I'd shaved for this!—and called down the flexible tunnel that had sucked onto the *Foxtrot*'s airlock. "Hello!" A dozen lonely echoes wafted back to me. "Yoohoo! I'm home!" I knew it was false bravado. And I hated it.

I ran down the corridor. It opened onto an expanse of stippled tile. A red sign along the far wall proclaimed *Welcome to Starport Toronto*. Some welcome. I placed hands on hips and took stock of the tableau before me. The journalists' lounge was much as I remembered it. I'd never seen it empty before, though. Nor so neat. No plastic Coca-Cola cups half-full of flat pop, no discarded hardcopy news sheets: nothing marred the gleaming curves of modular furniture. I began a slow circumnavigation of the room. The place had apparently been deserted for some time. But that didn't seem right, for there was no dust. No spider-webs, either, come to think of it. Someone must be maintaining things. I sighed. Maybe the janitor would show up to pin a medal on my chest.

I walked into an alcove containing a bay window and pressed my hands against the curving pane. Sunlight stung my eyes. The starport was built high on Oak Ridges moraine, north of Toronto. Highway 11, overgrown with brush, was deserted. The fake mountain over at Canada's Wonderland had caved in and the roller coasters had collapsed into heaps of intestines. The checkerboard-pattern of farmland that I remembered had disappeared under a blanket of uniform green. The view towards Lake Ontario was blocked by stands of young maples. The CN Tower, tallest free-standing structure in the world (when I left, anyway), still thrust high above everything else. But the Skypod with its revolving restaurant and night club had slipped far down the tapered spindle and was canted at an angle. "You go away for 140 years and they change everything," I muttered.

From behind me: "Most people prefer to live away from big cities these days." I wheeled. It was a strange, multitudinous voice, like a hundred people talking in unison. A machine rolled into the alcove. It was a cube, perhaps a meter on a side, translucent, like an aquarium filled with milk. The number 104 glowed on two opposing faces. Mounted on the upper surface was an assembly of lenses, which swung up to look at me.

"What are you?" I asked.

The same voice as before answered: a choir talking instead of singing. "An information robot. I was designed to display data, including launch schedules, bills of lading, and fluoroscopes of packages, as required."

I looked back out at where my city had been. "There were almost three million people in Toronto when I left," I said.

"You are Carl Hunt."

I paused. "I'm glad someone remembers."

"Of course." The tank cleared and amber letters glowed within: my name, date and place of birth, education and employment records—a complete dossier.

"That's me, all right: the 167-year-old man." I looked down at the strange contraption. "Where is everybody?"

The robot started moving away from me, out of the alcove, back into the journalists' lounge. "Much has happened since you left, Mr. Hunt."

I quickly caught up with the little machine. "You can call me Carl. And—damn; when I left there were no talking robots. What do I call you?"

We reached the mouth of a door-lined corridor. The machine was leading. I took a two-meter stride to pull out in front. "I have no individuality," it said. "Call me what you will."

I scratched my chin. "Raymo. I'll call you Raymo."

"Raymo was the name of your family's pet Labrador Retriever."

My eyes widened in surprise then narrowed in suspicion. "How did you know that?"

Raymo's many voices replied quickly. "I am a limb of the TerraComp Web—"

"The what?"

"The world computer network, if you prefer. I know all that is known." We continued down the hallway, me willing to go in the general direction Raymo wanted, so long as I, not the machine, could lead. Presently the robot spoke again. "Tell me about your mission."

"I prefer to report to the Director of Spaceflight."

Raymo's normally instantaneous reply was a long time in coming. "There is no person with that title anymore, Carl."

I turned around, blocking Raymo's path, and seized the top edges of the robot's crystalline body. "What?"

The bundle of lenses pivoted up to take stock of me. "This starport has been maintained solely for your return. All the other missions came back decades ago."

I felt moisture on my forehead. "What happened to the people? Did—did one of the other starprobes bring back a plague?"

"I *will* explain," said Raymo. "First, though, you must tell us about your mission."

We exited into the lobby. "Why do you want to know?" I could hear an edge on my words.

"You are something new under the sun."

Something new—? I shrugged. "Two years ship time to get to Zubenelgenubi, two years exploring the system. I found intelligent life—"

"Yes!" An excited robot?

"On a moon of the sixth planet were creatures of liquid light." I paused, remembering: two suns dancing in the green sky, living streams of gold splashing on the rocks, cascading uphill, singing their lifesongs. There was so much to tell; where to start? I waved my arm vaguely. "The data is in the *Terry Fox*'s computer banks."

"You must help us to interface, then. Tell me—"

Enough! "Look, Raymo, I've been gone for six years my time. Even a crusty misanthrope like me misses people eventually."

"Yet almost a century and a half have passed for Earth since you left—"

Across the lobby, I spied a door labeled *Station Master's office*. I bounded to it. Locked. I threw my shoulder against it. Nothing. Again. Still nothing. A third time. It popped back on its hinges. I stood on the threshold but did not enter. Inside were squat rows of gleaming computing equipment. My jaw dropped.

Raymo the robot rolled up next to me. "Pay no attention to that man behind the curtain."

I shuddered. "Is this what's become of everybody? Replaced by computers?"

"No, Carl. That system is simply one of many in the TerraComp Web."

"But what's it for?"

"It is used for a great many things."

"Used? Used by who?"

"By whom." A pause. "By all of us. It is the new order."

I pulled back. My adrenalin was flowing. To my left was the office. In front of me was Raymo, slipping slowly forward on casters. To my right, the lobby. Behind me . . . I shot a glance over my shoulder. Behind me was—what? Unknown territory. Maybe a way back to the *Terry Fox*.

"Do not be afraid," said Raymo.

I began to back away. The robot kept pace with me. The milky tank that made up most of Raymo's body grew clear again. A lattice of fluorescent lines formed within. Patterns of rainbow lightning flashed in time with my pounding heartbeat. Kaleidoscopic lights swirled, melded, merged. The lights seemed to go on forever and ever and ever, spiraling deeper and deeper and . . .

"A lot can happen in fourteen decades, Carl." The multitude that made up Raymo's voice had taken on a sing-song up-and-down quality. "The world is a better place than it has ever been before." A hundred mothers soothing a baby. "You can be a part of it." I knew that my backing was slowing, that I really should be trying to get away, but . . . but . . . but . . . Those lights were so pretty, so relaxing, so . . . A strobe began to wink in the center of Raymo's camera cluster. I usually find flashing lights irritating, but this one was so . . . interesting. I could stare at it forever . . .

Head over heels sharp jab of pain goddammit! I tripped as I backed, falling away from the lights. Scrabbling to my feet, I shielded my eyes. My fingers curled into a fist. I hauled back and rammed my arm into the center of Raymo's tank. As the glass shattered, the tank imploded. I ran through the lobby. Pausing at a juncture with two corridors, I looked at my carved and bleeding hand. I rubbed it, winced, and dug out a splinter of glass.

Left? Right? Which way to go? Dammit, it'd been six years since I'd last been in this building. Seemed to me the loading docks were back that way. My stride slowed as I ran, partly due to pain, partly because Raymo was already eating my dust.

"Believe in us, Carl." The same torrent of voices—but from up ahead. Out of the shadows rolled a second robot cube, identical to Raymo except that this one's sides glowed with the number 287. I looked over my shoulder. Raymo, sparks spitting from its shattered image tank, had castered into the end of the hallway. Sandwiched. "We have your best interests at heart," said Raymo.

I shouted: "Where are all the people?" *Easy, Carl. Panic's the last thing you need.*

The voices came in stereo now, from robot 287 in front and Raymo in the rear. "The people are *here*, Carl. All around you."

"There's nobody here!" Keep calm—dammit—calm! "What the hell's going on?"

Robot 287 was edging closer. I could hear the faint hum of Raymo moving in, as well. The voices surrounded me, soft, so very soft. "Join with us." Lights began to coalesce in 287's tank, all the colors of the starbow that had accompanied my ship on its long, lonely voyage. Swirling, dancing colors. I pivoted. Raymo was a dozen meters away, its tank dark and charred. I exploded down the corridor, legs pounding, pounding, pounding. I crouched low and leapt. Up, up, and over top of Raymo, my boot crashing through the jagged glass wall of the tank's far side. I ran back into the starport's lobby.

"Listen to us, Carl Hunt." Voices, like those the robots had spoken with, but clearer, more resonant, coming from nowhere, coming from everywhere. I halted, spreads my hands. "What do you want from me?"

"We want . . .you. Join us!"

I found myself shouting. "Who are you?"

The beautiful woman sitting opposite Carl tried to sink down in the crushed-velour upholstery. "Sssh, Carl. You're making a scene."

Carl slammed his fist onto the restaurant table. Wine sloshed out of his glass. "Dammit, Wendy, don't lie to me."

"Professor Cayman and I spent the entire weekend digging for arrowheads. I'm his research assistant—not his playmate."

"Then what were you doing sharing a tent with him?"

"You wouldn't believe me if I told you."

"You wouldn't believe me if I told you," said the voices. I ran through the lobby, swinging my right hand up to rub sweat from my forehead. Blood splattered across my face. My hand was more seriously hurt than I'd thought. A bloody archipelago of splotches trailed behind me across the lobby floor.

The voices again: "We're human, Hunt. A lot has happened since you left." I burst through a double doorway into the deserted press gallery. "We are the TerraComp Web. We are the sum of humanity." I ran past the tiered seating to the door at the other end. Locked. Breathing raggedly, I beat my hands against the mahogany, the injured one leaving a bloody mark each time it hit. "Think of it," said all the voices. "By joining with the global computer system, humankind has achieved everything it could ever want."

A woman's voice separated from the vocal melee. "Unlimited knowledge! Any fact instantly available. Any question instantly answered."

A man's voice followed, deep and hearty. "Immortality! Each of us lives forever as a free-floating consciousness in the memory banks."

And a child's voice: "Freedom from hunger and pain!"

Then, in unison, plus a hundred more voices on top: "Join with us!"

I slumped to the floor, my back against the door. I tried to shout but the words came out as hoarse whispers. "Leave me alone."

"We only want what's best for you."

"Go away, then! Just leave me the hell alone."

The lights in the gallery began to slowly dim. I lay back, too tired to even look to my slashed hand. Another robot, different in structure, rolled up quietly next to me. It was a long flatbed with forklift arms and lenses on a darting goose-neck. It spoke in the same whispering multitude. "Join with us."

I rallied some strength. "You're . . . not . . . human—"

"Yes, we are. In every way that counts."

"What . . . What about individuality?"

"There is no more loneliness. We are one."

I shook my head. "A man has to be himself; make his own mistakes."

"Individuality is childhood." The robot edged closer. "Community is adulthood."

With much effort, I managed to pull myself to my feet. "Can you love?"

"We have infinite intimacy. Each mind mingling—solute and solvent—into a collective consciousness. Join us!"

"And—sex?"

"We are immortal. There is no need."

I pushed off the wall and hobbled back the way I'd come. "Count me out!" I fell through the doors into the lobby. There had to be a way outside.

I turned into a darkened hallway. Bracing against a wall, I caught my breath. Suddenly, I became aware of a faint phosphorescent glow at the other end of the hall. It was another information robot, like Raymo, with the number 28 on its sides. I held my arm out in front of my body. "Stay back, demon."

"But you're hurt, Carl."

I looked at my mangled hand. "What's that to you?"

"Asimov's First Law of Robotics: 'A robot may not injure a human being, or, through inaction, allow a human being to come to harm.'" As the voices spoke, the words materialized in glowing amber within 28's tank. "If I do not tend to your hand, it may become infected. Indeed, if the bleeding is not stanched soon, you may suffer shock due to blood loss."

"So you respond like a classical robot?" My tone grew sharp. "I order you not to come any closer."

Twenty-eight continued to roll towards me. "Your health is my primary concern."

I peeled open a Velcro fastener on my hip and removed a metallic wedge. The thick end was peppered with the holes of a speaker grille and a numeric keypad checkerboarded one major face. I held it up in front of me, as if to ward off the approaching robot. "This is a remote tie-in to my landing module's onboard computer. If you come any closer, I will cause the landing module's fusion motors to overload. You, me, and what's left of the city of Toronto will go up in one giant ball of hellfire."

The robot stopped. I could hear the pounding of my heart. I stared fiercely at 28. The robot's crystalline eyes stared back. Stand-off. Five seconds. Ten. Fifteen.

The voices were plaintive: "I only wish to tend to your wounds." The box-like automaton eased forward slightly.

I hit keys in rapid succession. "Back off!"

Carl rolled off Wendy and she slipped into his arms. "You know," he said, gently stroking the small of her back, "they're going to announce who gets Starprobe 12 tomorrow. If it's me, I'm going to go."

Wendy stiffened ever so slightly. "Everybody you know will be dead when you get back."

"I know all that."

"And you still want to go?"

"More than anything."

Wendy moved to kiss him. "You're such a stubborn man."

The robot came to another halt. "You're such a stubborn man."

I looked quickly to my left and right. "How do I get out of here?"

Silence.

I fingered the tie-in wedge again. "Answer me, damn you."

"There are unlocked doors leading outside down the corridor on your left. But you must tend to your injury."

I looked down at my hand, caked with dried blood. Thick liquid still welled from shredded knuckles. Damn. I nodded slowly. "Where can I get a first-aid kit?"

"I brought one for you," said 28. A small slot opened in the base on which the robot's image cube rested. A hinged plastic box with a red cross flexographed on its lid clacked to the tiled floor. A dull hum, almost a white noise, issued from 28's twin speakers.

"Back away from it," I called. Twenty-eight retreated slightly. "Damn it, move right away. Fifteen meters back." Casters whirred as the robot receded perhaps a dozen meters. "More!" Twenty-eight slowly slid farther back. I stepped forward, crouched, set the interface wedge down, opened the box, and proceeded to mummify my hand in white gauze.

"You really should clean the wound first," said the multitude from 28's speakers. "And disinfect it. The plumbing isn't running anymore, but there is an old supply of bottled water in the men's room. If you should require—"

"I require nothing from you."

"As you wish, Carl. We only want to—" I whirled around, pivoting on my heel. Another robot had slipped up behind me, its approach masked by the droning noise from 28. It scooped up my remote control and wheeled across the lobby. Number 28 careened around to block my pursuit. I didn't know the damn things could move so fast. "We could not allow you to keep that device." The voices were almost apologetic. "We can allow no harm to come to you."

Football. I'd played some in high school. Deke right! The robot lurched to block. Deke left! The cube moved again, but ponderously, confused. Right! Left! Right! I barreled past the robot and ran down the corridor to my left. Golden sunlight poured in through glass doors at the end of the hall. I stretched out both arms as I ran, one to push open each of the double doors. Home free!

Another of the info cubes was waiting for me outside. This one was labeled 334. I wondered how high the bloody numbers went.

Like all the robots, this one spoke with the voice of hundreds. "Do not be alarmed, Carl."

One side was blocked by a high hedge. Number 334 stood too far in front for me to fake it out. In the distance I could see a pack of assorted robots rolling in from the loading area.

"There is really nothing to worry about." A few flashes of color appeared within the robot's tank.

"Why don't you leave me alone?"

The voices were soothing. "We will. Soon."

The lights began to dance more rapidly within the cube. Soon the seductive strobe began its hypnotic flashing. "There, now. Just relax, Carl."

Dammit, I'm a starprober! Keep a level head. Don't let them . . . Don't . . . Don't . . .

The image cube exploded in a shower of sparks. A brick lay in the center of the smoldering machine. "Over here, boy!"

From across the asphalt a ragged, filthy, old, old man beckoned wildly to me. I stared for a second in surprise, then hurried over to the bent figure. We ran on and scuttled under a concrete overhang. He and I both collapsed to catch our breaths. In the confined space I reeled at the man's smell. He reeked of sweat and wood smoke and more sweat: a rag doll made from ancient socks and rancid underwear.

He cut loose a cackling laugh showing popcorn-kernel teeth. "Bet you're surprised to see me, boy."

I regarded the old coot, crumpled and weather-hewn. "You bet. Who are you?"

"They call me String. Cap'n String."

I felt a broad grin spread across my face as I extended my hand. "I sure am glad to see you, String. My name's—"

"You're Hunt. Carl Hunt." String's knobby fingers shook my hand with surprising strength. "I've been waiting for you."

"Waiting for me?" I shook my head. Relativity is a crazy thing. "You weren't even born when I left."

String cackled again. "They talked about you in school. Last of the starprobes. Mission to Zubenelgenubi." The laugh again. "I'm a space buff, you know. You guys were my heroes."

For the first time, I noticed the filthy, tattered jacket String was wearing. It was covered with patches. Not mismatched pieces of cloth repairing rips and tears: space mission patches. *Friendship 7. Apollo 11. Apollo-Soyuz.* A host of *Vostoks.* The *Aurora* missions. *Ares. Glooscap.* And, yes, the Starprobes. A complete history of spaceflight. "String, what happened to Toronto? Where are all the people?"

String shook his grizzled head. "Ain't nobody else. Just me and the sandworms. Plenty of food around. No one to eat it."

"So it's true. The computers have taken over."

"Damned machines! Harlie! Colossus! P-1! Men got to be men, Hunt. Don't let them get you."

I smiled. "Don't worry about me."

String had a far-off, sad look. "They canceled the space program, you know. Your flight was the last." He shook his head. "Only thing kept me going all these years was knowing one of the spacers was going to return."

"Spacers?" I'd never heard that term before outside of a comic book.

String's gaze came home to roost above his bird's-nest beard. "What was it like . . . out there? Did you have a"—he lowered his voice—"sense of wonder?"

"It was beautiful. Desolate. Lonely. I met intelligent aliens."

He whooped and shoved his scrawny arm high. "All right!"

"But I'll tell you, String, I felt more at home with the liquid lights of Zubenelgenubi than I do here on Earth."

"Liquid lights! Dragons of Pern! Tharks of Barsoom!"

"What—?"

"The Final Frontier, boy! You were part of it! You—" String jumped to his feet. A robot had slipped up on us. "Run, boy! Run for all you're worth!"

We ran and ran through the starport grounds, past concrete bunkers and concrete towers, through concrete arches, down concrete tunnels, and along concrete sidewalks. Ahead, in the center of a vast concrete platter sat my boomerang-shaped landing module, the *Foxtrot*.

String stopped, rubbed his arm, and winced in pain. Two info robots and a cargo flatbed rolled out from behind the *Foxtrot*. The one in the middle, a cube labeled 101, moved slightly forward. "Let me tend to the old man. He requires medical aid."

"Leave me alone, machine," String shouted. "Hunt, don't let them have me!"

So near, so near. I turned away from my waiting ship and ran with String in the opposite direction. I could feel my own chest heaving and could hear a ragged, wet sound accompanying String's pained breathing. Once we were well away, I stopped running and reached out an arm to stop the old man, as well. We leaned against a gray wall for support. "String, you've got to tell me. What happened to everybody?"

He managed a faint cackle. "Future shock, boy! They built computers bigger than they could handle. It started before I was born; just after you left. Everybody was numbered, filed. A terminal in every home. No need to go to the office. No need to go shopping. No need to go to the bank. *No need!*"

I shook the man. "What about the people?"

"If you've got machines to do everything for you, you just fade away, boy. Obsolete. You end up as just a shell. The 'New Order,' they called it."

"People don't just 'fade away.' "

"I seen it with my own eyes, boy! It happened!"

I shook my head. "There's got to be more to it."

The voices spoke from the PA horns mounted high on the walls. "There is. Much more. Hear us out, Hunt."

String ran off and I followed. Suddenly, the old man stopped and grabbed at his chest. I put a hand on his shoulder. "Are you all right, String?"

"I don't feel so good."

"Let us help him," said the voices.

"Keep them away from me, Hunt." String forced the words out around clenched teeth.

"I—"

"Keep them away! Swear it!"

I looked up. An info robot was approaching fast. "I swear it."

The old man doubled over, clawing at his chest. He reached into a tattered pocket and pulled out an ornate, gaudy pistol. "Here, take my gun."

I grabbed it, turned, and aimed at the robot, now only a few meters away. My finger squeezed the trigger. A jet of water splashed against the robot's image cube.

I looked down, dumbfounded, at the dying old man. "A spacer," said String, almost incoherently. "I'd have given anything to have been you."

I felt my eyes stinging. "String . . ."

The crab-apple head lolled back, dead eyes staring up at the sky. The robot rolled slowly next to me. "I'm sorry, Carl," it said softly.

I exploded. "If you hadn't chased us, he wouldn't have had the heart attack."

The robot, number Four, responded quickly. "If you'd let us treat him, we could have prevented it."

I looked away and rubbed my eyes.

"What was Earth like when you left, Carl?"

"You seem to know everything," I snapped. "You tell me."

"It was filthy. Polluted. Dying. People starving across three-quarters of the globe. Petty wars raging in a dozen countries. The final conflict perhaps only days away."

"What's your point?"

"Look around you," said robot Four, its lens assembly swinging to and fro. "Things are better now. Cities are gardens and forests. Breathe the air: it's sweet and clean. There is no violence. No hate. No misery. Computers made this possible."

"By getting rid of the people! Some bargain!"

The symphony of voices grew deep, hard. "*You* left. You knew your mission would take a century and a half of Earth-time. You took a gamble. Some might say you hit the jackpot. You've come home to Utopia."

I measured my words evenly. "If there are no people, then this is Hell."

The robot rolled slightly closer. "Individual memory patterns are still separable from the whole." The image tank became transparent. "Recording began scant years after your departure." The tank filled with a matrix of glowing cubes, each perhaps ten centimeters on a side, each slightly tinged with a different color. "It took decades to process all seven billion humans." The cubes subdivided, like cells undergoing mitosis, each splitting into eight smaller cubes. Near the top of the tank the cubes were black, farther down, a rich almond. "Only a handful resisted in the end." The cubes divided again, tiny holographic pixels, making up the head and shoulders of a young woman. "The old man, String, was the last surviving holdout." The cubes split yet again, refining the grain, growing richer in color. "Now, all that is left is you . . . and your past."

I felt myself grow flush with excitement. "Wendy!"

The image remained still, but I tingled at the sound of that single, lyrical voice emanating from the robot's twin speakers. "Hello, Carl."

"Wendy, darling—" I shook myself. "No. It can't be you."

"It *is* me, Carl."

"But it's been a hundred and forty years since—since I left you. You're . . . dead."

"I was one of the first to transcend into the computer." She paused, ever so briefly. "I didn't want to lose you again. I would've tried almost anything."

"You waited over a century for me?"

"I would have waited a millennium."

"But how do I know it's really you?"

The voice laughed. "How do *I* know it's really *you?*"

I set my jaw. "Well?"

"You always wear your pajamas inside out."

"That damn robot even knew the name of my dog. Tell me something no one else could possibly know."

She paused for a moment. "Remember that night in High Park—"

New tears dissolved the yellow crystals String's passing had left at the corners of my eyes. "It is you!"

The voice laughed again. "In spirit if not in body."

But I shook my head. "How could you do this? Give up physical existence?"

"I did it for you. I did it for love."

"You weren't this romantic when I left. We used to fight."

"Over money. Over sex. Over all the things that don't matter anymore." Her tone grew warmer. "I love you, Carl."

"We said our goodbyes a long time ago. You didn't say 'I love you' then."

"But in your heart you must have known that I did. It would have been unfair for me to tell you how deeply I felt before you left. You were like String, your head in the stars. I couldn't ask you to give up the thing you wanted most: your one chance to visit another world." She was silent for a moment, then said, "If you love something, set it free . . ."

She'd sent me a card with that inscription once. Somehow it had hurt at the time: it was as if she was telling me to leave. I didn't understand then. But I did now. "If he comes back, he's yours . . ."

"If he doesn't, he never was."

"I love you, too, Wendy." I lightly touched the robot's image cube.

"Join with *me*," said the beautiful voice from the speakers.

"I—"

"Carl . . ."

"I'm—afraid. And . . ."

"Suspicious?"

"Yes." I turned from the image. "I've been chased all over and warned against you by the only living soul I've seen."

"The robots followed you for your own protection. String's warnings were those of a worn-out mind."

"But why did you try to—absorb—me without my consent?"

"You've seen what none of us have seen," said Wendy. "Other intelligent beings. We crave your memories. In our enthusiasm to know what you know, to feel what you have felt, we erred."

"You erred?"

" 'Tis human."

I looked deep into the image tank. "What if I choose not to transcend into the world computer network?"

"I'll cry."

"You'll—cry? That's it? I mean—I have the choice?"

"Of course. You can live the life of a scavenger, like String."

"What if I want to go back to Zubenelgenubi? Back to the liquid lights?"

Her voice was stiff. "That's up to you."

"Then that is what I choose." There was silence for a moment, then Wendy's image slowly began to break up into colored cubes. The little robot started to roll away. "Wait! Where are you going?"

It was the multitude of voices that answered. "To help prepare your ship for another journey."

I followed behind. Wendy, dear, sweet Wendy . . .

The cube rounded out onto the landing platter. A variety of robots—flatbeds, info cubes, and some kinds I hadn't seen before—were already at work on the *Foxtrot*; others were rolling in from various places around the starport. I looked at the ship, its sleek lines, its powerful engines. I thought of the giant, lonely *Terry Fox* up in orbit. I thought and thought and thought. "Stop," I said at last.

The robots did just that. "Yes, Carl?" said the multitude.

I hesitated. The words weren't easy. But they were the truth. "I—I just had to see for myself that it was *my* choice; that I still had my free will." I cleared my throat. "Wendy?"

The tank on the nearest info robot became transparent. Interference-pattern cubes coalesced into the pretty face within. "Yes, darling?"

"I love you."

"You know I love you, too, Carl."

I steeled myself. "And I'm staying."

Her voice sang with joy. "Just relax, darling. This won't hurt a bit."

Her image was replaced by dancing and whirling prismatic lights. I was aware of a new image forming in the tanks of the other info robots, an image growing more and more refined as cubic pixels divided and subdivided: an image of the two of us, side by side, together, forever. I let myself go.

I was home at last.

Lost in the Mail

Finalist for the Aurora Award
for Best Short Story of the Year

Author's Introduction

A writer is usually too modest to mention his own reviews, but I have a reason in this instance, so please bear with me: "Among the full-length stories in *TransVersions* #3, the standout is 'Lost in the Mail' "—*Tangent*; "This great and gimmicky story almost makes the whole package worth it all by itself"—*Scavenger's Newsletter*; "Excellent, imaginative, and well-written, further evidence of Sawyer's talents"—*NorthWords*; "If there is any justice in the world, Sawyer should win the Aurora Award for the emotive 'Lost in the Mail' "—*Sempervivum*.

Not too shabby, eh? And although I didn't win the Aurora—Canada's top honor in SF—that year (Robert Charles Wilson's fabulous "The Perseids" did), I did come in second. But the story in question was rejected *seventeen* times before it sold—which just goes to show that a writer shouldn't give up if he or she believes in a particular piece of work.

"Lost in the Mail" is not autobiographical—although I can see how people giving it a cursory read might think that it is. Like Jacob Coin, I used to want to be a paleontologist. And, again like him, I spent many years as a nonfiction writer. But Jacob is a sad man, and I am not. He decided not to pursue his dream, and instead settled into an uninteresting, uneventful life. Me, I did go after one of my dreams—being an SF writer. I'm pleased—and, frankly, a little surprised—that such a quiet, introspective, personal tale struck a responsive chord with so many people.

Lost in the Mail

The intercom buzzer sounded like a cardiac defibrillator giving a jump-start to a dying man. I sprang from my chair, not even pausing to save the article I was working on, threw back the dead-bolt, and hurried into the corridor. My apartment was next to the stairwell, so I swung through the fire door and bounded down the three flights to the lobby, through the inner glass door, and into the building's entry chamber.

The Pope was digging through his bag. Of course, he wasn't really the Pope—he probably wasn't even Catholic—but he bore a definite resemblance to John Paul II. The underarms of his pale blue Canada Post shirt were soaked and he was wearing those dark uniform shorts that made him look like an English school-boy. We exchanged greetings; he spoke in an obscure European accent.

A hole in the panel above the mailboxes puckered like an infected wound. John Paul inserted a brass key into it. The panel flopped forward the way a pull-down bed does, giving him access to a row of little cubicles. He began stuffing the day's round of junk mail into these—a bed of fertilizer for the first-class goodies. He left my mailbox empty, though, and instead dealt out a full set of leaflets and sale flyers onto the counter that jutted from the wall.

For most people the real mail amounted to one or two pieces, but I got a lot more than that—including a copy of the *Ryerson*

Rambler, the alumni magazine from Ryerson Polytechnic University. When he was finished, the Pope scooped up my pile and handed it to me. As usual, it was too much to fit comfortably into the box. "Thanks," I said, and headed back into the lobby.

I'd promised myself that I'd always take the stairs up to the third floor—one of these days I'd lose that spare tire—but, well, the elevator was right there, its door invitingly open...

Back in my apartment I sat in the angle of my L-shaped couch with my feet, as always, swung up on the right-hand section. The mail contained the usual round of press releases, several bills, and the *Ryerson Rambler*. The cover showed an alumnus dressed in African tribal gear. According to the caption on the contents page, some relative of his had abdicated as chief of a tribe in Ghana and he was off to take his place. Amazing how people's lives can change completely overnight.

I was surprised to find a second magazine stuck to the back of the *Rambler*. *University of Toronto Alumni Magazine*, it said. Down in the lower-right corner of its blue-and-white cover were three strips of adhesive partially covered with a frayed paper residue. Its address label must have torn off and the glue had stuck onto the back of my magazine.

Intriguing: I'd been accepted by U of T after high school, but had decided to go to Ryerson instead. If I'd stayed with U of T, I'd be a paleontologist today, sifting through the remains of ancient life. Instead, I'm a freelance journalist specializing in the petrochemical industry, a contributing editor of *Canadian Plastics*, an entirely competent writer, and the only life I sift through is my own.

I began thumbing through the magazine. Here, in thirty-two glossy pages, was my past that could have been but wasn't: graduation ceremonies at Convocation Hall, an article about the 115th year of the campus paper, *The Varsity*; a calendar of events at Hart House . . .

If I'd gone to U of T instead of Ryerson, the photos might have stirred nostalgic laughter and tears within me. Instead they lay there, halftone shadows, emotionless. Fossils of somebody else's life.

I continued leafing through the magazine until I came to the final pages. There, under the heading "Alumni Reports," were photos of graduates and blurbs on their careers and personal triumphs. I was surprised to find a paleo grad—it was such a small program—but at the bottom of page 30 there was an entry about a man named Zalmon Bernstein. The picture was hokey: Bernstein, a toothy grin splitting his features, holding up a geologist's pick. He'd finished his Ph.D. in 1983, it said, the same year I would have likely finished mine had I gone there. Doubtless we would have known each other; we might even have been friends.

I read his blurb two or three times. Married. Now living in Drumheller, Alberta. Research Associate with the Royal Tyrrell Museum of Paleontology. Working summers on the continuing excavations in Dinosaur Provincial Park.

He'd done all right for himself. I felt a twinge of sadness, and put the magazine aside. The other mail was nothing urgent, so I ambled back to my computer and continued poking at my article on polystyrene purification.

The next day, John Paul greeted me with his usual "Morning, Mr. Coin." As always, I felt at a disadvantage since I didn't know his name. When he'd begun this route two years ago, I'd wanted to ask what it was. I fancied it would be a mysterious, foreign-sounding thing ending in a vowel. But I'd missed my opportunity and now it was much too late. Anyway, he knows far more about me than I could ever hope to know about him. Because my bank insists on spelling out my name in full, he knows that my middle initial—which I use in my byline—stands for Horton (yuck). He knows what credit cards I have. He knows I'm a journalist, assuming he'd recognize a press kit when he saw one. He knows I read *Playboy* and *Canadian Geographic* and *Ellery Queen's Mystery Magazine*. He even knows who my doctor is. He could write my biography, all based on the things of mine he carries around in his heavy blue sack.

As usual, he was placing my mail in a separate pile. He topped it off with a thin white-and-orange book sealed in a polyethylene bag. I gathered my booty, wished him good day, and headed back. The elevator was only on two, so I called it down. I did that occasionally. If it was on three, I hardly ever waited for it and if it was on the top floor, well, once in a blue moon I might use it.

Someday I'm going to lose that spare tire.

As I rode up, I glanced at the white-and-orange book. It was a scholarly journal. My step-uncle, a university professor, had hundreds of such publications making neat rows of identical spines on the shelves of his musty den. This one looked interesting, though, at least to me: *The Journal of Vertebrate Paleontology*.

For some reason I swung my feet up to the left instead of the right on my L-couch. The *Journal*'s table of contents was printed on its cover. I recognized some of the words in the titles from my old interest in dinosaurs. *Ornithischian. Hadrosaurs. Cretaceous.*

I glanced at the piece of tractor-feed paper that had been slipped into the mailing bag: my name and address, all right. Who would have sent me such a thing? My birthday was rolling around—the big four-oh—so maybe somebody had got me a subscription as a semi-gag gift. The poly bag stretched as I yanked at it. Having written 750,000 words about plastics in my career, you'd think I'd be able to open those things easily.

Subscription rates were printed inside the journal's front cover. Eighty-five American dollars a year! I didn't have many friends and none of them would shell out that much on a gift for me, even if it was meant as a joke.

I closed the book and looked at the table of contents again. Dry stuff. Say, there's an article by that U of T guy, Zalmon Bernstein: *A New Specimen of* Lambeosaurus lambei *from the Badlands of Alberta, Canada*. I continued down the list of titles.

Correlations Between Crest Size and Shape of the Pre-Orbital Fenestra in Hadrosaurs. "Pre-orbital fenestra." What a great-sounding phrase. All those lovely Latin and Greek polysyllables. Here's another one—

I stopped dead. *Scrobiculated Fontanelle Margins in Pachyrhinosaurs and Other Centrosaurinae from the Chihuahuan Desert of Mexico,* by J. H. Coin.

By me.

My head swam for a moment. I was used to seeing my byline in print. It's just that I usually remembered writing whatever it was attached to, that's all.

It must be somebody with the same name, of course. Hell, Coin wasn't that unusual. Besides, this guy was down in Mexico. I turned to the indicated page. There was the article, the writer's name, and his institutional affiliation: Research Associate, Department of Vertebrate Paleontology, Royal Ontario Museum, Toronto, Canada.

It came back in a deluge of memory. The ROM had undertaken a dig in Mexico a few summers ago. A local newspaper, *The Toronto Sun,* had sponsored it. I remembered it as much because of my dormant interest in dinosaurs as because it seemed so out-of-character for the tabloid *Sun*—best known for its bikini-clad Sunshine Girls—to foot the bill for a scientific expedition.

I was disoriented for several seconds. What was going on? Why did I even have a copy of this publication? Then it hit me. Of course. All so simple, really. There must be someone at the ROM with the same initials and last name as me. He (or she, maybe) had written this article. The *Journal* had somehow lost his address, so they'd looked him up in the phone book to send a contributor's copy. They'd gotten the wrong J. H. Coin, that's all.

I decided I'd better return the guy's *Journal* to him. Besides, this other Coin would probably get a kick out of the story of how his copy had ended up with me. I know I would.

I phoned the Royal Ontario Museum and spoke to a receptionist who had a pleasant Jamaican accent. "Hello," I said. "J. H. Coin, please."

"Can you tell me which department?" she asked.

He can't have made a big name for himself if the receptionist didn't know where he worked. "Paleontology."

"Vert or invert?"

For a second I didn't understand the question. "Oh—vertebrate."

"I'll put you through to the departmental assistant." I often had to contact presidents of petrochemical firms for quotes, so I knew that how difficult it was to get hold of someone could be a sign of how important he or she was. But this shunting struck me as different. It wasn't that J. H. Coin had to be shielded from annoying calls. Rather, it was more like he was a fossil, lost in layers of sediment.

"Vert paleo," said a woman's voice.

"Hello. J. H. Coin, please."

There was a pause, as though the departmental assistant was momentarily confused. "Ah, just a second."

At first I thought that she, too, hadn't heard of J. H. Coin, but when the next person came on I knew that wasn't it. The voice seemed slightly alien to me: deeper, less resonant, more nasal than my own—at least than my own sounds to me. "Hello," he said, politely, but sounding somewhat surprised at being called at work. "Jacob Coin speaking."

Jacob and Coin. Sure, some names go together automatically, like John and Smith, or Tom and Sawyer or, if you believe the Colombian Coffee Growers' commercials, Juan and Valdez. But Jacob and Coin weren't a natural pair. I was named after my mother's father. Not some literary allusion, not some easy assonance, just a random line of circumstances.

I wanted to ask this Jacob Coin what his "H" stood for. I wanted to ask him what his mother's maiden name was. I wanted to know his birth date, his social insurance number, whether his left leg gave him trouble when it was about to rain, whether he was allergic to cheese, if he had managed to keep his weight under control. But I didn't have to. I already knew the answers.

I hung up the phone. I hated doing it only because I know how much I hate it when that happens to me—how much he must hate it, too.

I heeded John Paul's buzz again on Friday. This time, though, I didn't wait for him to assemble my pile of mail. Instead, I snapped up each envelope as he placed it on the counter. The first three really were for me: a check from one of my publishers, a birthday card from my insurance agent, and my cable-TV bill. But the fourth was bogus: a gray envelope addressed to J. H. Coin, Ph.D. The return address was *Royal Ontario Museum Staff Association*.

"Wait a minute," I said.

The Pontiff was busy dealing out lives into the little mailboxes. "Hmm?"

"This one isn't for me."

"Oh, sorry." He reached out to take it. For a moment I thought about keeping it, holding on to that piece of what might have been, but, no, I let him have it.

He looked at it, then frowned. "You're J. H. Coin, ain't you?"

"Well, yes."

"Then it is for you." He proffered the envelope, but now that I'd let it go I couldn't bring myself to take it back.

"No. I mean, I'm not *that* J. H. Coin." The Pope said nothing. He just stood there holding the letter out towards me. I shook my head. "I don't have a Ph.D."

"Take that up with whoever wrote you," he said. "I worry about apartment numbers and postal codes, not diplomas."

"But I don't want it. It's not mine. I don't work at the Museum."

John Paul let out a heavy sigh. "Mr. Coin, it's addressed correctly. It's got sufficient postage. I have to deliver it to you."

"Can't you send it back?"

"I've been doing you a big favor all this time, calling you down instead of stuffing your things into that little box. Don't make me sorry that I've been nice to you." He looked me straight in the eye. "Take the letter."

"But yesterday you brought me *The Journal of Vertebrate Paleontology*. And the day before, the *University of Toronto Alumni Magazine*. None of those things were meant for me."

"Who's to say what's meant for any of us, Mr. Coin? All I know is I've got to deliver the mail. It's my job."

He went back to his bag. The next thing he pulled out happened to be for me, too. Sort of. Instead of placing it on the counter, he tried to hand it to me directly. It was a letter hand-addressed to Mr. and Mrs. Jake Coin.

I shook my head again, more in wonder than negation this time. "There is no Mrs. Coin."

"You have to take it," he said.

It was tempting, in a way. But no, she wasn't *my* wife. She wasn't part of my world. I didn't move.

He shrugged and put the envelope in the empty cubicle that had my apartment number on it.

I didn't want this other Coin's life forced upon me. "Take that out of there," I said.

John Paul continued distributing mail, ignoring me the way he might ignore a stranger who tried to strike up a conversation on the subway. I grabbed his arms and attempted to swing him around. The old guy was a lot stronger than he looked—thanks, I guess, to hauling that great sack of letters around. He pushed me away easily and I fell backward against the vestibule's inner glass door. For a horrible instant I thought the pane was going to break and come tumbling down on me, but it held solid. The Pontiff had wheeled around and was now aiming a tiny aerosol can of Mace at me.

"Don't ever try that again," he said in his mysterious European voice, not shouting, really, but with a firmness that made the words sound loud.

"Just tell me what's going on," I said. "Please."

We held our eye contact for a moment. His expression wasn't the indignation of a man who has suffered an unprovoked attack. Rather, it was more like the quiet turmoil of a father who's had to spank his child. "I'm sorry," he said.

Damn the man's infinite patience. I was angry and I wanted him to be angry, too. "Look," I said at last, "you keep bringing me the wrong mail." I hated the quaver my voice had taken on. "I—I don't want to have to report you to your supervisor."

The threat seemed stupid and my words hung in the air between us. John Paul stared at me, his face waxing reflective. Finally, he laughed and shook his head. He hefted his bag, as if to gauge how much mail he had left to deliver. Then he glanced at his watch. "All right," he said at last. "After all, I don't want to get in trouble with the boss." He laughed again—not hard, really, but there were tears at the corners of his eyes.

I slowly brought myself to my feet, wiping dirt off the bum of my cutoffs. "Well?"

"You're out of place, Mr. Coin," he said, slowly. "You don't belong here."

That's the story of my life, I thought. But I said, "What do you mean?"

"You think you can just up and say you're going to be a journalist?" He put the can of Mace back in his bag.

"I didn't just up and say it. I worked hard to get my degree."

"That's not what I meant. You were supposed to be a"—he paused, then pronounced his next word carefully—"paleontologist."

"What do you mean, 'supposed to be'?"

"You can't just do whatever you want in this life. You've got to play the hand that's dealt to you. You think I wanted to be a letter carrier? It's just the way it worked out for me. You don't get any choice." His voice sounded far away and sad. "Still, it ain't so bad for me. I get to do this extra stuff as a sideline—putting people like you back on the right course."

"The right course?" The old guy was insane. I should run, get away, hide.

"When did you decide to become a journalist instead of a . . . paleontologist?"

"I don't remember for sure," I said. "Sometime during my last year in high school. I got bored; didn't want to spend the rest of my life being a student."

"That was a big decision," he said. "I'd think you'd remember it more clearly." The Pope smiled. "It was April 22nd, 1973, at 10:27 in the evening. That's when the universe split. You ripped up your acceptance letter from U of T—"

"The universe did what?"

"It split, became two universes. That happens once in a while. See, they used to think that every time somebody made a decision, instead of things going one way or the other, they went *both* ways. The universe splitting a million times a second, each one going on forever along its separate path."

I didn't understand what he was talking about. "Parallel universes?" I said, the phrase coming to me out of dimly remembered *Star Trek* reruns. "I guess that's possible . . ."

"It's hogwash, man. Couldn't happen that way. Ain't enough matter to constantly be spinning off new universes at that rate. Any fool can see that. No, most of the times the decisions iron themselves out within a few minutes or days—everything is exactly the same as if the decision had never been taken. The two universes join up, matter is conserved, the structure is sound, and I get to knock off early."

Although he sounded cavalier, he didn't look it. Of course, maybe he was always like this. After all, in the twenty-odd months that I'd known the Pope we'd never exchanged more than a dozen words at a time. "So?" I said at last.

"So, every now and then there's a kind of cosmic hiccup. The universes get so out of joint that they just keep moving farther apart. Can't have that. It weakens the fabric of existence, so they tell me. We've got to get things back on course."

"What are you talking about?"

"You ever hear of Ronald Reagan?"

"No. Wait—you mean the actor? Guy who did a bunch of pictures with a chimp?"

"That's him. There was a hiccup almost forty years ago. He got it into his head to be a politician, don't you know. I won't even tell you how high up he made it in the American government—you'd never believe me. It took an army of posties to get the world back on track after that one."

"So you're saying I'm supposed to be a paleontologist, not a plastics writer."

"Uh huh."

"Why?"

"That's just the way it was meant to be, that's all."

My head was spinning. None of this made sense. "But I don't want to be a paleontologist. I'm happy as a journalist." That wasn't really true, and I had a feeling John Paul knew it wasn't, but he let it pass.

"I'm sorry," he said for the second time.

This was craziness. But he sounded so serious, so much like he really believed it himself, that it made me nervous. "But other people get to choose their lives," I said at last.

"No," he said, looking very old. "No, they don't. They think they choose them, but they don't."

"So—so I'm supposed to do some great thing as a paleontologist? Something that makes a difference in the scheme of things?" That wouldn't be so bad, I thought. To make a difference, to count, maybe to be remembered after I'm dead.

"Perhaps," said the Pope, but I knew in an instant that he was lying.

"Well, it's too late for me to go back to school now, anyway," I said, folding my arms across my chest. "I mean, I'd practically be ready to retire by the time I could get a Ph.D. in paleontology."

"You've got a Ph.D. Don't ask me what your thesis was on, though. I can't pronounce most of the words in its title."

"No. I've got a Bachelor of Applied Arts from the School of Journalism, Ryerson Polytechnic University." I hadn't said that with such pride in years.

"Yes. That, too." He glanced at his watch again. "For the time being."

I didn't believe a word of it but I decided to humor the old man. "Well, how's this change supposed to take place?"

"The two universes are mingling even now. We're just suturing up the rift between them. When the posties have everything in place, they'll automatically rejoin into one universe."

"How long until that happens?"

"Soon. Today, maybe, if I finish my route on time."

"And I don't get a say in any of this?"

"No. I'm sorry." He sounded like he really meant it. "None of us gets a say. Now, excuse me, but I really must get on with my work." And with that, the Bishop of Rome scurried out the glass door.

Lubomir Dudek, member of the Toronto Local of the Canadian Union of Postal Workers, came to the last house on his route, a large side-split with a two-car garage. He didn't want to finish, didn't want to drop off a copy of the Jesuit journal *Compass* for a man who was now, because of that fateful day in 1973, one of Toronto's better-known podiatrists instead of a Father in the Society of Jesus. Lubo envied the foot doctor, just as he envied Jacob Coin, writer-about-to-turn-fossil-hunter. They went on from this point, with new vistas ahead of them. Their alternative lives beat the hell out of his own.

Lubo had known that the two realities would have to be reconciled. He, too, had made a fateful decision two decades ago, back when he was a press operator in a printing plant, a time when his own hiccups had drowned out those of the universe. He'd been pissed to the gills, celebrating—for the life of him he couldn't remember what. Wisely, or so it had seemed at the time, he had decided to call a cab instead of driving home from the Jolly Miller. It should have been the right choice, he thought sadly, but we play the hand that we're dealt.

For a long time he had wondered why he had been selected to be one of those helping to set things right. He'd tried to convince himself that it was because he was an honest man (which he was), a good man (which was also true), a man with a sense of duty (that, too). He'd waited patiently for his own letter carrier to bring him some exotic mail: a copy of a trade magazine from some new profession, maybe, or a dues notice from some union he didn't belong to, or even a dividend check from a stock he didn't own. But nothing of the kind came and finally Lubo was forced to consciously face what he supposed he had really known all along. His one brief moment of free will had let him live when he should not have. In the reunited universe, Jacob Coin would have his thunder lizards, the podiatrist would have his brethren, but Lubo would have only rest.

He came to the end of the driveway and lifted the lid of the foot doctor's mailbox, its black metal painfully hot in the summer sun. Slowly, sadly, he dropped in the sale flyers, bills, and letters. He hesitated for a moment before depositing the copy of *Compass*, then, with a concern not usually lavished on the mails, he gingerly inserted the slim magazine, taking care not to dog-ear its glossy white pages.

Just Like Old Times

Winner of the Aurora Award
for Best Short Story of the Year

Winner of the Crime Writers of Canada's Arthur Ellis Award
for Best Short Story of the Year

Finalist for Japan's Seiun Award
for Best Foreign Short Story of the Year

Author's Introduction

In 1987, I gave up writing short fiction: the pay rates were a tiny fraction of what I was getting for nonfiction, response times from SF magazines were ridiculously long, and I was mightily discouraged by having been unable to sell "Lost in the Mail." Five years went by during which the only fiction I wrote was novel-length.

And then came Mike Resnick.

In July 1992, Mike asked me if I'd agree to write a story for the anthology *Dinosaur Fantastic* he and Martin H. Greenberg were putting together.

Note what Mike was doing: he was *commissioning* a story.

My work wouldn't have to languish for the better part of a year in a magazine's slush pile.

This was a very appealing notion. Throughout the 1980s, I had made my living as a freelance nonfiction writer, specializing in high technology and personal finance. I'd done over 200 articles for Canadian and American magazines and newspapers, almost all of which were commissioned in advance of my writing them . . . and I liked it that way.

I accepted Mike's offer, but with trepidation. I hadn't written a short story for half a decade now. What if I'd forgotten how? Or, even worse, what if, as the apparent failure of "Lost in the Mail" had demonstrated, I never really knew how in the first place?

"Just Like Old Times" turned out to be quite a success: Mike and Marty used it as the lead story in *Dinosaur Fantastic*, and I also sold it to *On Spec: The Canadian Magazine of Speculative Writing*. The *On Spec* people reprinted it in their "best-of" anthology, *On Spec: The First Five Years*; Marty Greenberg scooped it up for his unrelated hardcover anthology *Dinosaurs*; Jack Dann and Gardner Dozois reprinted it in their *Dinosaurs II*; and David G. Hartwell and Glenn Grant bought it for their anthology *Northern Stars*.

After that, there was no turning back: I knew writing short fiction would always be a part of my life. Still, since that day in 1992, I haven't written any short fiction without a specific commission; I just don't seem to find the time for short work otherwise.

Just Like Old Times

The transference went smoothly, like a scalpel slicing into skin.

Cohen was simultaneously excited and disappointed. He was thrilled to be here—perhaps the judge was right, perhaps this was indeed where he really belonged. But the gleaming edge was taken off that thrill because it wasn't accompanied by the usual physiological signs of excitement: no sweaty palms, no racing heart, no rapid breathing. Oh, there was a heartbeat, to be sure, thundering in the background, but it wasn't Cohen's.

It was the dinosaur's.

Everything was the dinosaur's: Cohen saw the world now through tyrannosaur eyes.

The colors seemed all wrong. Surely plant leaves must be the same chlorophyll green here in the Mesozoic, but the dinosaur saw them as navy blue. The sky was lavender; the dirt underfoot ash gray.

Old bones had different cones, thought Cohen. Well, he could get used to it. After all, he had no choice. He would finish his life as an observer inside this tyrannosaur's mind. He'd see what the beast saw, hear what it heard, feel what it felt. He wouldn't be able to control its movements, they had said, but he would be able to experience every sensation.

The rex was marching forward.

Cohen hoped blood would still look red.

It wouldn't be the same if it wasn't red.

"And what, Ms. Cohen, did your husband say before he left your house on the night in question?"

"He said he was going out to hunt humans. But I thought he was making a joke."

"No interpretations, please, Ms. Cohen. Just repeat for the court as precisely as you remember it, exactly what your husband said."

"He said, 'I'm going out to hunt humans.'"

"Thank you, Ms. Cohen. That concludes the Crown's case, my lady."

The needlepoint on the wall of the Honorable Madam Justice Amanda Hoskins's chambers had been made for her by her husband. It was one of her favorite verses from *The Mikado*, and as she was preparing sentencing she would often look up and re-read the words:

My object all sublime
I shall achieve in time—
To let the punishment fit the crime—
The punishment fit the crime.

This was a difficult case, a horrible case. Judge Hoskins continued to think.

It wasn't just colors that were wrong. The view from inside the tyrannosaur's skull was different in other ways, too.

The tyrannosaur had only partial stereoscopic vision. There was an area in the center of Cohen's field of view that showed true depth perception. But because the beast was somewhat wall-eyed, it had a much wider panorama than normal for a human, a kind of saurian Cinemascope covering 270 degrees.

The wide-angle view panned back and forth as the tyrannosaur scanned along the horizon.

Scanning for prey.

Scanning for something to kill.

The Calgary Herald, Thursday, October 16, 2042, hardcopy edition: Serial killer Rudolph Cohen, 43, was sentenced to death yesterday.

Formerly a prominent member of the Alberta College of Physicians and Surgeons, Dr. Cohen was convicted in August of thirty-seven counts of first-degree murder.

In chilling testimony, Cohen had admitted, without any signs of remorse, to having terrorized each of his victims for hours before slitting their throats with surgical implements.

This is the first time in eighty years that the death penalty has been ordered in this country.

In passing sentence, Madam Justice Amanda Hoskins observed that Cohen was "the most cold-blooded and brutal killer to have stalked Canada's prairies since *Tyrannosaurus rex . . .*"

From behind a stand of dawn redwoods about ten meters away, a second tyrannosaur appeared. Cohen suspected tyrannosaurs might be fiercely territorial, since each animal would require huge amounts of meat. He wondered if the beast he was in would attack the other individual.

His dinosaur tilted its head to look at the second rex, which was standing in profile. But as it did so, almost all of the dino's mental picture dissolved into a white void, as if when concentrating on details the beast's tiny brain simply lost track of the big picture.

At first Cohen thought his rex was looking at the other dinosaur's head, but soon the top of other's skull, the tip of its muzzle and the back of its powerful neck faded away into snowy nothingness. All that was left was a picture of the throat. Good, thought Cohen. One shearing bite there could kill the animal.

The skin of the other's throat appeared gray-green and the throat itself was smooth. Maddeningly, Cohen's rex did not attack. Rather, it simply swiveled its head and looked out at the horizon again.

In a flash of insight, Cohen realized what had happened. Other kids in his neighborhood had had pet dogs or cats. He'd had lizards and snakes—cold-blooded carnivores, a fact to which expert psychological witnesses had attached great weight. Some kinds of male lizards had dewlap sacks hanging from their necks. The rex he was in—a male, the Tyrrell paleontologists had believed—had looked at this other one and seen that she was smooth-throated and therefore a female. Something to be mated with, perhaps, rather than to attack.

Perhaps they would mate soon. Cohen had never orgasmed except during the act of killing. He wondered what it would feel like.

"We spent a billion dollars developing time travel, and now you tell me the system is useless?"

"Well—"

"That is what you're saying, isn't it, professor? That chrono-transference has no practical applications?"

"Not exactly, Minister. The system *does* work. We can project a human being's consciousness back in time, superimposing his or her mind overtop of that of someone who lived in the past."

"With no way to sever the link. *Wonderful.*"

"That's not true. The link severs automatically."

"Right. When the historical person you've transferred consciousness into dies, the link is broken."

"Precisely."

"And then the person from our time whose consciousness you've transferred back dies as well."

"I admit that's an unfortunate consequence of linking two brains so closely."

"So I'm right! This whole damn chronotransference thing is useless."

"Oh, not at all, Minister. In fact, I think I've got the perfect application for it."

The rex marched along. Although Cohen's attention had first been arrested by the beast's vision, he slowly became aware of its other senses, too. He could hear the sounds of the rex's footfalls, of twigs and vegetation being crushed, of birds or pterosaurs singing, and, underneath it all, the relentless drone of insects. Still, all the sounds were dull and low; the rex's simple ears were incapable of picking up high-pitched noises, and what sounds they did detect were discerned without richness. Cohen knew the late Cretaceous must have been a symphony of varied tone, but it was as if he was listening to it through earmuffs.

The rex continued along, still searching. Cohen became aware of several more impressions of the world both inside and out, including hot afternoon sun beating down on him and a hungry gnawing in the beast's belly.

Food.

It was the closest thing to a coherent thought that he'd yet detected from the animal, a mental picture of bolts of meat going down its gullet.

Food.

The Social Services Preservation Act of 2022: Canada is built upon the principle of the Social Safety Net, a series of entitlements and programs designed to ensure a high standard of living for every citizen. However, ever-increasing life expectancies coupled with constant lowering of the mandatory retirement age have placed an untenable burden on our social-welfare system and, in particular, its cornerstone program of universal health care. With most taxpayers ceasing to work at the age of 45, and with average Canadians living to be 94 (males) or 97 (females), the system is in danger of complete collapse. Accordingly, all social programs will henceforth be available only to those below the age of 60, with one exception: all Canadians, regardless of age, may take advantage, at no charge to themselves, of government-sponsored euthanasia through chronotransference.

There! Up ahead! Something moving! Big, whatever it was: an indistinct outline only intermittently visible behind a small knot of fir trees.

A quadruped of some sort, its back to him/it/them.

Ah, there. Turning now. Peripheral vision dissolving into albino nothingness as the rex concentrated on the head.

Three horns.

Triceratops.

Glorious! Cohen had spent hours as a boy pouring over books about dinosaurs, looking for scenes of carnage. No battles were better than those in which *Tyrannosaurus rex* squared off against *Triceratops*, a four-footed Mesozoic tank with a trio of horns projecting from its face and a shield of bone rising from the back of its skull to protect the neck.

And yet, the rex marched on.

No, thought Cohen. Turn, damn you! Turn and attack!

Cohen remembered when it had all begun, that fateful day so many years ago, so many years from now. It should have been a routine operation. The patient had supposedly been prepped properly. Cohen brought his scalpel down toward the abdomen, then, with a steady hand, sliced into the skin. The patient gasped. It had been a *wonderful* sound, a beautiful sound.

Not enough gas. The anesthetist hurried to make an adjustment.

Cohen knew he had to hear that sound again. He had to.

The tyrannosaur continued forward. Cohen couldn't see its legs, but he could feel them moving. Left, right, up, down.

Attack, you bastard!

Left.

Attack!

Right.

Go after it!

Up.

Go after the *Triceratops*.

Dow—

The beast hesitated, its left leg still in the air, balancing briefly on one foot.

Attack!

Attack!

And then, at last, the rex changed course. The ceratopsian appeared in the three-dimensional central part of the tyrannosaur's field of view, like a target at the end of a gun sight.

"Welcome to the Chronotransference Institute. If I can just see your government benefits card, please? Yup, there's always a last time for everything, heh heh. Now, I'm sure you want an exciting death. The problem is finding somebody interesting who hasn't been used yet. See, we can only ever superimpose one mind onto a given historical personage. All the really obvious ones have been done already, I'm afraid. We still get about a dozen calls a week asking for Jack Kennedy, but he was one of the first to go, so to speak. If I may make a suggestion, though, we've got thousands of Roman legion officers cataloged. Those tend to be very satisfying deaths. How about a nice something from the Gallic Wars?"

The *Triceratops* looked up, its giant head lifting from the wide flat gunnera leaves it had been chewing on. Now that the rex had focussed on the plant-eater, it seemed to commit itself.

The tyrannosaur charged.

The hornface was sideways to the rex. It began to turn, to bring its armored head to bear.

The horizon bounced wildly as the rex ran. Cohen could hear the thing's heart thundering loudly, rapidly, a barrage of muscular gunfire.

The *Triceratops*, still completing its turn, opened its parrot-like beak, but no sound came out.

Giant strides closed the distance between the two animals. Cohen felt the rex's jaws opening wide, wider still, mandibles popping from their sockets.

The jaws slammed shut on the hornface's back, over the shoulders. Cohen saw two of the rex's own teeth fly into view, knocked out by the impact.

The taste of hot blood, surging out of the wound . . .

The rex pulled back for another bite.

The *Triceratops* finally got its head swung around. It surged forward, the long spear over its left eye piercing into the rex's leg . . .

Pain. Exquisite, beautiful pain.

The rex roared. Cohen heard it twice, once reverberating within the animal's own skull, a second time echoing back from distant hills. A flock of silver-furred pterosaurs took to the air. Cohen saw them fade from view as the dinosaur's simple mind shut them out of the display. Irrelevant distractions.

The *Triceratops* pulled back, the horn withdrawing from the rex's flesh.

Blood, Cohen was delighted to see, still looked red.

"If Judge Hoskins had ordered the electric chair," said Axworthy, Cohen's lawyer, "we could have fought that on Charter grounds. Cruel and unusual punishment, and all that. But she's authorized full access to the chronotransference euthanasia program for you." Axworthy paused. "She said, bluntly, that she simply wants you dead."

"How thoughtful of her," said Cohen.

Axworthy ignored that. "I'm sure I can get you anything you want," he said. "Who would you like to be transferred into?"

"Not who," said Cohen. "What."

"I beg your pardon?"

"That damned judge said I was the most cold-blooded killer to stalk the Alberta landscape since *Tyrannosaurus rex*." Cohen shook his head. "The idiot. Doesn't she know dinosaurs were warm-blooded? Anyway, that's what I want. I want to be transferred into a *T. rex*."

"You're kidding."

"Kidding is not my forte, John. *Killing* is. I want to know which was better at it, me or the rex."

"I don't even know if they can do that kind of thing," said Axworthy.

"Find out, damn you. What the hell am I paying you for?"

The rex danced to the side, moving with surprising agility for a creature of its bulk, and once again it brought its terrible jaws down on the ceratopsian's shoulder. The plant-eater was hemorrhaging at an incredible rate, as though a thousand sacrifices had been performed on the altar of its back.

The *Triceratops* tried to lunge forward, but it was weakening quickly. The tyrannosaur, crafty in its own way despite its trifling intellect, simply retreated a dozen giant paces. The hornface took one tentative step toward it, and then another, and, with great and ponderous effort, one more. But then the dinosaurian tank teetered and, eyelids slowly closing, collapsed on its side. Cohen was briefly startled, then thrilled, to hear it fall to the ground with a *splash*—he hadn't realized just how much blood had poured out of the great rent the rex had made in the beast's back.

The tyrannosaur moved in, lifting its left leg up and then smashing it down on the *Triceratops*'s belly, the three sharp toe claws tearing open the thing's abdomen, entrails spilling out into the harsh sunlight. Cohen thought the rex would let out a victorious roar, but it didn't. It simply dipped its muzzle into the body cavity, and methodically began yanking out chunks of flesh.

Cohen was disappointed. The battle of the dinosaurs had been fun, the killing had been well engineered, and there had certainly been enough blood, but there was no *terror*. No sense that the *Triceratops* had been quivering with fear, no begging for mercy. No feeling of power, of control. Just dumb, mindless brutes moving in ways preprogrammed by their genes.

It wasn't enough. Not nearly enough.

Judge Hoskins looked across the desk in her chambers at the lawyer.

"A *Tyrannosaurus*, Mr. Axworthy? I was speaking figuratively."

"I understand that, my lady, but it was an appropriate observation, don't you think? I've contacted the Chronotransference people, who say they can do it, if they have a rex specimen to work from. They have to back-propagate from actual physical material in order to get a temporal fix."

Judge Hoskins was as unimpressed by scientific babble as she was by legal jargon. "Make your point, Mr. Axworthy."

"I called the Royal Tyrrell Museum of Paleontology in Drumheller and asked them about the *Tyrannosaurus* fossils available worldwide. Turns out there's only a handful of complete skeletons, but they were able to provide me with an annotated list, giving as much information as they could about the individual probable causes of death." He slid a thin plastic printout sheet across the judge's wide desk.

"Leave this with me, counsel. I'll get back to you."

Axworthy left, and Hoskins scanned the brief list. She then leaned back in her leather chair and began to read the needlepoint on her wall for the thousandth time:

My object all sublime
I shall achieve in time—

She read that line again, her lips moving slightly as she subvocalized the words: "I shall achieve *in time* . . ."

The judge turned back to the list of tyrannosaur finds. Ah, that one. Yes, that would be perfect. She pushed a button on her phone. "David, see if you can find Mr. Axworthy for me."

There had been a very unusual aspect to the *Triceratops* kill—an aspect that intrigued Cohen. Chronotransference had been performed countless times; it was one of the most popular forms of euthanasia. Sometimes the transferee's original body would give an ongoing commentary about what was going on, as if talking during sleep. It was clear from what they said that transferees couldn't exert any control over the bodies they were transferred into.

Indeed, the physicists had claimed any control was impossible. Chronotransference worked precisely because the transferee could exert no influence, and therefore was simply observing things that had already been observed. Since no new observations were being made, no quantum-mechanical distortions occurred. After all, said the physicists, if one could exert control, one could change the past. And that was impossible.

And yet, when Cohen had willed the rex to alter its course, it eventually had done so.

Could it be that the rex had so little brains that Cohen's thoughts *could* control the beast?

Madness. The ramifications were incredible.

Still . . .

He had to know if it was true. The rex was torpid, flopped on its belly, gorged on ceratopsian meat. It seemed prepared to lie here for a long time to come, enjoying the early evening breeze.

Get up, thought Cohen. *Get up, damn you!*

Nothing. No response.

Get up!

The rex's lower jaw was resting on the ground. Its upper jaw was lifted high, its mouth wide open. Tiny pterosaurs were flitting in and out of the open maw, their long needle-like beaks apparently yanking gobbets of hornface flesh from between the rex's curved teeth.

Get up, thought Cohen again. *Get up!*

The rex stirred.

Up!

The tyrannosaur used its tiny forelimbs to keep its torso from sliding forward as it pushed with its powerful legs until it was standing.

Forward, thought Cohen. *Forward!*

The beast's body felt different. Its belly was full to bursting. *Forward!*

With ponderous steps, the rex began to march.

It was wonderful. To be in control again! Cohen felt the old thrill of the hunt.

And he knew exactly what he was looking for.

"Judge Hoskins says okay," said Axworthy. "She's authorized for you to be transferred into that new *T. rex* they've got right here in Alberta at the Tyrrell. It's a young adult, they say. Judging by the way the skeleton was found, the rex died falling, probably into a fissure. Both legs and the back were broken, but the skeleton remained almost completely articulated, suggesting that scavengers couldn't get at it. Unfortunately, the chronotransference people say that back-propagating that far into the past they can only plug you in a few hours before the accident occurred. But you'll get your wish: you're going to die as a tyrannosaur. Oh, and here are the books you asked for: a complete library on Cretaceous flora and fauna. You should have time to get through it all; the chronotransference people will need a couple of weeks to set up."

As the prehistoric evening turned to night, Cohen found what he had been looking for, cowering in some underbrush: large brown eyes, long, drawn-out face, and a lithe body covered in fur that, to the tyrannosaur's eyes, looked blue-brown.

A mammal. But not just any mammal. *Purgatorius,* the very first primate, known from Montana and Alberta from right at the end of the Cretaceous. A little guy, only about ten centimeters long, excluding its ratlike tail. Rare creatures, these days. Only a precious few.

The little furball could run quickly for its size, but a single step by the tyrannosaur equaled more than a hundred of the mammal's. There was no way it could escape.

The rex leaned in close, and Cohen saw the furball's face, the nearest thing there would be to a human face for another sixty million years. The animal's eyes went wide in terror.

Naked, raw fear.

Mammalian fear.

Cohen saw the creature scream.

Heard it scream.

It was beautiful.

The rex moved its gaping jaws in toward the little mammal, drawing in breath with such force that it sucked the creature into its maw. Normally the rex would swallow its meals whole, but Cohen prevented the beast from doing that. Instead, he simply had it stand still, with the little primate running around, terrified, inside the great cavern of the dinosaur's mouth, banging into the giant teeth and great fleshy walls, and skittering over the massive, dry tongue.

Cohen savored the terrified squealing. He wallowed in the sensation of the animal, mad with fear, moving inside that living prison.

And at last, with a great, glorious release, Cohen put the animal out of its misery, allowing the rex to swallow it, the fur-ball tickling as it slid down the giant's throat.

It was just like old times.

Just like hunting humans.

And then a wonderful thought occurred to Cohen. Why, if he killed enough of these little screaming balls of fur, they wouldn't have any descendants. There wouldn't ever be any *Homo sapiens*. In a very real sense, Cohen realized he *was* hunting humans— every single human being who would ever exist.

Of course, a few hours wouldn't be enough time to kill many of them. Judge Hoskins no doubt thought it was wonder-fully poetic justice, or she wouldn't have allowed the transfer: sending him back to fall into the pit, damned.

Stupid judge. Why, now that he could control the beast, there was no way he was going to let it die young. He'd just—

There it was. The fissure, a long gash in the earth, with a crumbling edge. Damn, it *was* hard to see. The shadows cast by neighboring trees made a confusing gridwork on the ground that obscured the ragged opening. No wonder the dull-witted rex had missed seeing it until it was too late.

But not this time.

Turn left, thought Cohen.

Left.

His rex obeyed.

He'd avoid this particular area in future, just to be on the safe side. Besides, there was plenty of territory to cover. Fortunately, this was a young rex—a juvenile. There would be decades in which to continue his very special hunt. Cohen was sure that Axworthy knew his stuff: once it became apparent that the link had lasted longer than a few hours, he'd keep any attempt to pull the plug tied up in the courts for years.

Cohen felt the old pressure building in himself, and in the rex. The tyrannosaur marched on.

This was *better* than old times, he thought. Much better.

Hunting all of humanity.

The release would be *wonderful.*

He watched intently for any sign of movement in the underbrush.

The Contest

Author's Introduction

This is the oldest story in the book. It was written in November 1978—my last year in high school—for my English teacher William Martyn, a man who encouraged me enormously and remains a friend to this day. The story was first published (for no pay) in 1980 in *White Wall Review*, the literary journal put out by Ryerson Polytechnic Institute, edited that year by Ed Greenwood, who went on to be a major force in Dungeons and Dragons. (I was a student at Ryerson from 1979 to 1982, and co-edited *White Wall Review* myself in 1982).

In 1982, I sold reprint rights to Isaac Asimov, Terry Carr, and Martin H. Greenberg for their anthology *100 Great Fantasy Short Short Stories*—and this time I was paid!

In 1985, I wrote and narrated three hour-long documentaries about science fiction for CBC Radio's *Ideas* series; for that project, I got to interview Asimov in his Manhattan penthouse.

I brought along just one book for him to sign: not one of his famous novels, but rather a copy of *100 Great Fantasy Short Short Stories*, the book that contained this, my first professional fiction publication.

The Contest

"It's getting too much for me," said the leader of the Party in Power, his voice thundering through the sky. "I propose a simple contest, winner take all."

"Oh?" replied the leader of the Opposition, the syllable materializing as a puff of flame. "This intrigues me. The terms?"

"We select a mutually agreeable subject, an average man, and measure his tendencies toward our respective sides. The party whose ideology he leans to will gain custody of the species for all time. I'm getting too old to fight over each individual with you. Do you agree to the contest?"

"It sounds like a Hell of an idea."

"It is done, then."

John Smith was, of course, the perfect choice. He was of average height and average weight, of average intellect and income. Even his name was average. He went to work that morning just another one of four billion people, but, during his lunch hour, he became the sole object of attention of two great minds.

"Aha!" proclaimed the leader of the Party in Power, whom henceforth we shall call G. "Observe his generosity: his gratuity is over twenty percent of the total bill. My point."

"Not so fast," interposed the leader of the Opposition, D. "Look into his mind for his motive. The magnitude of the tip is intended to impress the buxom secretary he is dining with. His wife, I suspect, would not approve. The point is mine."

John Smith left the table with his secretary and proceeded through the streets to their place of employment. Catching sight of a matronly woman ahead soliciting donations for a worthwhile charity, he crossed the road early.

"Generosity, you said?" D smiled. "My point."

Returning to his office ten minutes late, Smith settled to his work. His secretary buzzed him to say that his wife was on the phone.

"Tell her I'm in a meeting," Smith commanded.

"Three zip," said D.

Smith next entered his purely personal luncheon date on his company expense account.

"You're lagging behind," said D, satisfied. "I would say he is a staunch supporter of my party. Four."

"Perhaps," said G, "perhaps."

At 4:50, Smith left his office to go home. "Don't worry. I won't count that against him," said D, comfortable in his lead.

On the subway, Smith read over the shoulder of the man sitting beside him, averting his eyes from the old woman standing nearby.

"Five."

Walking from the subway station to his house, he threw a candy bar wrapper onto his neighbor's lawn.

"Is littering a sin?" asked D.

"I'm not sure," allowed G.

"It's unimportant. The outcome is inevitable."

Entering his house, Smith called a greeting to his fat wife and sat down to read the newspaper before dinner. His wife asked him to take the dog for a walk before they ate. He left something else on his neighbor's lawn this time.

"Well, I'm certainly entitled to a point for that," said D.

"Crudity. Six to nothing."

"Perhaps a more definitive test?"

"For instance?"

D waved his red arms and screams rose from an alley near Smith. "Help! Somebody help!" D chalked up another point as Smith turned deliberately away from the noise. G sent a police officer running past Smith.

"Did you hear anything?" shouted the cop.

"No. I don't want to be involved."

G frowned. D smiled.

Smith headed quickly back to his house, hurrying up the driveway as he heard the phone ringing. "It's for you," called out his wife.

He picked up the receiver. "Why, Christopher! I'll be damned!"

"Would you care to play the best two out of three?" sighed G.

Stream of Consciousness

Winner of the Aurora Award
for Best Short Story of the Year

Author's Introduction

Julie E. Czerneda is one of Canada's newest, and best, SF novelists, but she has also worked for years in educational publishing. She commissioned me to write a biologically themed short story for an anthology that would be used to teach science through science fiction; the book, eventually entitled *Packing Fraction*, also contained stories by Julie, Charles Sheffield, Josepha Sherman, and Jan Stirling, plus poetry by my wife Carolyn Clink and illustrations by my friend Larry Stewart. Sudbury, Ontario, where this story is set, went on to feature prominently in my *Neanderthal Parallax* novels.

Stream of Consciousness

The roar of the helicopter blades pounded in Raji's ears—he wished the university could afford a hoverjet. The land below was rugged Canadian shield. Pine trees grew where there was soil; lichen and moss covered the Precambrian rocks elsewhere. Raji wore a green parka, its hood down. He continued to scan the ground, and—

There! A path through the wilderness, six meters wide and perhaps half a kilometer long: trees knocked over, shield rocks scraped clean, and, at the end of it—

Incredible. Absolutely incredible.

A large dark-blue object, shaped like an arrowhead.

Raji pointed, and the pilot, Tina Chang, banked the copter to take it in the direction he was indicating. Raji thumbed the control for his microphone. "We've found it," he said, shouting to be heard above the noise of the rotor. "And it's no meteorite." As the copter got closer, Raji could see that the front of the arrowhead was smashed in. He paused, unsure what to say next. Then: "I think we're going to need the air ambulance from Sudbury."

Raji Sahir was an astronomer with Laurentian University. He hadn't personally seen the fireball that streaked across the Ontario sky last night, flanked by northern lights, but calls about it had flooded the university. He'd hoped to recover a meteorite intact; meteors were a particular interest of his, which is why he'd come to Sudbury from Vancouver twenty years ago, in 1999. Sudbury was situated on top of an ancient iron-nickel meteorite; the city's economy had traditionally been based on mining this extraterrestrial metal.

The helicopter set down next to the dark-blue arrowhead. There could be no doubt: it was a spaceship, with its hull streamlined for reentry. On its port side were white markings that must have been lettering, but they were rendered in an alphabet of triangular characters unlike anything Raji had ever seen before.

Raji was cross-appointed to the biology department; he taught a class called "Life on Other Worlds," which until this moment had been completely theoretical. He and Tina clambered out of the copter, and they moved over to the landing craft. Raji had a Geiger counter with him; he'd expected to use it on a meteorite, but he waved it over the ship's hull as he walked around it. The clicks were infrequent; nothing more than normal background radiation.

When he got to the pointed bow of the lander, Raji gasped. The damage was even more severe than it looked from above. The ship's nose was caved in and crumpled, and a large, jagged fissure was cut deep into the hull. If whatever lifeforms were inside didn't already breathe Earthlike air, they were doubtless dead. And, of course, if the ship carried germs dangerous to life on Earth, well, they were already free and in the air, too. Raji found himself holding his breath, and—

"Professor!"

It was Tina's voice. Raji hurried over to her. She was pointing at a rectangular indentation in the hull, set back about two centimeters. In its center was a circular handle.

A door.

"Should we go inside?" asked Tina.

Raji looked up at the sky. Still no sign of the air ambulance. He thought for a moment, then nodded: "First, though, please get the camcorder from the helicopter."

The woman nodded, hustled off to the chopper, and returned a moment later. She turned on the camera, and Raji leaned in to examine the door's handle. It was round, about twenty centimeters across. A raised bar with fluted edges crossed its equator. Raji thought perhaps the fluting was designed to allow fingers to grip it—but, if so, it had been built for a six-fingered hand.

He grasped the bar, and began to rotate it. After he'd turned it through 180 degrees, there was a sound like four gunshots. Raji's heart jumped in his chest, but it must have been restraining bolts popping aside; the door panel—shorter and wider than a human door—was suddenly free, and falling forward toward Raji. Tina surged in to help Raji lift it aside and set it on the ground. The circular handle was likely an emergency way of opening the panel. Normally, it probably slid aside into the ship's hull; Raji could see a gap on the right side of the opening that looked like it would have accommodated the door.

Raji and Tina stepped inside. Although the outer hull was opaque, the inner hull seemed transparent—Raji could see the gray-blue sky vaulting overhead. Doubtless there were all kinds of equipment in between the outer and inner hulls, so the image was perhaps conveyed inside via bundles of fibre optics, mapping points on the exterior to points on the interior. There was plenty of light; Raji and Tina followed the short corridor from the door into the ship's main habitat, where—

Tina gasped.

Raji felt his eyes go wide.

There was an alien being, dead or unconscious, slumped over in a bowl-shaped chair in the bow of the ship. The fissure Raji had seen outside came right through here as a wide gap in the hull; a cool breeze was blowing in from outside.

Raji rushed over to the strange creature. There was, at once, no doubt in his mind that this creature had come from another world. It was clearly a vertebrate—it had rigid limbs, covered over with a flexible greenish-gray hide. But every vertebrate on Earth had evolved from the same basic body plan, an ancestral creature with sensory organs clustered around the head, and four limbs. Oh, there were creatures that had subsequently dispensed with some or all of the limbs, but there were no terrestrial vertebrates with more than four.

But this creature had *six* limbs, in three pairs. Raji immediately thought of the ones at the top of the tubular torso as arms, and the much thicker ones at the bottom as legs. But he wasn't sure what the ones in the middle, protruding halfway between hips and shoulders, should be called. They were long enough that if the creature bent over, they could serve as additional legs, but they ended in digits complex and supple enough that it seemed they could also be used as hands.

Raji counted the digits—there were indeed six at the end of each limb. Earth's ancestral vertebrate had five digits, not six, and no Earthly animal had ever evolved with more than five. The alien's digits were arranged as four fingers flanked on either side by an opposable thumb.

The alien also had a head protruding above the shoulders—at least that much anatomy it shared with terrestrial forms. But the head seemed ridiculously small for an intelligent creature. Overall, the alien had about the same bulk as Raji himself did, but its head was only the size of a grapefruit. There were two things that might have been eyes covered over by lids that closed from either side, instead of from the top and bottom. There were two ears, as well, but they were located on top of the head, and were triangular in shape, like the ears of a fox.

The head had been badly banged up. Although the alien was strapped into its seat, a large hunk of hull material had apparently hit it, cutting into one side of its head; the debris that had likely done the damage was now lying on the floor behind the being's chair. Interestingly, though, the head wound showed no signs of bleeding: the edges of it were jagged but dry.

At first Raji could see nothing that might be a mouth, but then he looked more closely at the middle limbs. In the center of each circular palm was a large opening—perhaps food was drawn in through these. In place of peristalsis, perhaps the creature flexed its arms to move its meals down into the torso.

Assuming, of course, that the alien was still alive. So far, it hadn't moved or reacted to the presence of the two humans in any way.

Raji placed his hand over one of the medial palms, to see if he could detect breath being expelled. Nothing. If the creature still breathed, it wasn't through its mouths. Still, the creature's flesh was warmer than the surrounding air—meaning it was probably warm blooded, and, if dead, hadn't been dead very long.

A thought occurred to Raji. If the breathing orifices weren't on the middle hands, maybe they were on the upper hands. He looked at one of the upper hands, spreading the semi-clenched fingers. The fingers seemed to be jointed in many more places than human fingers were.

Once he'd spread the fingers, he could see that there were holes about a centimeter in diameter in the center of each palm. Air was indeed alternately being drawn in and expelled through these—Raji could feel that with his own hand.

"It's alive," he said excitedly. As he looked up, he saw the air ambulance hoverjet through the transparent hull, coming in for a landing.

The ambulance attendants were a white man named Bancroft and a Native Canadian woman named Cardinal. Raji met them at the entrance to the downed ship.

Bancroft looked absolutely stunned. "Is this—is this what I think it is?"

Raji was grinning from ear to ear. "It is indeed."

"Who's injured?" asked Cardinal.

"The alien pilot," said Raji.

Bancroft's jaw dropped, but Cardinal grinned. "Sounds fascinating." She hustled over to the hoverjet and got a medical kit.

The three of them went inside. Raji led them to the alien; Tina had remained with it. She had the palm of her hand held about five centimeters in front of one of the alien's breathing holes. "Its respiration is quite irregular," she said, "and it's getting more shallow."

Raji looked anxiously at the two ambulance attendants.

"We could give it oxygen . . ." suggested Bancroft tentatively.

Raji considered. Oxygen only accounted for 21% of Earth's atmosphere. Nitrogen, which makes up 78%, was almost inert—it was highly unlikely that N_2 was the gas the alien required. Then again, plants took in carbon dioxide and gave off oxygen—perhaps giving it oxygen would be a mistake.

No, thought Raji. No energetic life forms had ever appeared on Earth that breathed carbon dioxide; oxygen was simply a much better gas for animal physiology. It seemed a safe bet that if the alien were indeed gasping, it was O_2 that it was gasping for. He motioned for the ambulance attendants to proceed.

Cardinal got a cylinder of oxygen, and Bancroft moved in to stand near the alien. He held the face mask over one of the alien's palms, and Cardinal opened the valve on the tank.

Raji had been afraid the creature's palm orifices would start spasming, as if coughing at poisonous gas, but they continued to open and close rhythmically. The oxygen, at least, didn't seem to be hurting the being.

"Do you suppose it's cold?" asked Tina.

The creature had naked skin. Raji nodded, and Tina hustled off to get a blanket from her helicopter.

Raji bent over the creature's small head and gently pried one of its pairs of eyelids apart at their vertical join. The eye was yellow-gold, shot through with reddish orange veins. It was a relief seeing those—the red color implied that the blood did indeed transport oxygen using hemoglobin, or a similar iron-containing pigment.

In the center of the yellow eye was a square pupil. But the pupil didn't contract at all in response to being exposed to light. Either the eye worked differently—and the square pupil certainly suggested it might—or the alien was very deeply unconscious.

"Is it safe to move it?" asked Cardinal.

Raji considered. "I don't know—the head wound worries me. If it's got anything like a human spinal cord, it might end up paralyzed if we moved it improperly." He paused. "What sort of scanning equipment have you got?"

Cardinal opened her medical kit. Inside was a device that looked like a flashlight with a large LCD screen mounted at the end opposite the lens. "Standard class-three Deepseer," she said.

"Let's give it a try," said Raji.

Cardinal ran the scanner over the body. Raji stood next to her, looking over her shoulder. The woman pointed to the image. "That dark stuff is bone—or, at least, something as dense as bone," she said. "The skeleton is very complex. We've got around 200 bones, but this thing must have twice that number. And see that? The material where the bones join is darker—meaning it's denser—than the actual bones; I bet these beasties never get arthritis."

"What about organs?"

Cardinal touched a control on her device, and then waved the scanner some more. "That's probably one there. See the outline? And—wait a sec. Yup, see there's another one over here, on the other side that's a mirror image of the first one. Bilateral symmetry."

Raji nodded.

"All of the organs seem to be paired," said Cardinal, as she continued to move the scanner over the body. "That's better than what we've got, of course, assuming they can get by with just one in a pinch. See that one there, inflating and deflating? That must be one of the lungs—you can see the tube that leads up the arm to the breathing hole."

"If all the organs are paired," asked Raji, "does it have two hearts?"

Cardinal frowned, and continued to scan. "I don't see anything that looks like a heart," she said. "Nothing that's pumping or beating, or . . ."

Raji quickly checked the respiratory hole that wasn't covered by the oxygen mask. "It *is* still breathing," he said, with relief. "Its blood must be circulating somehow."

"Maybe it doesn't have any blood," said Bancroft, pointing at the dry head wound.

"No," said Raji. "I looked at its eyes. I could see blood vessels on their surface—and if you've got blood, you've got to make it circulate somehow; otherwise, how do you get the oxygen taken in by the lungs to the various parts of the body?"

"Maybe we should take a blood sample," said Bancroft. "Cardy's scanner can magnify it."

"All right," said Raji.

Bancroft got a syringe out of the medical kit. He felt the alien's hide, and soon found what looked like a distended blood vessel. He pushed the needle in, and pulled the plunger back. The glass cylinder filled with a liquid more orange than red. He then moved the syringe over to the scanner, and put a drop of the alien blood into a testing compartment.

Cardinal operated the scanner controls. An image of alien blood cells appeared on her LCD screen.

"Goodness," she said.

"Incredible," said Raji.

Tina jockeyed for position so that she, too, could see the display. "What?" she said. "What is it?"

"Well, the blood cells are much more elaborate than human blood cells. Our red cells don't even have nuclei, but these ones clearly do—see the dark, peanut-shaped spot there? But they also have cilia—see those hair-like extensions?"

"And that means?" asked Tina.

"It means the blood cells are self-propelled," said Cardinal. "They swim in the blood vessels, instead of being carried along by the current; that's why the creature has no heart. And look at all the different shapes and sizes—there's much more variety here than what's found in our blood."

"Can you analyze the chemical makeup of the blood?" asked Raji.

Cardinal pushed some buttons on the side of her scanner. The LCD changed to an alphanumeric readout.

"Well," said Cardinal, "just like our blood, the major constituent of the alien's plasma is water. It's a lot saltier than our plasma, though."

"Human blood plasma is a very close match for the chemical composition of Earth's oceans," said Raji to Tina. "Our component cells are still basically aquatic lifeforms—it's just that we carry a miniature ocean around inside us. The alien must come from a world with more salt in its seas."

"There are lots of protein molecules," said Cardinal, "although they're using some amino acids that we don't. And—my goodness, that's a complex molecule."

"What?"

"That one there," she said, pointing to a chemical formula being displayed on her scanner's screen. "It looks like—incredible."

"What?" asked Tina, sounding rather frustrated at being the only one with no medical or biological training.

"It's a neurotransmitter," said Raji. "At least, I think it is, judging by its structure. Neurotransmitters are the chemicals that transmit nerve impulses."

"There's lots of it in the blood," said Cardinal, pointing at a figure.

"Can you show me some blood while it's still in the body?" asked Raji.

Cardinal nodded. She pulled a very fine fibre optic out of the side of her scanner, and inserted it into the same distended blood vessel Bancroft had extracted the sample from earlier.

On the scanner's screen, blood cells could be seen moving along in unison.

"They're all going the same way," said Raji. "Even without a heart to pump them along, they're all traveling in the same direction."

"Maybe that's why there are neurotransmitters in the blood-stream," said Bancroft. "The blood cells communicate using them, so that they can move in unison."

"What about the head injury?" asked Tina. "If it's got all that blood, why isn't it bleeding?"

Cardinal moved the scanner up to the alien's small, spherical head. The eyes were still closed. On the LCD screen, the skull was visible beneath the skin, and, beneath the skull, the scanner outlined the organ that was presumably the brain within.

"It's so tiny," said Raji.

Bancroft indicated the spaceship around them. "Well, despite that, it's obviously very advanced intellectually."

"Let's have a look at the wound," said Raji.

Cardinal repositioned the scanner.

"There seem to be valves in the broken blood vessels that have closed off," she said.

Raji turned to Tina. "We've got valves in our veins, to keep blood from flowing backwards. It looks like this creature has valves in both its veins *and* its arteries." He paused, then turned to Cardinal. "I still don't know if we can or should move the alien."

"Well, the oxygen bottle is almost empty," said Bancroft. "Who knows if it was doing it any good, anyway, but—"

"Oh, God," said Tina. She'd still been holding her hand near one of the respiratory orifices. "It's stopped breathing!"

"We could try artificial respiration," said Bancroft.

"You mean blowing into its hands?" said Tina incredulously.

"Sure," said Bancroft. "It might work." He lifted one of the arms, but, as he did so, orange liquid began to spill from the breathing hole.

"Yuck!" said Tina.

Raji pulled back, too. The head wound had started to bleed as well.

"It's bleeding from the mouths, too," said Cardinal, looking at the medial limbs.

"We can't let it die," said Raji. "Do something!"

Bancroft reached into the medical kit and brought out a roll of gauze. He began packing it into the mouth located in the palm of the right medial hand. Cardinal grabbed a larger roll of gauze and tried to stanch the flow from the head.

But it was no good. Orange liquid was seeping out of previously unnoticed orifices in the torso, too, as well as from the soles of the feet.

"It's dying!" said Tina.

Blood was pooling on the spaceship's floor, which was canted at a bit of an angle.

"Maybe one of our viruses has the same effect on it that *Ebola* has on us," said Bancroft.

But Raji shook his head. "Viruses evolve in tandem with their hosts. I find it hard to believe any of our viruses or germs would have any effect on something from another ecosystem."

"Well, then, what's happening to it?" asked Bancroft. And then his eyes went wide. Raji followed Bancroft's gaze.

The orange blood wasn't pooling in the lowest part of the floor. Rather, it was remaining in a puddle in the middle of the floor—and the puddle's edges were rippling visibly. The middle of the pool started to dry up. As the four humans watched, the opening in the middle grew bigger and bigger. But it wasn't round—rather, it had straight edges. Meanwhile, the outside of the puddle was also taking on definite shape, forming straight edges parallel to those on the inside.

"It's—it's a *triangle*," said Tina.

"The orange pigment in the blood—it's probably iron-based," said Raji. "Maybe it's magnetic; maybe the blood is pooling along the field lines formed by magnetic equipment beneath the hull . . ."

But then pairs of liquid arms started extending from the vertices of the central triangle. The four humans watched dumbfounded while the blood continued to move. Suddenly, the six growing arms turned in directions perpendicular to the way they'd previously been expanding.

Finally, the outline was complete: the central object was a right-angle triangle, and off of each face of the triangle was a square.

Suddenly, lines started to cross diagonally through two of the squares—one square was crossed from the lower-left to the upper-right; another from the upper-left to the lower right; and the third—

—the third square was *crosshatched*, as if the patterns from the other squares had been overlain on top of each other.

"The square of the hypotenuse," said Tina, her voice full of wonder, "equals the sum of the squares of the other two sides."

"What?" said Bancroft.

"The Pythagorean theorem," said Raji, absolutely astonished. "It's a diagram illustrating one of the basic principles of geometry."

"A diagram made by *blood*?" said Bancroft incredulously.

A sudden thought hit Raji. "Can your scanner sequence nucleic acids?" he asked, looking at Cardinal.

"Not quickly."

"Can it compare strands? See if they're the same?"

"Yes, it can do that."

"Compare the nucleic acid from a body cell with that from one of the blood cells."

Cardinal set to work. "They don't match," she said after a few minutes.

"Incredible," said Raji shaking his head.

"What?" said Tina.

"In all Earth lifeforms, the DNA is the same in every cell of the body, including in those blood cells that do contain DNA—non-mammalian red corpuscles, as well as white corpuscles in all types of animals. But the alien's blood doesn't contain the same genetic information as the alien's body."

"So?"

"Don't you see? The blood and the body aren't even related! They're separate lifeforms. *Of course* the body has a tiny brain—it's just a vehicle for the blood. The blood is the intelligent lifeform, and the body is only a host." Raji pointed at the orange diagram on the floor. "That's what it's telling us, right there, on the floor! It's telling us not to worry about saving the body—we should be trying to save the blood!"

"That must be why the host has built-in valves to shut off cuts," said Cardinal. "If the blood cells collectively form an intelligent creature, obviously that creature wouldn't want to give up part of itself just to clot wounds."

"And when the host dies, the orifices and valves open up, to let the blood escape," said Bancroft. "The host doesn't hate the blood—this isn't an enslavement; it's a partnership."

"What do we do now?" asked Tina.

"Collect all the blood and take it somewhere safe," said Raji. "Then see how much we can communicate with it."

"And then?"

"And then we wait," said Raji, looking up at the transparent ceiling. It was getting dark; soon the stars would be visible. "We wait for other aliens to come on a rescue mission."

Raji dropped his gaze. The alien blood was forming a new pattern on the floor: the outlines of two large circles, separated by about twenty centimeters of space.

"What's it trying to say?" asked Cardinal.

Lines started to squiggle across the circles. The lines on the right-hand circle seemed random, but suddenly Raji recognized the ones on the left: the coastlines of North America. It was a picture of Earth and of another planet, presumably the alien's home world.

As the four humans watched, the two circles moved closer together, closer still, the gap between them diminishing, until at last they gently touched.

Raji smiled. "I think that means we're going to be friends."

Forever

Author's Introduction

Mike Resnick and Marty Greenberg, who had re-energized my short-fiction career by commissioning "Just Like Old Times" for their *Dinosaur Fantastic*, decided to do a second volume of dinosaur-related stories, and once again I was asked to participate.

Although the dinosaur culture in this piece bears some resemblance to that portrayed in my novels *Far-Seer*, *Fossil Hunter*, and *Foreigner*, the Shizoo are definitely *not* Quintaglios.

Attentive readers will note that the Jacob Coin who is quoted at the beginning of this story is also the main character in my "Lost in the Mail."

This story received an honorable mention in Gardner Dozois's *Year's Best Science Fiction*.

Forever

Everything we know about dinosaurs comes from a skewed sample: the only specimens we have are of animals who happened to die at locations in which fossilization could occur; for instance, we have no fossils at all from areas that were mountainous during the Mesozoic.

Also, for us to find dinosaur fossils, the Mesozoic rocks have to be re-exposed in the present day—assuming, of course, that the rocks still exist; some have been completely destroyed through subduction beneath the Earth's crust.

From any specific point in time—such as what we believe to be the final million years of the age of dinosaurs—we have at most only a few hundred square miles of exposed rock to work with. It's entirely possible that forms of dinosaurs wildly different from those we're familiar with did exist, and it's also quite reasonable to suppose that some of these forms persisted for many millions of years after the end of the Cretaceous.

But, of course, we'll never know for sure.

—Jacob Coin, Ph.D.
Keynote Address,
A.D. 2018 Annual Meeting of the
Society of Vertebrate Paleontology

Five planets could be seen with the naked eye: Sunhugger, Silver, Red, High, and Slow; all five had been known since ancient times. In the two hundred years since the invention of the telescope, much had been discovered about them. Tiny Sunhugger and bright Silver went through phases, just like the moon did; Red had visible surface features, although exactly what they were was still open to considerable debate. High was banded, and had its own coterie of at least four moons, and Slow—Slow was the most beautiful of all, with a thin ring orbiting around its equator.

Almost a hundred years ago, Ixoor the Scaly had discovered a sixth planet—one that moved around the Sun at a more indolent pace than even Slow did; Slow took twenty-nine years to make an orbit, but Ixoor's World took an astonishing eighty-four.

Ixoor's World—yes, she had named it after herself, assuring her immortality. And ever since that discovery, the search had been on for more planets.

Cholo, an astronomer who lived in the capital city of Beskaltek, thought he'd found a new planet himself, about ten years ago. He'd been looking precisely where Raymer's law predicted an as-yet-undiscovered planet should exist, between the orbits of Red and High. But it soon became apparent that what Cholo had found was nothing more than a giant rock, an orbiting island. Others soon found additional rocks in approximately the same orbit. That made Cholo more determined than ever to continue scanning the heavens each night; he'd rather let a meatscooper swallow him whole than have his only claim to fame be the discovery of a boulder in space . . .

He searched and searched and searched, hoping to discover a seventh planet. And, one night, he did find something previously uncatalogued in the sky. His tail bounced up and down in delight, and he found himself hissing "Cholo's world" softly over and over again—it had a glorious sound to it.

But, as he continued to plot the object's orbit over many months, making notes with a claw dipped in ink by the light of a lamp burning sea-serpent oil, it became clear that it wasn't another planet at all.

Still, he had surely found his claim to immortality.

Assuming, of course, that anyone would be left alive after the impact to remember his name.

"You're saying this flying mountain will hit the Earth?" said Queen Kava, looking down her long green-and-yellow muzzle at Cholo.

The Queen's office had a huge window overlooking the courtyard. Cholo's gaze was momentarily distracted by the sight of a large, furry winger gliding by. He turned back to the queen. "I'm not completely thirty-six thirty-sixths certain, Your Highness," he said. "But, yes, I'd say it's highly likely."

Kava's tail, which, like all Shizoo tails, stuck straight out behind her horizontally held body, was resting on an intricately carved wooden mount. Her chest, meanwhile, was supported from beneath by a padded cradle. "And what will happen to the Earth when this giant rock hits us?"

Cholo was standing freely; no one was allowed to sit in the presence of the Queen. He tilted his torso backward from the hips, letting the tip of his stiff tail briefly touch the polished wooden floor of the throne room. "Doubtless Your Highness has seen sketches of the moon's surface, as observed through telescopes. We believe those craters were made by the impacts of similar minor planets, long ago."

"What if your flying rock hits one of our cities?"

"The city would be completely destroyed, of course," said Cholo. "Fortunately, Shizoo civilization only covers a tiny part of the globe. Anyway, odds are that it will impact the ocean. But if it does hit on land, the chances are minuscule that it will be in an inhabited area."

The Shizoo lived on an archipelago of equatorial islands. Although many kinds of small animals existed on the islands, the greatest beasts—wild shieldhorns, meatscoopers, the larger types of shovelbills—were not found here. Whenever the Shizoo had tried to establish a colony on the mainland, disaster ensued. Even those who had never ventured from the islands knew of the damage a lone meatscooper or a marauding pack of terrorclaws could inflict.

A nictitating membrane passed in front of Kava's golden eyes. "Then we have nothing to worry about," she said.

"If it hits the land," replied Cholo, "yes, we are probably safe. But if it hits the ocean, the waves it kicks up may overwhelm our islands. We have to be prepared for that."

Queen Kava's jaw dropped in astonishment, revealing her curved, serrated teeth.

Cholo predicted they had many months before the flying mountain would crash into the Earth. During that time, the Shizoo built embankments along the perimeters of their islands. Stones had to be imported from the mainland—Shizoo usually built with wood, but something stronger would be needed to withstand the waves.

There was much resistance at first. The tiny dot, visible only in a telescope, seemed so insignificant. How could it pose a threat to the proud and ancient Shizoo race?

But the dot grew. Eventually, it became visible with the naked eye. It swelled in size, night after night. On the last night it was seen, it had grown to rival the apparent diameter of the moon.

Cholo had no way to know for sure when the impact would occur. Indeed, he harbored a faint hope that the asteroid would disintegrate and vaporize in the atmosphere—he was sure that friction with the air was what caused shooting stars to streak across the firmament. But, of course, Cholo's rock was too big for that.

The sound of the asteroid's impact was heard early in the morning—a great thunderclap, off in the distance. But Cholo knew sound took time to travel—it would take three-quarters of a day for a sound to travel halfway around the world.

Most of the adult population had stayed up, unable to sleep. When the sound did come, some of the Shizoo hissed in contempt. A big noise; that was all. Hardly anything to worry about. Cholo had panicked everyone for no good reason; perhaps his tail should be cut off in punishment . . .

But within a few days, Cholo was vindicated—in the worst possible way.

The storms came first—great gale-force winds that knocked down trees and blew apart huts. Cholo had been outdoors when the first high winds hit; he saw wingers crumple in the sky, and barely made it to shelter himself, entering a strongly built wooden shop.

A domesticated shieldhorn had been wandering down the same dirt road Cholo had been on; it dug in its four feet, and tipped its head back so that its neck shield wouldn't catch the wind. But five of its babies had been following along behind it, and Cholo saw them go flying into the air like so many leaves. The shieldhorn opened her mouth and was doubtless bellowing her outrage, but not even the cry of a great crested shovelbill would have been audible over the roar of this storm.

The wind was followed by giant waves, which barreled in toward the Shizoo islands; just as Cholo had feared, the asteroid had apparently hit the ocean.

The waves hammered the islands. On Elbar, the embankments gave way, and most of the population was swept out to sea. Much damage was done to the other islands, too, but—thank the Eggmother!—overall, casualties were surprisingly light.

It was half a month before the seas returned to normal; it was even longer before the heavens completely cleared. The sunsets were spectacular, stained red as though a giant meatscooper had ripped open the bowl of the sky.

"You have done the Shizoo people a great service," said Queen Kava. "Without your warning, we would all be dead." The monarch was wearing a golden necklace; it was the only adornment on her yellowish-gray hide. "I wish to reward you."

Cholo, whose own hide was solid gray, tilted his head backward, exposing the underside of his neck in supplication. "Your thanks is reward enough." He paused, then lowered his head. "However . . ."

Kava clicked the claws on her left hand against those on her right. "Yes?"

"I wish to go in search of the impact site."

The waves had come from the west. Dekalt—the continent the Shizoo referred to as "the mainland"—was to the east. There was a land mass to the west, as well, but it was more than five times as far away. Shizoo boats had sailed there from time to time; fewer than half ever returned. There was no telling how far away the impact site was, or if there would be anything to see; the crater might be completely submerged, but Cholo hoped its rim might stick up above the waves.

Queen Kava flexed her claws in surprise. "We are recovering from the worst natural disaster in our history, Cholo. I need every able body here, and every ship for making supply runs to the mainland." She fell silent, then: "But if this is what you want . . ."

"It is."

Kava let air out in a protracted hiss. "It's not really a suitable reward. Yes, you may have the use of a ship; I won't deny you that. But while on your voyage, think of what you really want—something lasting, something of value."

"Thank you, Your Highness," said Cholo. "Thank you."

Kava disengaged her tail from the wooden mount, stepped away from her chest cradle, and walked over to the astronomer, placing the back of a hand, her claws bent up and away, gently on his shoulder. "Travel safely, Cholo."

They sailed for almost two months without finding any sign of the impact site. Cholo had tried to determine the correct heading based on the apparent direction from which the huge waves had come, plus his knowledge of the asteroid's path through the sky, but either he had miscalculated, or the ocean really had covered over all evidence of the impact. Still, they had come this far; he figured they might as well push on to the western continent.

The ship deployed its anchor about thirty-six bodylengths from the shore, and Cholo and two others rowed in aboard a small boat. The beach was covered with debris obviously washed in by giant waves—mountains of seaweed, millions of shells, coral, driftwood, several dead sea serpents, and more. Cholo had a hard time walking over all the material; he almost lost his balance several times.

The scouting party continued on, past the beach. The forest was charred and blackened—a huge fire had raged through here recently, leaving burnt-out trunks and a thick layer of ash underfoot. The asteroid would have heated up enormously coming through the atmosphere; even if it did hit the ocean, the air temperature might well have risen enough to set vegetation ablaze. Still, there were already signs of recovery: in a few places, new shoots were poking up through the ash.

Cholo and his team hiked for thousands of bodylengths. The crew had been looking forward to being on solid ground again, but there was no joy in their footsteps, no jaunty bouncing of tails; this burned-out landscape was oppressive.

Finally, they came to a river; its waters had apparently held back the expanding fire. On the opposite side, Cholo could see trees and fields of flowers. He looked at Garsk, the captain of the sailing ship. Garsk bobbed from her hips in agreement. The river was wide, but not raging. Cholo, Garsk, and three others entered its waters, their tails undulating from side to side, their legs and arms paddling until they reached the opposite shore.

As Cholo clambered up the river's far bank and out onto dry land, he startled a small animal that had been lurking in the underbrush.

It was a tiny mammal, a disgusting ball of fur.

Cholo had grown sick of sea serpent and fish on the long voyage; he was hoping to find something worth killing, something worth eating.

After about a twelfth of a day spent exploring, Cholo came across a giant shieldhorn skull protruding from the ground. At first he thought it was a victim of the recent catastrophe, but closer examination revealed the skull was ancient—hundreds, if not thousands, of years old. Shizoo legend said that long ago great herds of shieldhorns had roamed this continent, their footfalls like thunder, their facial spears glaring in the sunlight, but no one in living memory had seen such a herd; the numbers had long been diminishing.

Cholo and Garsk continued to search.

They saw small mammals.

They saw birds.

But nowhere did they see any greater beasts. At least, none that were still alive.

At one point, Cholo discovered the body of a meatscooper. From its warty snout to the tip of its tail, it measured more than four times as long as Cholo himself. When he approached the body, birds lifted into the air from it, and clouds of insects briefly dispersed. The stench of rotting meat was overpowering; the giant had been dead for a month or more. And yet there were hundreds of stoneweights worth of flesh still on the bones. If there had been any mid-sized scavengers left alive in the area, they would have long since picked the skeleton clean.

"So much death," said Garsk, her voice full of sadness.

Cholo bobbed in agreement, contemplating his own mortality.

Months later, Cholo at last returned to Queen Kava's chambers.

"And you found no great beasts at all?" said the Queen.

"None."

"But there are lots of them left on the mainland," said Kava. "While you were away, countless trips were made there to find wood and supplies to repair our cities."

"'Lots' is a relative term, Your Highness. If the legends are to believed—not to mention the fossil record—great beasts of all types were much more plentiful long ago. Their numbers have been thinning for some time. Perhaps, on the eastern continent, the aftermath of the asteroid was the gizzard stone that burst the thunderbeast's belly, finishing them off."

"Even the great may fall," said the Queen.

Cholo was quiet for a time, his own nictitating membranes dancing up and down. Finally, he spoke: "Queen Kava, before I left, you promised me another reward—whatever I wanted—for saving the Shizoo people."

"I did, yes."

"Well, I've decided what I'd like . . ."

The unveiling took place at noon six months later, in the large square outside the palace. The artist was Jozaza—the same Jozaza who had assured her own immortality through her stunning frieze on the palace wall depicting the Eggmother's six hunts.

Only a small crowd gathered for the ceremony, but that didn't bother Cholo. This wasn't for today—it was for the ages. It was for immortality.

Queen Kava herself made a short speech—there were many reasons why Kava was popular, and her brevity was certainly one of them. Then Jozaza came forward. As she turned around to face the audience, her tail swept through a wide arc. She made a much longer speech; Cholo was growing restless, hopping from foot to foot.

Finally the moment came. Jozaza bobbed her torso at four of her assistants. They each took hold of part of the giant leather sheet, and, on the count of three, they pulled it aside, revealing the statue.

It was made of white marble veined with gold that glistened in the sunlight. The statue was almost five times life size, rivaling the biggest meatscooper's length. The resemblance to Cholo was uncanny—it was him down to the very life; no one could mistake it for anyone else. Still, to assure that the statue fulfilled its purpose for generations to come, Cholo's name was carved into its base, along with a description of what he'd done for the Shizoo people.

Cholo stared up at the giant sculpture; the white stone was almost painfully bright in the glare of the sun.

A statue in his honor—a statue bigger than any other anywhere in the world. His nictitating membranes danced up and down.

He *would* be remembered. Not just now, not just tomorrow. He would be remembered for all time. A million years from now—nay, a hundred million hence, the Shizoo people would still know his name, still recall his deeds.

He would be remembered forever.

The Abdication of Pope Mary III

Author's Introduction

Scientists dream of having their work published in either *Science* (the leading American scientific journal) or *Nature* (the great British one).

Imagine my surprise, then, when I received a commission from Dr. Henry Gee, the Senior Editor of *Nature*, to write an original 800-word science-fiction story for that magazine (a commission that concluded, in delightful British fashion, by proffering "apologies for this intrusion"). *Nature* was publishing a series of short stories, beginning with a contribution from my favorite SF writer, Sir Arthur C. Clarke, in celebration of the dawn of the new millennium.

I was thrilled to contribute the following. I deliberately touched on the theme of my twelfth novel *Calculating God*, since that book would be hitting the bookstore shelves just as this story saw print in the summer of 2000.

The Abdication of Pope Mary III

Darth Vader's booming voice, still the network's trademark 600 years after its founding: "This is CNN."

And then the news anchor: "Our top story: Pope Mary III abdicated this morning. Giancarlo DiMarco, our correspondent in Vatican City, has the details. Giancarlo?"

"Thanks, Lisa. The unprecedented has indeed happened: after 312 years of service, Pope Mary III stepped down today. Traditionally, the conclave of Roman Catholic cardinals waits 18 days after the death of a pope before beginning deliberations to choose a successor, but Mary—who has returned to her birth name of Sharon Cheung—is alive and well, and so the members of the conclave have already been sealed inside the Vatican Palace, where they will remain until they've chosen Mary's replacement. Although no new pope has been elected for over 300 years, the traditional voting method will be used. We are now watching the Sistine Chapel for the smoke that indicates the ballots have been burned following a round of voting. And—Lisa, Lisa, it's happening right now! There's smoke coming out, and—no, you can hear the disappointment of the crowd. It's black smoke; that means no candidate has yet received the required majority of two-thirds plus one. But we'll keep watching."

"Thank you, Giancarlo. Let's take a look at Pope Mary's press conference, given earlier today."

Tight shot on Mary, looking only a tenth of her four hundred years: "Since Vatican IV reaffirmed the principle of papal infallibility," she said, "and since I now believe that I was indeed in error 216 years ago when I issued a bull instructing Catholics to reject the evidence of the two Benmergui experiments, I feel compelled to step down . . ."

"We're joined now in studio by Joginder Singh, professor of physics at the University of Toronto. Dr. Singh, can you explain the Benmergui experiments for our viewers?"

"Certainly, Lisa," said Singh. "The first proved that John Cramer's transactional interpretation of quantum mechanics, proposed in the late 20th century, is in fact correct."

"And that means . . . ?"

"It means that the many-worlds interpretation is flat-out wrong: new parallel universes are not spawned each time a quantum event could go multiple ways. This is the one and only extant iteration of reality."

"And Dr. Benmergui's second experiment?"

"It proved the current cycle of creation was only the *seventh* such ever; just six other big-bang / big-crunch oscillations preceded our current universe. The combined effect of these two facts led directly to Pope Mary's crisis of faith, specifically because they proved the existence of—one might as well use the word—God."

"How? I'm sure our viewers are scratching their heads . . ."

"Well, you see, the observation, dating back to the 20th century, that the fundamental parameters of the universe seem fine-tuned to an almost infinite degree specifically to give rise to life, could previously be dismissed as a statistical artifact caused by the existence of many contemporaneous parallel universes or a multitude of previous ones. In all of that, every possible combination would crop up by chance, and so it wouldn't be remarkable that there was a universe like this one—one in which the force of gravity is just strong enough to allow stars and planets to coalesce but not just a little bit stronger, causing the universe to collapse long before life could have developed. Likewise the value of the strong nuclear force, which holds atoms together, seems finely tuned, as do the thermal properties of water, and on and on."

"So our universe is a very special place?"

"Exactly. And since, as Kathryn Benmergui proved, this is the *only* current universe, and one of just a handful that have ever existed, then the life-generating properties of the very specific fundamental constants that define reality are virtually impossible to explain except as the results of deliberate design."

"But then why would Pope Mary resign? Surely if science has proven the existence of a creator . . . ?"

Singh smiled. "Ah, but that creator is clearly not the God of the Bible or the Torah or the Qur'an. Rather, the creator is a physicist, and we are one of his or her experiments. Science hasn't reconciled itself with religion; it has *superseded* it, and—"

"I'm sorry to interrupt, Dr. Singh, but our reporter in Vatican City has some breaking news. Giancarlo, over to you . . ."

"Lisa, Lisa—the incredible is happening. At first I thought they were just tourists coming out of the Sistine Chapel, but they're not—I recognize Fontecchio and Leopardi and several of the others. But none of them are wearing robes; they're in street clothes. I haven't taken my eyes off the chapel: there's been no plume of white smoke, meaning they haven't elected a new leader of the church. But the cardinals *are* coming out. They're coming outside, heading into St. Peter's Square. The crowd is stunned, Lisa—it can only mean one thing . . ."

Star Light, Star Bright

Author's Introduction

Ever since reading Larry Niven's essay "Bigger Than Worlds" in 1974, I've been fascinated by artificial habitats larger than the planet Earth—but I never wrote about one until a quarter-century later, when I penned this story for Marty Greenberg and Larry Segriff's anthology *Far Frontiers*.

In 1997, I happened to run into *WKRP in Cincinnati* star Gordon Jump at a deli in Los Angeles; I introduced myself by saying I wanted to shake the hand of the man who had uttered the funniest line in sitcom history—a line that was echoing gently in my mind as I wrote this story.

Star Light, Star Bright

"Daddy, what are those?" My young son, Dalt, was pointing up. We'd floated far away from the ancient buildings, almost to where the transparent dome over our community touches the surface of the great sphere.

Four white hens were flying across the sky, their little wings propelling them at a good clip. "Those are chickens, Dalt. You know—the birds we get eggs from."

"Not the *chickens*," said Dalt, as if I'd offended him greatly by suggesting he didn't know what they were. "Those lights. Those points of light."

I squinted a bit. "I don't see any lights," I replied. "Where are they?"

"Everywhere," he said. He swung his head in an arc, taking in the whole sky. "Everywhere."

"How many points do you see?"

"Hundreds. Thousands."

I felt my back bumping gently against the surface; I pushed off with my palm, rising into the air again. The ancient texts I'd been translating said human beings were never really meant to live in such low gravity, but it was all I, and countless generations of my ancestors, had ever known. "There aren't any points of light, Dalt."

"Yes, there are," he insisted. "There are thousands of them, and—look!—there's a band of light across the sky there."

I faced in the direction he was pointing. "I don't see anything except another chicken."

"No, Daddy," insisted Dalt. "Look!"

Dalt was a good boy. He almost never lied to me—and I couldn't see why he would lie to me about something like this. I maneuvered so that we were hovering face to face, then extended my hand.

"Can you see my hand clearly?" I said.

"Sure."

"How many fingers am I holding up?"

He rolled his eyes. "Oh, Daddy . . ."

"How many fingers am I holding up?"

"Two."

"And do you see lights on them, as well?"

"On your fingers?" asked Dalt incredulously.

I nodded.

"Of course not."

"You don't see any lights in front of my fingers? Do you see any on my face?"

"Daddy!"

"Do you?"

"Of course not. The lights aren't down here. They're up there!"

I touched my boy's shoulder reassuringly. "Tomorrow, we'll go see Doc Tadders about your eyes."

We hadn't built the protective dome—the clear blister on the outer surface of the *Dyson* sphere (to use the ancient name our ancestors had given to our home, a term we could transliterate but not translate). Rather, the dome was already here when we'd come outside. Adjacent to it was a large, black pyramidal structure that didn't seem to be part of the sphere's outer hull; instead, it appeared to be clamped into place. No one was exactly sure what the pyramid was for, although you could enter it from an access tube extending from the dome. The pyramid was filled with corridors and rooms, and lots of control consoles marked in the script of the ancients.

The transparent dome was much larger than the pyramid—plenty big enough to cover the thirty-odd buildings the ancients had built here, as well as the concentric circles of farming fields we'd created by importing soil from within the interior of the Dyson sphere. Still, if the dome hadn't been transparent, I probably would have felt claustrophobic within it; it wasn't even a pimple on the vastness of the sphere.

We'd been fortunate that the ancients had constructed all these buildings under the protective dome; they served as homes and work spaces for us. In many cases, we could only guess at the original purposes of the buildings, but the one that housed Dr. Tadders's office had likely been a warehouse.

After sleeptime, I took Dalt to see Tadders. He seemed more fascinated by the wall diagram the doctor had of a human skeleton than he was by her eye chart, but we'd finally got him to spin around in midair to face it.

I was floating freely beside my son. For an instant, I found myself panicking because there was no anchor rope looped around my wrist; the habits of a lifetime were hard to break, even after being here, on the outside of the Dyson sphere, for all this time. I'd lived from birth to middle age on the inside of the sphere, where things tended to float up if they weren't anchored. Of course, you couldn't drift all the way up to the sun. You'd eventually bump against the glass roof that held the atmosphere in. But no one wanted to be stuck up there, waiting to be rescued; it was humiliating.

Out here, though, under our clear, protective dome, things floated *down*, not up; both Dalt and I would eventually settle to the padded floor.

"Can you read the top row of letters?" asked Doc Tadders, indicating the eye chart. She was about my age, with pale blue eyes and red hair just beginning to turn gray.

"Sure," said Dalt. "Eet, bot, doo, shuh, kee."

Tadders nodded. "What about the next row?"

"Hih, fah, roo, shuh, puh, ess."

"Can you read the last row?"

"Ayt, doo, tee, nuh, tee, ess, guh, hih, fah, roo."

"Are you sure about the second letter?"

"It's a doo, no?" said Dalt.

If there's any letter my son should know, it should be that one, since it was the first in his own name. But the character on the chart wasn't a doo; it was a fah.

Dr. Tadders jotted a note in the book she was holding, then said, "What about the last letter?"

"That's a roo."

"Are you sure?"

Dalt squinted. "Well, if it's not a roo, then it's an shuh, no?"

"Which do you think it is?"

"A shuh . . . or a roo." Dalt shrugged. "It's so tiny, I can't be sure."

I could see that it was a roo; I was surprised that I had better vision than my son did.

"Thanks," said Tadders. She looked at me. "He's a tiny bit nearsighted," she said. "Nothing to worry about." She faced Dalt again. "What about the lights in front of your eyes? Do you see any of them now?"

"No," said Dalt.

"None at all?"

"You can only see them in the dark," he said.

Tadders pushed against the padded wall with her palm, which was enough to send her drifting across the room toward the light switch; the ancients had made switches that were little rockers, instead of the click-in/click-out buttons we build. She rocked the switch, and the lighting strips at the edges of the padded roof went dark. "What about now?"

Dalt sounded puzzled. "No."

"Let's give your eyes a few moments to adjust," she said.

"It won't make any difference," said Dalt, exasperated. "You can only see the lights outside."

"Outside?" repeated Tadders.

"That's right," said Dalt. "Outside. In the dark. Up in the sky."

Dalt was the first child born after our group left the interior of the Dyson sphere. Our little town had a population of 240 now, of which fifteen had been born since we'd come outside. Dalt's usual playmate was Suzto, the daughter of the couple who lived next door to my wife and me in a building that had clearly been designed by the ancients to be living quarters.

All adults spent half their days working on their particular area of expertise, which for me was translating ancient documents stored in the computers inside the buildings and the pyramid, and the other half doing the chores that were needed to support a fledgling society. But after work, I took Dalt and Suzto for a float. We drifted away from the lights of the ancient buildings, across the fields of crops, and out toward the access tunnel that led to the pyramid.

I knew that the surface of the sphere, beneath us, was curved, of course, and, here on the outside, that it curved down. But the sphere was so huge that everything seemed flat. Oh, one could make out the indentations that were hills on the other side of the sphere's shell, and the raised plateaus that water collected in. Although we *were* on the frontier—the outside of the sphere!—we were still only one bodylength away from the world we'd left behind; that's how thick the sphere's shell was. But the double-doored portal that led back inside had been sealed off; the people on the interior had welded it shut after we'd left. They wanted nothing to do with whatever we might find out here, calling our quest for knowledge of the exterior universe a sacrilege against the wisdom of the ancients.

As we floated in the darkness, Dalt looked up again and said, "See! The lights!"

Suzto looked up, too. I expected her to scrunch her face in puzzlement, baffled by Dalt's words, but instead, near as I could make out in the darkness, she was smiling in wonder.

"Can—can you see the lights, too?" I asked Suzto.

"Sure."

I was astonished. "How big are they?"

"Tiny. Like this." She held up her hand, but if there was any space between her finger and thumb, I couldn't make it out.

"Are they arranged in some sort of pattern?"

Suzto's vocabulary wasn't yet as big as Dalt's. She looked at me, and I tried again. "Do they make shapes?"

"Maybe," said Suzto. "Some are brighter than others. There are three over there that make a straight line."

I frowned. "Dalt, please cover your eyes."

He did so, with elaborate hand gestures.

"Suzto, point to the brightest light in the sky."

"There're so many," she said.

"All right, all right. Point to the brightest one in this part of the sky over here."

She didn't hesitate. "That one."

"Okay," I said, "now put your hand down, please."

She drew her arm back in toward her body.

"Dalt, uncover your eyes."

He did so.

"Now, Dalt, point to the brightest light in this part of the sky over here."

He lifted his arm, then seemed to vacillate for a moment between two possible choices.

"Not that one, silly," said Suzto's voice. She pointed. "This one's brighter."

"Oh, yeah," said Dalt. "I guess it is." He pointed at it, too. I couldn't see anything, but it seemed in the darkness that if I could draw lines from the two children's outstretched fingers, they would converge at infinity.

Dr. Tadders was an old friend, and with both Suzto and Dalt seeing the lights, I decided to join her for lunch. We grew wheat, corn, and other crops under lamps here on the outside of the sphere, and raised chickens and pigs; if you wanted the eggs to hatch, you had to put low roofs over the hens, because they needed to be in constant contact with their clutches, and their own body movements were enough to propel them into flight; chickens really seemed to love flying. Tadders and I both knew that we'd have had more interesting meals if we'd stayed inside the sphere, but the ancient texts said that although the interior was huge, there was still much, much more to the universe.

Most of those on the interior didn't care about such things; they knew that the sphere's inner surface could accommodate over a million trillion human beings—a vastly larger number than the current population—and that our ancestors had shut us off from the rest of the universe for a reason. But some of us had decided to venture outside, starting a new settlement on our world's only real frontier. I didn't miss much about the inside—but I did miss the food.

"All right, Rodal," Dr. Tadders said, gesturing with a sandwich triangle, "here's what I think is happening." She took a deep breath, as if reviewing her thoughts once more before giving them voice, then: "We know that a long, long time ago, our ancestors built a double-walled shell around our sun. The outer wall is opaque, and the inner wall, fifty bodylengths above that, is transparent. The area between the two walls is the habitat, where all those who still live on the interior of the sphere reside."

I nodded, and kicked gently off the floor to keep myself afloat. We drifted out of the dining hall, heading outdoors.

"Well," she continued, "we also know that there was a war generations ago that knocked humanity back into a primitive state. We've been rebuilding our civilization for a long time, but we're nowhere near as advanced as our ancestors who constructed our world were."

That was certainly true. "So?"

"So, what about that story you translated a while ago? The one about where we supposedly came from?"

I'd found a story in the ancient computers that claimed that before we lived on the interior of the Dyson sphere, our ancestors had made their home on the outer surface of a small, solid, rocky globe. "But that was probably just a myth," I said.

"I mean, such a globe would have been impossibly tiny. The myth said the homeworld was six million bodylengths in diameter. Kobost"—a physicist in our community—"worked out that if it were made of the elements the myth described, even a globe that small would have had a crushingly huge gravitational attraction: five bodylengths per heartbeat squared. That's more than ten thousand times what we experience here."

Of course, the gravitational attraction on any point on the interior of a hollow sphere is zero. When we lived inside the sphere, the only gravity we felt was the pull from our sun, gently tugging things upwards. Here, on the outside of the sphere, the gravitational pull is downward, toward the sphere's surface—and the sun at its center.

I continued. "Although Kobost thinks human muscle could perhaps be built up enough to withstand such an overwhelming gravity, his own studies prove that the globe described in the myth can't be our homeworld."

"Why not?" asked Tadders.

"Because of the chickens. There are several ancient texts that show that chickens have been essentially the same since before our ancestors built the Dyson sphere. But with an acceleration due to gravity of five bodylengths per heartbeat squared, their wings wouldn't be strong enough to let them fly. So that globe in the myth couldn't possibly have been our ancestral home."

"Well, I agree that's puzzling about the chickens," said Tadders, "but wherever our ancestors came from, you have to admit it wasn't another Dyson sphere. And the inside of a Dyson sphere forms a very special kind of sky. Remember what it was like when we lived in there? Wherever you looked over your head, you saw—well, you saw the sun, of course, if you looked directly overhead. But everywhere else, you saw other parts of the sphere. Some of those parts are a long, long way off—the far side of the sphere is a hundred and fifty billion bodylengths away, isn't it? But, regardless, wherever you looked, you saw either the sun or the surface of the sphere."

"So?"

"So the surface of the sphere is reflective—even the dull, grass-covered parts reflect back a lot of light. Indeed, on average the surface reflects back about a third of the light it receives from the sun, making the whole sky glaringly bright."

People in there did have a tendency to float facing the ground instead of the sky. I nodded for her to go on.

"Well, our eyes didn't evolve here," continued Tadders. "If we did come from a rocky world, the sun would have been seen against an empty, non-reflective sky. It must be much, much brighter inside the Dyson sphere than it ever was on the original homeworld."

"Surely our eyes would have adapted to deal with the brighter light here."

"How?" asked Tadders. "Even after the great war, we regained a measure of civilization fairly quickly. There was no period during which we were reduced to survival of the fittest. Human beings haven't undergone any appreciable evolution since long before our ancestors built the sphere. Which means our eyes are as they originally were: suited for much dimmer light. Of course, the ancients may have had drugs or other things that made the interior light seem more comfortable to them, but whatever they used must have been lost in the war."

"I suppose," I said.

"But you, me, and everyone else in our settlement who has lived inside the sphere—we've damaged our retinas, without even knowing it."

I saw what she was getting at. "But the children—the children born here, on the outside of the sphere—"

She nodded. "The children born here, after we left the interior, have never been exposed to the brightness inside, and so they see just as well in the dark as our distant, distant ancestors did, back on the homeworld. The points of light the children are seeing really do exist, but they're simply too faint to register on the damaged retinas we adults have."

My head was swimming. "Maybe," I said. "Maybe. But—but what *are* those lights?"

Tadders pursed her lips, then lifted her shoulders a bit. "You want my best guess? I think they're other suns, like the one our ancestors encased in the sphere, but so incredibly far away that they're all but invisible." She looked up, out the clear roof of the dome covering our town, out at the uniform blackness, which was all either of us could make out. She then used one of the words I'd taught her, a word transliterated from the ancient texts—a word we could pronounce but whose meaning we'd never really understood. "I think," she said, "that the points of light are *stars*."

There were thousands of documents stored in the ancient computers; my job was to try to make sense of as many of them as I could. And I made much progress as Dalt continued to grow up. Eventually, he and the other children were able to match the patterns of stars they could see in the sky to those depicted in ancient charts I'd found. The patterns didn't correspond exactly; the stars had apparently drifted in relation to each other since the charts had been made. But the kids—the adolescents, now—were indeed able to discern the *constellations* shown in the old texts; ironically, this was easier to do, they said, when some of the lights of our frontier town were left on, drowning out all but the brightest stars.

According to the charts, our sun—the sun enclosed in the Dyson sphere—was the star the ancients had called Tau Ceti. It was not the original home to humanity, though; our ancestors were apparently unwilling to cannibalize the worlds of their own system to make their Dyson sphere. Instead, they—we—had come from another star, the closest similar one that wasn't part of a multiple system, a sun our ancestors had called Sol.

And the *planet*—that was the term—we had evolved on was, in the infinite humility of our wise ancestors, called by a simple, unassuming name, one I could easily translate: Dirt.

Old folks like me couldn't live on Dirt now, of course. Our muscles—including our hearts—were weak compared to what our ancestors must have had, growing up under the stupendous gravity of that tiny, rocky world.

But—

But locked in our genes, as if for safekeeping, were all the potentials we'd ever had as a species. The ability to see dim sources of light, and—

Yes, it must be there, too, still preserved in our DNA.

The ability to produce muscles strong enough to withstand much, much higher gravity.

You'd have to grow up under such a gravity, have to live with it from birth, said Dr. Tadders, to really be comfortable with it, but if you did—

I'd seen Kobost's computer animation showing how we might have moved under a much greater gravity, how we might have deployed our bodies vertically, how our spines would have supported the weight of our heads, how our legs might have worked back and forth, hinging at knee and ankle, producing sustained forward locomotion. It all seemed so bizarre, and so inefficient compared to spending most of one's life floating, but—

But there were new worlds to explore, and old ones, too, and to fully experience them would require being able to stand on their surfaces.

Dalt was growing up to be a fine young man. There wasn't a lot of choice for careers in a small community: he could have apprenticed with his mother, Delar, who worked as our banker, or with me. He chose me, and so I did my best to teach him how to read the ancient texts.

"I've finished translating that file you gave me," he said on one occasion. "It was what you suspected: just a boring list of supplies." I guess he saw that I was only half-listening to him. "What's got you so intrigued?" he asked. I looked up, and smiled at his face, with its bits of fuzz; I'd have to teach him how to shave soon. "Sorry," I said. "I've found some documents related to the pyramid. But there are several words I haven't encountered before."

"Such as?"

"Such as this one," I said, pointing at a string of eight letters on the computer screen. "*'Starship.'* The first part is obviously the word for those lights you can see in the sky: *stars*. And the second part, *hip*, well—" I slapped my haunch—"that's their name for where the leg joins the torso. They often made compound words in this fashion, but I can't for the life of me figure out what a 'stars hip' might be."

I always say nothing is better than a fresh set of eyes. "Yes, they often used that hissing sound for plurals," said Dalt. "But those two letters there—can't they also be transliterated jointly as shuh, instead of separately as ess and hih?"

I nodded.

"So maybe it's not 'stars hip,'" he said. "Maybe it's 'star ship.'"

"*Ship,*" I repeated. "Ship, ship, ship—I've seen that word before." I riffled through a collection of papers, searching my notes; the sheets fluttered around the room, and Dalt dutifully began collecting them for me. "Ship!" I exclaimed. "Here it is: 'a kind of vehicle that could float on water.'"

"Why would you want to float on water when you can float on air?" asked Dalt.

"On the homeworld," I said, "water didn't splash up in great clouds every time you touched it. It stayed in place." I frowned. "Star ship. Starship. A—a vehicle of stars?" And then I got it. "No," I said, grabbing my son's arm in excitement. "No—a vehicle for traveling to the stars!"

Dalt and Suzto eventually married, to no one's surprise.

But I *was* surprised by my son's arms. He and Suzto had been exercising for ages now, and when Dalt bent his arm at the elbow, the upper part of it *bulged*. Doc Tadders said she'd never seen anything like it, but assured us it wasn't a tumor. It was *meat*. It was muscle.

Dalt's legs were also much, much thicker than mine. Suzto hadn't bulked up quite as much, but she, too, had developed great strength.

I knew what they were up to, of course. I admired them both for it, but I had one profound regret.

Suzto had gotten pregnant shortly after she and Dalt had married—at least, they told me that the conception had occurred after the wedding, and, as a parent, it's my prerogative to believe them. But I'd never know for sure. And *that* was my great regret: I'd never get to see my own grandchild.

Dalt and Suzto would be able to *stand* on Dirt, and, indeed, would be able to endure the journey there. The starship was designed to accelerate at a rate of five bodylengths per heartbeat squared, simulating Dirt's gravity. It would accelerate for half its journey, reaching a phenomenal speed by so doing, then it would turn around and decelerate for the other half.

They were the logical choices to go. Dalt knew the ancient language as well as I did now; if there were any records left behind by our ancestors on the homeworld, he should be able to read them.

He and Suzto had to leave soon, said Doc Tadders; it would be best for the child if it developed under the fake gravity of the starship's acceleration. Dalt and Suzto would be able to survive on Dirt, but their child should actually be comfortable there.

My wife and I came to see them off, of course—as did everyone else in our settlement. We wondered what people in the sphere would make of it when the pyramid lifted off—it would do so with a kick that would doubtless be detectable on the other side of the shell.

"I'll miss you, son," I said to Dalt. Tears were welling in my eyes. I hugged him, and he hugged me back, so much harder than I could manage.

"And, Suzto," I said, moving to my daughter-in-law, while my wife moved to hug our son. "I'll miss you, too." I hugged her, as well. "I love you both."

"We love you, too," Suzto said.

And they entered the pyramid.

I was hovering over a field, harvesting radishes. It was tricky work; if you pulled too hard, you'd get the radish out, all right, but then you and it would go sailing up into the air.

"Rodal! Rodal!"

I looked in the direction of the voice. It was old Doc Tadders, hurtling toward me, a white-haired projectile. At her age, she should be more careful—she could break her bones slamming into even a padded wall at that speed.

"Rodal!"

"Yes?"

"Come! Come quickly! A message has been received from Dirt!"

I kicked off the ground, sailing toward the communication station next to the access tube that used to lead to the starship. Tadders managed to turn around without killing herself and she flew there alongside me.

A sizable crowd had already gathered by the time we arrived.

"What does the message say?" I asked the person closest to the computer monitor.

He looked at me in irritation; the ancient computer had displayed the text, naturally enough, in the ancient script, and few besides me could understand that. He moved aside and I consulted the screen, reading aloud for the benefit of everyone.

"It says, 'Greetings! We have arrived safely at Dirt.'"

The crowd broke into cheers and applause. I couldn't help reading ahead a bit while waiting or them to quiet down, so I was already misty-eyed when I continued. "It goes on to say, 'Tell Rodal and Delar that they have a grandson; we've named him Madar.'"

My wife had passed on some time ago—but she would have been delighted at the choice of Madar; that had been her father's name.

"'Dirt is beautiful, full of plants and huge bodies of water,'" I read. "'And there are other human beings living here. It seems those people interested in technology moved to the Dyson sphere, but a small group who preferred a pastoral lifestyle stayed on the homeworld. We're mastering their language—it's deviated a fair bit from the one in the ancient texts—and are already great friends with them.'"

"Amazing," said Doc Tadders.

I smiled at her, wiped my eyes, then went on: "'We will send much more information later, but we can clear up at least one enduring mystery right now.'" I grinned as I read the next part. "'Chickens can't fly here. Apparently, just because you have wings doesn't mean you were meant to fly.'"

That was the end of the message. I looked up at the dark sky, wishing I could make out Sol, or any star. "And just because you don't have wings," I said, thinking of my son and his wife and my grandchild, far, far away, "doesn't mean you weren't."

Above It All

Winner of the CompuServe SF&F Forum's HOMer Award
for Best Short Story of the Year

Author's Introduction

The first anthology Edward E. Kramer invited me to write for was *Dante's Disciples*, which he co-edited with Peter Crowther; it was a book about literal or figurative encounters with the devil. "Ed," I'd said upon receiving the invitation, "I'm a hard-SF writer—I don't know anything about any devil." But Ed said, "Why not try something set aboard a spaceship?"—and from that suggestion this story was born.

"Above It All" turned out to be a rather controversial tale, since many read it as a condemnation of the space program (although I did get a wonderful fan letter praising it from someone at NASA); if it *is* a condemnation, I think "The Shoulders of Giants" (the last story in this book) more than makes up for it.

Above It All

Rhymes with fear.

The words echoed in Colonel Paul Rackham's head as he floated in *Discovery's* airlock, the bulky Manned Maneuvering Unit clamped to his back. Air was being pumped out; cold vacuum was forming around him.

Rhymes with fear.

He should have said no, should have let McGovern or one of the others take the spacewalk instead. But Houston had suggested that Rackham do it, and to demur he'd have needed to state a reason.

Just a dead body, he told himself. Nothing to be afraid of.

There was a time when a military man couldn't have avoided seeing death—but Rackham had just been finishing high school during Desert Storm. Sure, as a test pilot, he'd watched colleagues die in crashes, but he'd never actually seen the bodies. And when his mother passed on, she'd had a closed casket. His choice, that, made without hesitation the moment the funeral director had asked him—his father, still in a nursing home, had been in no condition to make the arrangements.

Rackham was wearing liquid-cooling long johns beneath his spacesuit, tubes circulating water around him to remove excess body heat. He shuddered, and the tubes moved in unison, like a hundred serpents writhing.

He checked the barometer, saw that the lock's pressure had dropped below 0.2 psi—just a trace of atmosphere left. He closed his eyes for a moment, trying to calm himself, then reached out a gloved hand and turned the actuator that opened the outer circular hatch. "I'm leaving the airlock," he said. He was wearing the standard "Snoopy Ears" communications carrier, which covered most of his head beneath the space helmet. Two thin microphones protruded in front of his mouth.

"Copy that, Paul," said McGovern, up in the shuttle's cockpit. "Good luck."

Rackham pushed the left MMU armrest control forward. Puffs of nitrogen propelled him out into the cargo bay. The long space doors that normally formed the bay's roof were already open, and overhead he saw Earth in all its blue-and-white glory. He adjusted his pitch with his right hand control, then began rising up. As soon as he'd cleared the top of the cargo bay, the Russian space station *Mir* was visible, hanging a hundred meters away, a giant metal crucifix. Rackham brought his hand up to cross himself.

"I have *Mir* in sight," he said, fighting to keep his voice calm. "I'm going over."

Rackham remembered when the station had gone up, twenty years ago in 1986. He first saw its name in his hometown newspaper, the Omaha *World Herald. Mir*, the Russian word for peace—as if peace had had anything to do with its being built. Reagan had been hemorrhaging money into the Strategic Defense Initiative back then. If the Cold War turned hot, the high ground would be in orbit.

Even then, even in grade eight, Rackham had been dying to go into space. No price was too much. "Whatever it takes," he'd told Dave—his sometimes friend, sometimes rival—over lunch. "One of these days, I'll be floating right by that damned *Mir*. Give the Russians the finger." He'd pronounced *Mir* as if it rhymed with *sir*.

Dave had looked at him for a moment, as if he were crazy. Then, dismissing all of it except the way Paul had spoken, he smiled a patronizing smile and said, "It's *meer*, actually. Rhymes with fear."

Rhymes with fear.

Paul's gaze was still fixed on the giant cross, spikes of sunlight glinting off it. He shut his eyes and let the nitrogen exhaust push against the small of his back, propelling him into the darkness.

"I've got a scalpel," said the voice over the speaker at mission control in Kaliningrad. "I'm going to do it."

Flight controller Dimitri Kovalevsky leaned into his mike. "You're making a mistake, Yuri. You don't want to go through with this." He glanced at the two large wall monitors. The one showing *Mir*'s orbital plot was normal; the other, which usually showed the view inside the space station, was black. "Why don't you turn on your cameras and let us see you?"

The speaker crackled with static. "You know as well as I do that the cameras can't be turned off. That's our way, isn't it? Still—even after the reforms—cameras with no off switches."

"He's probably put bags or gloves over the lenses," said Metchnikoff, the engineer seated at the console next to Kovalevsky's.

"It's not worth it, Yuri," said Kovalevsky into the mike, while nodding acknowledgment at Metchnikoff. "You want to come on home? Climb into the *Soyuz* and come on down. I've got a team here working on the re-entry parameters."

"*Nyet*," said Yuri. "It won't let me leave."

"What won't let you leave?"

"I've got a knife," repeated Yuri, ignoring Kovalevsky's question. "I'm going to do it."

Kovalevsky slammed the mike's off switch. "Dammit, I'm no expert on this. Where's that bloody psychologist?"

"She's on her way," said Pasternak, the scrawny orbital-dynamics officer. "Another fifteen minutes, tops."

Kovalevsky opened the mike again. "Yuri, are you still there?"

No response.

"Yuri?"

"They took the food," said the voice over the radio, sounding even farther away than he really was, "right out of my mouth."

Kovalevsky exhaled noisily. It had been an international embarrassment the first time it had happened. Back in 1994, an unmanned *Progress* rocket had been launched to bring food up to the two cosmonauts then aboard *Mir*. But when it docked with the station, those cosmonauts had found its cargo hold empty—looted by ground-support technicians desperate to feed their own starving families. The same thing had happened again just a few weeks ago. This time the thieves had been even more clever—they'd replaced the stolen food with sacks full of dirt to avoid any difference in the rocket's pre-launch weight.

"We got food to you eventually," said Kovalevsky.

"Oh, yes," said Yuri. "We reached in, grabbed the food back—just like we always do."

"I know things haven't been going well," said Kovalevsky, "but—"

"I'm all alone up here," said Yuri. He was quiet for a time, but then he lowered his voice conspiratorially. "Except I discover I'm not alone."

Kovalevsky tried to dissuade the cosmonaut from his delusion. "That's right, Yuri—we're here. We're always here for you. Look down, and you'll see us."

"No," said Yuri. "No—I've done enough of that. It's time. I'm going to do it."

Kovalevsky covered the mike and spoke desperately. "What do I say to him? Suggestions? Anyone? Dammit, what do I say?"

"I'm doing it," said Yuri's voice. There was a grunting sound. "A stream of red globules . . . floating in the air. Red—that was our color, wasn't it? What did the Americans call us? The Red Menace. Better dead than Red . . . But they're no better, really. They wanted it just as badly."

Kovalevsky leaned forward. "Apply pressure to the cut, Yuri. We can still save you. *Come on, Yuri*—you don't want to die! Yuri!"

Up ahead, *Mir* was growing to fill Rackham's view. The vertical shaft of the crucifix consisted of the *Soyuz* that had brought Yuri to the space station sixteen months ago, the multiport docking adapter, the core habitat, and the Kvant-1 science module, with a green *Progress* cargo transport docked to its aft end.

The two arms of the cross stuck out of the docking adapter. To the left was the Kvant-2 biological research center, which contained the EVA airlock through which Rackham would enter. To the right was the Kristall space-production lab. Kristall had a docking port that a properly equipped American shuttle could hook up to—but *Discovery* wasn't properly equipped; the *Mir* adapter collar was housed aboard *Atlantis*, which wasn't scheduled to fly again for three months.

Rackham's heart continued to race. He wanted to swing around, return to the shuttle. Perhaps he could claim nausea. That was reason enough to abort an EVA; vomiting into a space helmet in zero-g was a sure way to choke to death.

But he couldn't go back. He'd fought to get up here, clawed, competed, cheated, left his parents behind in that nursing home. He'd never married, never had kids, never found time for anything but *this*. He couldn't turn around—not now, not here.

Rackham had to fly around to the Kvant-2's backside to reach the EVA hatch. Doing so gave him a clear view of *Discovery*. He saw it from the rear, its three large and two small engine cones looking back at him like a spider's cluster of eyes.

He cycled through the space station's airlock. The main lights were dark inside the biology module, but some violet-white fluorescents were on over a bed of plants. Shoots were growing in strange circular patterns in the microgravity. Rackham disengaged the Manned Maneuvering Unit and left it floating near the airlock, like a small refrigerator with arms. Just as the Russians had promised, a large pressure bag was clipped to the wall next to Yuri's own empty spacesuit. Rackham wouldn't be able to get the body, now undoubtedly stiff with *rigor mortis*, into the suit, but it would fit easily into the pressure bag, used for emergency equipment transfers.

Mir's interior was like everything in the Russian space program—rough, metallic, ramshackle, looking more like a Victorian steamworks than space-age technology. Heart thundering in his ears, he pushed his way down Kvant-2's long axis toward the central docking adapter to which all the other parts of the station were attached.

Countless small objects floated around the cabin. He reached out with his gloved hand and swept a few up in his palm. They were six or seven millimeters across and wrinkled like dried peas. But their color was a dark rusty brown.

Droplets of dried blood. *Jesus Christ.* Rackham let go of them, but they continued to float in midair in front of him. He used the back of his glove to flick them away, and continued on deeper into the station.

"Discovery, this is Houston."

"Rackham here, Houston. Go ahead."

"We—ah—have an errand for you to run."

Rackham chuckled. "Your wish is our command, Houston."

"We've had a request from the Russians. They, ah, ask that you swing by *Mir* for a pickup."

Rackham turned to his right and looked at McGovern, the pilot. McGovern was already consulting a computer display. He gave Rackham a thumbs-up signal.

"Can do," said Rackham into his mike. "What sort of pick up?"

"It's a body."

"Say again, Houston."

"A body. A dead body."

"My God. Was there an accident?"

"No accident, *Discovery*. Yuri Vereshchagin has killed himself."

"Killed . . ."

"That's right. The Russians can't afford to send another manned mission up to get him." A pause. "Yuri was one of us. Let's bring him back where he belongs."

Rackham squeezed through the docking adapter and made a right turn, heading down into *Mir*'s core habitat. It was dark except for a few glowing LEDs, a shaft of earthlight coming in through one window, and one of sunlight coming in through the other. Rackham found the light switch and turned it on. The interior lit up, revealing beige cylindrical walls. Looking down the module's thirteen-meter length, he could see the main control console, with two strap-in chairs in front of it, storage lockers, the exercise bicycle, the dining table, the closet-like sleeping compartments, and, at the far end, the round door leading into Kvant-1, where Yuri's body was supposedly floating.

He pushed off the wall and headed down the chamber. It widened out near the eating table. He noticed that the ceiling there had writing on it. Rackham looked at the cameras, one fore, one aft, both covered over with spacesuit gloves, and realized that even if they were uncovered, that part of the ceiling was perpetually out of their view. Each person who had visited the station had apparently written his or her name there in bold Magic Marker strokes: Romanenko, Leveykin, Viktorenko, Krikalev, dozens more. Foreign astronauts names' appeared, too, in Chinese characters, and Arabic, and English.

But Yuri Vereshchagin's name was nowhere to be seen. Perhaps the custom was to sign off just before leaving the station. Rackham easily found the Magic Marker, held in place on the bulkhead with Velcro. His Cyrillic wasn't very good—he had to carefully copy certain letters from the samples already on the walls—but he soon had Vereshchagin's name printed neatly across the ceiling.

Rackham thought about writing his own name, too. He touched the marker to the curving metal, but stopped, pulling the pen back, leaving only a black dot where it had made contact. Vereshchagin's name *should* be here—a reminder that he had existed. Rackham remembered all the old photographs that came to light after the fall of the Soviet Union: the original versions, before those who had fallen out of favor had been airbrushed out. Surely no cosmonaut would ever remove Vereshchagin's name, but there was no need to remind those who might come later that an American had stopped by to bring his body home.

The dried spheres of blood were more numerous in here. They bounced off Rackham's faceplate with little pinging sounds as he continued down the core module through the circular hatch into Kvant-1.

Yuri's body was indeed there, floating in a semi-fetal position. His skin was as white as candle wax, bled dry. He'd obviously rotated slowly as his opened wrist had emptied out—there was a ring of dark brown blood stains all around the circumference of the science module. Many pieces of equipment also had blood splatters on them where drops had impacted before they'd desiccated. Rackham could taste his lunch at the back of his throat. He desperately fought it down.

And yet he couldn't take his eyes off Yuri. A corpse, a body without a soul in it. It was mesmerizing, terrifying, revolting. The very face of death.

He'd met Yuri once, in passing, years ago at an IAU conference in Montreal. Rackham had never known anyone before who had committed suicide. How could Yuri have killed himself? Sure, his country was in ruins. But billions of—of rubles—had been spent building this station and getting him up here. Didn't he understand how special that made him? How, quite literally, he was above it all?

As he drifted closer, Rackham saw that Yuri's eyes were open. The pupils were dilated to their maximum extent, and a pale gray film had spread over the orbs. Rackham thought that the decent thing to do would be to reach over and close the eyes. His gloves had textured rubber fingertips, to allow as much feedback as possible without compromising his suit's thermal insulation, but even if he could work up the nerve, he didn't trust them for something as delicate as moving eyelids.

His breathing was growing calmer. He was facing death—facing it directly. He regretted now not having seen his mother one last time, and—

There was something here. Something else, inside Kvant-1 with him. He grabbed hold of a projection from the bulkhead and wheeled around. He couldn't see it. Couldn't hear any sound conducted through the helmet of his suit. But he felt its presence, knew it was there.

There was no way to get out; Kvant-1's rear docking port was blocked by the *Progress* ferry, and the exit to the core module was blocked by the invisible presence.

Get a grip on yourself, Rackham thought. *There's nothing here.* But there was. He could feel it. "What do you want?" he said, a quaver in his tones.

"Say again, Paul." McGovern's voice, over the headset.

Rackham reached down, switched his suit radio from VOX to OFF. "What do you want?" he said again.

There was no answer. He waved his arms, batting around hundreds of dried drops of blood. They flew all over the cabin—except for an area, up ahead, the size of a man. In that area, they deflected before reaching the walls. Something *was* there—something unseen. Paul's stomach contracted. He felt panic about to overtake him, when—

A hand on his shoulder, barely detectable through the bulky suit.

His heart jumped, and he swung around. He'd been floating backwards, moving away from the unseen presence, and had bumped into the corpse. He stopped dead—revolted by the prospect of touching the body again, terrified of moving in the other direction toward whatever was up ahead.

But he had to get out—somebody else could come back for Yuri. He'd find some way to explain it all later, but for now he had to escape. He grabbed hold of a handle on the wall and pushed off the bulkhead, trying to fly past the presence up ahead. He made it through into the core module. But something cold as space reached out and stopped him directly in front of the small window that looked down on the planet.

Look below, said a voice in Rackham's head. *What do you see?*

He looked outside, saw the planet of his birth. "Africa."

Millions of children starving to death.

Rackham moved his head left and right. "Not my fault."

The view changed, faster than any orbital mechanics would allow. *Look below,* said the voice again. *What do you see?*

"China."

A billion people living without freedom.

"Nothing I can do."

Again, the world spun. *Look below.*

"The west coast of America. There's San Francisco."

The plague is everywhere, but nowhere is it worse than there.

"Someday they'll find a cure."

What else do you see?

"Los Angeles."

The inner city. Slums. Poverty. They haven't abandoned hope, those who live there . . . Hope has abandoned them.

"They can get out. They just need help."

Whose help? Where will the money come from?

"I don't know."

Don't you? Look below.

"No."

Look. Your eyes have been closed too long. Open them. What do you see?

"Russia. Ah, now—Russia! Free! We defeated the Evil Empire. We defeated the Communist menace."

The people are starving.

"But they're free."

They have nothing to eat. Twice now they've taken food destined for this station.

"I read about that. Terrible, unthinkable. Like committing murder."

To take food from the mouths of the hungry. It is like committing murder, isn't it?

"Yes. No. No, wait—that's not what I meant."

Isn't it? The people need food.

"No. The space program provides jobs. And don't forget the spinoffs—advanced plastics and pharmaceuticals and . . . and . . ."

Microwave ovens.

"Yes, and—"

And dehydrated ice cream.

"No, important stuff. Medical equipment. And all kinds of new electronic devices."

That's why you go into space, then? To make life better on Earth?

"Yes. Yes. Exactly."

Look below.

"No. No, dammit, I won't."

Yuri looked below.

"Yuri was a cosmonaut—a Russian. Maybe—maybe Russia shouldn't be spending all this money on space. But I'm an American. My country is rich."

Los Angeles, said the voice that wasn't a voice. *San Francisco. And don't forget New York. Slums, plague, a populace at war with itself.*

Rackham felt his gloved fists clenching. He ground his teeth. "Damn you!"

Or you.

He closed his eyes, tried to think. Any price, he'd said—and now it was time to pay. For the good of everyone, he said—but the road was always paved with good intentions.

Starvation. Enslavement. Poverty. War.

He couldn't go back to *Discovery*—he had no choice in the matter. It wouldn't let him leave. But he'd be damned if he'd end up like Yuri, bait for yet another spacefarer.

He slipped into the control station just below the entrance portal that led from the docking adapter. He looked at the cameras fore and aft, the bulky white gloves covering them like beckoning hands. An ending, yes—and with the coffin closed. He scanned the controls, consulted the onboard computer, made his preparations. He couldn't see the entity, couldn't see its grin— but he knew they both were there.

"—in the hell, Paul?" McGovern's voice, as Rackham turned his suit radio back on. "Why are you firing the ACS jets?"

"It—it must be a malfunction," Rackham said, his finger still firmly on the red activation switch.

"Then get out of there. Get out before the delta-V gets too high. We can still pick you up if you get out now."

"I can't get out," said Rackham. "The—the way to the EVA airlock is blocked."

"Then get into the *Soyuz* and cast off. God's sake, man, you're accelerating down toward the atmosphere."

"I—I don't know how to fly a *Soyuz.*"

"We'll get Kaliningrad to talk you through the separation sequence."

"No—no, that won't work."

"Sure it will. We can bring the *Soyuz* descent capsule into our cargo bay, if need be—but hurry, man, hurry!"

"Goodbye, Charlie."

"What do you mean, 'Goodbye'? Jesus Christ, Paul—" Rackham's brow was slick with sweat. "Goodbye."

The temperature continued to rise. Rackham reached down and undogged his helmet, the abrupt increase in air pressure hurting his ears. He lifted the great fishbowl off his head, letting it fly across the cabin. He then took off the Snoopy-eared headset array. It undulated up and away, a fabric bat in the shaft of earthlight, ending up pinned by acceleration to the ceiling.

Paint started peeling off the walls, and the plastic piping had a soft, unfocused look to it. The air was so hot it hurt to breathe. Yuri's body was heating up, too. The smell from that direction was overpowering.

Rackham was close to one of the circular windows. Earth had swollen hugely beneath him. He couldn't make out the geography for all the clouds—was that China or Africa, America or Russia below? It was all a blur. And all the same.

An orange glow began licking at the port as paint on the station's hull burned up in the mesosphere. The water in the reticulum of tubes running over his body soon began to boil.

Flames were everywhere now. Atmospheric turbulence was tearing the station apart. The winglike solar panels flapped away, crisping into nothingness. Rackham felt his own flesh blistering.

The roar from outside the station was like a billion screams. Screams of the starving. Screams of the poor. Screams of the shackled. Through the port, he saw the Kristall module sheer clean off the docking adapter and go tumbling away.

Look below, the voice had said. *Look below.*

And he had.

Into space, at any price.

Into space—above it all.

The station disintegrated around him, metal shimmering and tearing away. Soon nothing was left except the flames. And they never stopped.

Ours to Discover

Author's Introduction

John Robert Colombo edited the first-ever anthology of Canadian science fiction, *Other Canadas*; it came out in 1979, my last year in high school.

In 1981, the special SF collection of the Toronto Public Library system was known as the Spaced-Out Library (it was later renamed The Merril Collection of Science Fiction, Speculation and Fantasy—the precise wording of which was my coinage). Back then the Friends of SOL held its first-ever public event: readings by local writers Terence M. Green, Andrew Weiner, and Robert Priest, all introduced by John Colombo. I met all four gentlemen for the first time that day, and Terry, Andrew, and John went on to become close friends (my novel *Frameshift* is dedicated to Terry and his wife; this collection is dedicated to Andrew; and *Tesseracts 6*, an anthology of Canadian SF I co-edited with my wife, is dedicated to John).

John remembered me in 1982, when he sold *Leisure Ways*, a glossy magazine for members of the Canadian Automobile Association, on the idea of running three short-short stories set in Ontario's future. He tapped Terry and Andrew for two of the stories—excellent choices, as they had both already published in *The Magazine of Fantasy & Science Fiction*—and he took a chance by asking me for the third. The result is "Ours to Discover" (the slogan on Ontario license plates is "Yours to Discover"). It may leave non-Canadians scratching their heads, but I confess I still get misty-eyed whenever I read this one aloud.

Ours to Discover

Old man Withers was crazy. Everybody said so, everybody but that boy Eric. "Mr. Withers is an archeologist," Eric would say—whatever an archeologist might be. Remember that funny blue-and-white sweater Withers found? He claimed he could look at the markings on it and hear the words "Toronto Maple Leafs" in his head. Toronto was the name of our steel-domed city, of course, so I believed that much, but I'd never heard of a maple leaf before. The same maple leaf symbol was in the center of all those old flags people kept finding in the ruins. Some thought a maple leaf must have been a horrendous beast like a moose or a beaver or a trudeau. Others thought it was a kind of crystal. But crystals make people think of rocks and uranium and bombs and, well, those are hardly topics for polite conversation.

Eric wanted to know for sure. He came around to the museum and said, "Please, Mr. Curator, help me find out what a maple leaf is."

Truth to tell, I wasn't the real curator. I'd moved into the museum, or *rom* (as some called it), because it was such a nice building. No one ever used it, after all, and with so few of us under the Dome you could live just about anywhere you chose. Well, we looked, but Eric and I didn't have any luck finding a real maple leaf among the few intact exhibits. "It must have been something very special," Eric said. "It must have meant something to our ancestors, back When Times Were Good." He looked up at me with innocent eyes. "If we could find out what a maple leaf was, maybe times would be good again."

Who was I to tell him he was dreaming? "You've looked everywhere there is to look."

"We haven't looked *outside* of the Dome."

"Outside? There's nothing outside, lad."

"There has to be."

"Why?" I'd never heard such nonsense.

"There just has to be, that's all."

Well, you can't argue with that kind of logic. "Even if there is," I said, "there's no way to go outside, so that's that."

"Yes there is," said Eric. "Mr. Withers found a door, way up in North York. It's all rusted shut. If we took some of the tools from here we might be able to open it."

Well, the boy insisted on going, and I couldn't let him hike all that way alone, could I? We set out the next day. It'd been years since I'd been to Dome's edge. They called it Steels Avenue up there, which seemed an appropriate name for where the iron Dome touched the ground. Sure enough, there was a door. I felt sure somebody would have had the good sense to jam it closed, so I didn't worry when I gave it a healthy pry with a crowbar. Damned if the thing didn't pop right open. We stepped cautiously through.

There was magic out there. A huge ball of light hung up over our heads. Tall and proud brown columns stretched as far as the eye could see. On top they were like frozen fire: orange and red and yellow. Little things were flying to and fro—and they were *singing*! Suddenly Eric fell to his knees. "Look, Mr. Curator! Maple leafs!" There were millions of them, covering the ground. More fluttered down from above, thin and veined and beautiful. Eric looked up at me. "This must have been what it was like When Times Were Good: people living outside with the maple leafs. I think we should live out here, Mr. Curator." I laughed and cried and hugged the boy. We turned our backs on the dome and marched forward.

When it came time to fly a flag over our new town everyone agreed it should be the maple leaf, forever.

You See But You Do Not Observe

Winner of France's *Le Grand Prix de l'Imaginaire*
for Best Foreign Short Story of 1996

Winner of the CompuServe SF&F Forum's HOMer Award
for Best Short Story of the Year

Author's Introduction

Okay, time for a big confession: I'd only read one Sherlock Holmes story ("Silver Blaze," at age 13) when Mike Resnick sent me an E-mail commissioning a story for his anthology *Sherlock Holmes in Orbit*.

But there was plenty of time before the story was due, and my lovely wife is a huge Holmes fan, so I said yes, then dived into not only reading the entire canon, but also watching various film and TV adaptations of Holmes.

I felt kinship with Arthur Conan Doyle, constantly receiving exhortations to bring back Holmes; on a smaller scale, I was inundated with similar requests to go back to writing about Afsan, the hero of my Quintaglio trilogy.

"You See But You Do Not Observe" missed making it to the

Hugo Award ballot by just four nominations. In 1996, my *The Terminal Experiment* won the Science Fiction and Fantasy Writers of America's Nebula Award for Best Novel of the Year. Rather than publishing an excerpt from that book in the anthology *Nebula Awards 31*, I chose instead to be represented there by this story.

You See But You Do Not Observe

I had been pulled into the future first, ahead of my companion. There was no sensation associated with the chronotransference, except for a popping of my ears which I was later told had to do with a change in air pressure. Once in the 21st century, my brain was scanned in order to produce from my memories a perfect reconstruction of our rooms at 221B Baker Street. Details that I could not consciously remember or articulate were nonetheless reproduced exactly: the flock-papered walls, the bearskin hearthrug, the basket chair and the armchair, the coal-scuttle, even the view through the window—all were correct to the smallest detail.

I was met in the future by a man who called himself Mycroft Holmes. He claimed, however, to be no relation to my companion, and protested that his name was mere coincidence, although he allowed that the fact of it was likely what had made a study of my partner's methods his chief avocation. I asked him if he had a brother called Sherlock, but his reply made little sense to me: "My parents weren't *that* cruel."

In any event, this Mycroft Holmes—who was a small man with reddish hair, quite unlike the stout and dark ale of a fellow with the same name I had known two hundred years before—wanted all details to be correct before he whisked Holmes here from the past. Genius, he said, was but a step from madness, and although I had taken to the future well, my companion might be quite rocked by the experience.

When Mycroft did bring Holmes forth, he did so with great stealth, transferring him precisely as he stepped through the front exterior door of the real 221 Baker Street and into the simulation that had been created here. I heard my good friend's voice down the stairs, giving his usual glad tidings to a simulation of Mrs. Hudson. His long legs, as they always did, brought him up to our humble quarters at a rapid pace.

I had expected a hearty greeting, consisting perhaps of an ebullient cry of "My Dear Watson," and possibly even a firm clasping of hands or some other display of bonhomie. But there was none of that, of course. This was not like the time Holmes had returned after an absence of three years during which I had believed him to be dead. No, my companion, whose exploits it has been my honor to chronicle over the years, was unaware of just how long we had been separated, and so my reward for my vigil was nothing more than a distracted nodding of his drawn-out face. He took a seat and settled in with the evening paper, but after a few moments, he slapped the newsprint sheets down. "Confound it, Watson! I have already read this edition. Have we not *today's* paper?"

And, at that turn, there was nothing for it but for me to adopt the unfamiliar role that queer fate had dictated I must now take: our traditional positions were now reversed, and I would have to explain the truth to Holmes.

"Holmes, my good fellow, I am afraid they do not publish newspapers anymore."

He pinched his long face into a scowl, and his clear, gray eyes glimmered. "I would have thought that any man who had spent as much time in Afghanistan as you had, Watson, would be immune to the ravages of the sun. I grant that today was unbearably hot, but surely your brain should not have addled so easily."

"Not a bit of it, Holmes, I assure you," said I. "What I say is true, although I confess my reaction was the same as yours when I was first told. There have not been any newspapers for seventy-five years now."

"Seventy-five years? Watson, this copy of *The Times* is dated August the fourteenth, 1899—yesterday."

"I am afraid that is not true, Holmes. Today is June the fifth, *anno Domini* two thousand and ninety-six."

"Two thou—"

"It sounds preposterous, I know—"

"It *is* preposterous, Watson. I call you 'old man' now and again out of affection, but you are in fact nowhere near two hundred and fifty years of age."

"Perhaps I am not the best man to explain all this," I said.

"No," said a voice from the doorway. "Allow me."

Holmes surged to his feet. "And who are you?"

"My name is Mycroft Holmes."

"Impostor!" declared my companion.

"I assure you that that is not the case," said Mycroft. "I grant I'm not your brother, nor a habitué of the Diogenes Club, but I do share his name. I am a scientist—and I have used certain scientific principles to pluck you from your past and bring you into my present."

For the first time in all the years I had known him, I saw befuddlement on my companion's face. "It is quite true," I said to him.

"But why?" said Holmes, spreading his long arms. "Assuming this mad fantasy is true—and I do not grant for an instant that it is—why would you thus kidnap myself and my good friend, Dr. Watson?"

"Because, Holmes, the game, as you used to be so fond of saying, is afoot."

"Murder, is it?" asked I, grateful at last to get to the reason for which we had been brought forward.

"More than simple murder," said Mycroft. "Much more. Indeed, the biggest puzzle to have ever faced the human race. Not just one body is missing. Trillions are. *Trillions.*"

"Watson," said Holmes, "surely you recognize the signs of

madness in the man? Have you nothing in your bag that can help him? The whole population of the Earth is less than two thousand millions."

"In your time, yes," said Mycroft. "Today, it's about eight thousand million. But I say again, there are trillions more who are missing."

"Ah, I perceive at last," said Holmes, a twinkle in his eye as he came to believe that reason was once again holding sway. "I have read in *The Illustrated London News* of these *dinosauria*, as Professor Owen called them—great creatures from the past, all now deceased. It is their demise you wish me to unravel."

Mycroft shook his head. "You should have read Professor Moriarty's monograph called *The Dynamics of an Asteroid*," he said.

"I keep my mind clear of useless knowledge," replied Holmes curtly.

Mycroft shrugged. "Well, in that paper Moriarty quite cleverly guessed the cause of the demise of the dinosaurs: an asteroid crashing into Earth kicked up enough dust to block the sun for months on end. Close to a century after he had reasoned out this hypothesis, solid evidence for its truth was found in a layer of clay. No, that mystery is long since solved. This one is much greater."

"And what, pray, is it?" said Holmes, irritation in his voice.

Mycroft motioned for Holmes to have a seat, and, after a moment's defiance, my friend did just that. "It is called the Fermi paradox," said Mycroft, "after Enrico Fermi, an Italian physicist who lived in the twentieth century. You see, we know now that this universe of ours should have given rise to countless planets, and that many of those planets should have produced intelligent civilizations. We can demonstrate the likelihood of this mathematically, using something called the Drake equation. For a century and a half now, we have been using radio—wireless, that is— to look for signs of these other intelligences. And we have found nothing—*nothing!* Hence the paradox Fermi posed: if the universe is supposed to be full of life, then where are the aliens?"

"Aliens?" said I. "Surely they are mostly still in their respective foreign countries."

Mycroft smiled. "The word has gathered additional uses since your day, good doctor. By aliens, I mean extraterrestrials—creatures who live on other worlds."

"Like in the stories of Verne and Wells?" asked I, quite sure that my expression was agog.

"And even in worlds beyond the family of our sun," said Mycroft.

Holmes rose to his feet. "I know nothing of universes and other worlds," he said angrily. "Such knowledge could be of no practical use in my profession."

I nodded. "When I first met Holmes, he had no idea that the Earth revolved around the sun." I treated myself to a slight chuckle. "He thought the reverse to be true."

Mycroft smiled. "I know of your current limitations, Sherlock." My friend cringed slightly at the overly familiar address. "But these are mere gaps in knowledge; we can rectify that easily enough."

"I will not crowd my brain with useless irrelevancies," said Holmes. "I carry only information that can be of help in my work. For instance, I can identify one hundred and forty different varieties of tobacco ash—"

"Ah, well, you can let that information go, Holmes," said Mycroft. "No one smokes anymore. It's been proven ruinous to one's health." I shot a look at Holmes, whom I had always warned of being a self-poisoner. "Besides, we've also learned much about the structure of the brain in the intervening years. Your fear that memorizing information related to fields such as literature, astronomy, and philosophy would force out other, more relevant data, is unfounded. The capacity for the human brain to store and retrieve information is almost infinite."

"It is?" said Holmes, clearly shocked.

"It is."

"And so you wish me to immerse myself in physics and

astronomy and such all?"

"Yes," said Mycroft.

"To solve this paradox of Fermi?"

"Precisely!"

"But why me?"

"Because it is a *puzzle*, and you, my good fellow, are the greatest solver of puzzles this world has ever seen. It is now two hundred years after your time, and no one with a facility to rival yours has yet appeared."

Mycroft probably could not see it, but the tiny hint of pride on my longtime companion's face was plain to me. But then Holmes frowned. "It would take years to amass the knowledge I would need to address this problem."

"No, it will not." Mycroft waved his hand, and amidst the homely untidiness of Holmes's desk appeared a small sheet of glass standing vertically. Next to it lay a strange metal bowl. "We have made great strides in the technology of learning since your day. We can directly program new information into your brain." Mycroft walked over to the desk. "This glass panel is what we call a *monitor*. It is activated by the sound of your voice. Simply ask it questions, and it will display information on any topic you wish. If you find a topic that you think will be useful in your studies, simply place this helmet on your head" (he indicated the metal bowl), "say the words 'load topic,' and the information will be seamlessly integrated into the neural nets of your very own brain. It will at once seem as if you know, and have always known, all the details of that field of endeavor."

"Incredible!" said Holmes. "And from there?"

"From there, my dear Holmes, I hope that your powers of deduction will lead you to resolve the paradox—and reveal at last what has happened to the aliens!"

"Watson! Watson!"

I awoke with a start. Holmes had found this new ability to

effortlessly absorb information irresistible and he had pressed on long into the night, but I had evidently fallen asleep in a chair. I perceived that Holmes had at last found a substitute for the sleeping fiend of his cocaine mania: with all of creation at his fingertips, he would never again feel that emptiness that so destroyed him between assignments.

"Eh?" I said. My throat was dry. I had evidently been sleeping with my mouth open. "What is it?"

"Watson, this physics is more fascinating than I had ever imagined. Listen to this, and see if you do not find it as compelling as any of the cases we have faced to date."

I rose from my chair and poured myself a little sherry—it was, after all, still night and not yet morning. "I am listening."

"Remember the locked and sealed room that figured so significantly in that terrible case of the Giant Rat of Sumatra?"

"How could I forget?" said I, a shiver traversing my spine. "If not for your keen shooting, my left leg would have ended up as gamy as my right."

"Quite," said Holmes. "Well, consider a different type of locked-room mystery, this one devised by an Austrian physicist named Erwin Schrödinger. Imagine a cat sealed in a box. The box is of such opaque material, and its walls are so well insulated, and the seal is so profound, that there is no way anyone can observe the cat once the box is closed."

"Hardly seems cricket," I said, "locking a poor cat in a box."

"Watson, your delicate sensibilities are laudable, but please, man, attend to my point. Imagine further that inside this box is a triggering device that has exactly a fifty-fifty chance of being set off, and that this aforementioned trigger is rigged up to a cylinder of poison gas. If the trigger is tripped, the gas is released, and the cat dies."

"Goodness!" said I. "How nefarious."

"Now, Watson, tell me this: without opening the box, can you say whether the cat is alive or dead?"

"Well, if I understand you correctly, it depends on whether

the trigger was tripped."

"Precisely!"

"And so the cat is perhaps alive, and, yet again, perhaps it is dead."

"Ah, my friend, I knew you would not fail me: the blindingly obvious interpretation. But it is wrong, dear Watson, totally wrong."

"How do you mean?"

"I mean the cat is neither alive nor is it dead. It is a *potential* cat, an unresolved cat, a cat whose existence is nothing but a question of possibilities. It is neither alive nor dead, Watson—neither! Until some intelligent person opens the box and looks, the cat is unresolved. Only the act of looking forces a resolution of the possibilities. Once you crack the seal and peer within, the potential cat collapses into an actual cat. Its reality is *a result of* having been observed."

"That is worse gibberish than anything this namesake of your brother has spouted."

"No, it is not," said Holmes. "It is the way the world works. They have learned so much since our time, Watson—so very much! But as Alphonse Karr has observed, *Plus ça change, plus c'est la même chose.* Even in this esoteric field of advanced physics, it is the power of the qualified observer that is most important of all!"

I awoke again hearing Holmes crying out, "Mycroft! Mycroft!"

I had occasionally heard such shouts from him in the past, either when his iron constitution had failed him and he was feverish, or when under the influence of his accursed needle. But after a moment I realized he was not calling for his real brother but rather was shouting into the air to summon the Mycroft Holmes who was the 21st-century savant. Moments later, he was rewarded: the door to our rooms opened and in came the red-haired fellow.

"Hello, Sherlock," said Mycroft. "You wanted me?"

"Indeed I do," said Holmes. "I have absorbed much now on

not just physics but also the technology by which you have recreated these rooms for me and the good Dr. Watson."

Mycroft nodded. "I've been keeping track of what you've been accessing. Surprising choices, I must say."

"So they might seem," said Holmes, "but my method is based on the pursuit of trifles. Tell me if I understand correctly that you reconstructed these rooms by scanning Watson's memories, then using, if I understand the terms, holography and micro-manipulated force fields to simulate the appearance and form of what he had seen."

"That's right."

"So your ability to reconstruct is not just limited to rebuilding these rooms of ours, but, rather, you could simulate anything either of us had ever seen."

"That's correct. In fact, I could even put you into a simulation of someone else's memories. Indeed, I thought perhaps you might like to see the Very Large Array of radio telescopes, where most of our listening for alien messages—"

"Yes, yes, I'm sure that's fascinating," said Holmes, dismissively. "But can you reconstruct the venue of what Watson so appropriately dubbed 'The Final Problem'?"

"You mean the Falls of Reichenbach?" Mycroft looked shocked. "My God, yes, but I should think that's the last thing you'd want to relive."

"Aptly said!" declared Holmes. "Can you do it?"

"Of course."

"Then do so!"

And so Holmes and my brains were scanned and in short order we found ourselves inside a superlative recreation of the Switzerland of May 1891, to which we had originally fled to escape Professor Moriarty's assassins. Our re-enactment of events began at the charming Englischer Hof in the village of Meiringen. Just as the original innkeeper had done all those years ago, the reconstruction of him exacted a promise from us that we would not miss the spectacle of the falls of Reichenbach. Holmes and I set out for the Falls, him walking with the aid of an alpenstock. Mycroft, I was given to understand, was somehow observing all this from afar.

"I do not like this," I said to my companion. " 'Twas bad enough to live through this horrible day once, but I had hoped I would never have to relive it again except in nightmares."

"Watson, recall that I have fonder memories of all this. Vanquishing Moriarty was the high point of my career. I said to you then, and say again now, that putting an end to the very Napoleon of crime would easily be worth the price of my own life."

There was a little dirt path cut out of the vegetation running halfway round the falls so as to afford a complete view of the spectacle. The icy green water, fed by the melting snows, flowed with phenomenal rapidity and violence, then plunged into a great, bottomless chasm of rock black as the darkest night. Spray shot up in vast gouts, and the shriek made by the plunging water was almost like a human cry.

We stood for a moment looking down at the waterfall, Holmes's face in its most contemplative repose. He then pointed further ahead along the dirt path. "Note, dear Watson," he said, shouting to be heard above the torrent, "that the dirt path comes to an end against a rock wall there." I nodded. He turned in the other direction. "And see that backtracking out the way we came is the only way to leave alive: there is but one exit, and it is coincident with the single entrance."

Again I nodded. But, just as had happened the first time we had been at this fateful spot, a Swiss boy came running along the path, carrying in his hand a letter addressed to me which bore the mark of the Englischer Hof. I knew what the note said, of course: that an Englishwoman, staying at that inn, had been overtaken by a hemorrhage. She had but a few hours to live, but doubtless would take great comfort in being ministered to by an English doctor, and would I come at once?

"But the note is a pretext," said I, turning to Holmes. "Granted,

I was fooled originally by it, but, as you later admitted in that letter you left for me, you had suspected all along that it was a sham on the part of Moriarty." Throughout this commentary, the Swiss boy stood frozen, immobile, as if somehow Mycroft, overseeing all this, had locked the boy in time so that Holmes and I might consult. "I will not leave you again, Holmes, to plunge to your death."

Holmes raised a hand. "Watson, as always, your sentiments are laudable, but recall that this is a mere simulation. You will be of material assistance to me if you do exactly as you did before. There is no need, though, for you to undertake the entire arduous hike to the Englischer Hof and back. Instead, simply head back to the point at which you pass the figure in black, wait an additional quarter of an hour, then return to here."

"Thank you for simplifying it," said I. "I am eight years older than I was then; a three-hour round trip would take a goodly bit out of me today."

"Indeed," said Holmes. "All of us may have outlived our most useful days. Now, please, do as I ask."

"I will, of course," said I, "but I freely confess that I do not understand what this is all about. You were engaged by this twenty-first-century Mycroft to explore a problem in natural philosophy—the missing aliens. Why are we even here?"

"We are here," said Holmes, "because I have solved that problem! Trust me, Watson. Trust me, and play out the scenario again of that portentous day of May 4th, 1891."

And so I left my companion, not knowing what he had in mind. As I made my way back to the Englischer Hof, I passed a man going hurriedly the other way. The first time I had lived through these terrible events I did not know him, but this time I recognized him for Professor Moriarty: tall, clad all in black, his forehead bulging out, his lean form outlined sharply against the green backdrop of the vegetation. I let the simulation pass, waited fifteen minutes as Holmes had asked, then returned to the falls.

Upon my arrival, I saw Holmes's alpenstock leaning against

a rock. The black soil of the path to the torrent was constantly re-moistened by the spray from the roiling falls. In the soil I could see two sets of footprints leading down the path to the cascade, and none returning. It was precisely the same terrible sight that greeted me all those years ago.

"Welcome back, Watson!"

I wheeled around. Holmes stood leaning against a tree, grinning widely.

"Holmes!" I exclaimed. "How did you manage to get away from the falls without leaving footprints?"

"Recall, my dear Watson, that except for the flesh-and-blood you and me, all this is but a simulation. I simply asked Mycroft to prevent my feet from leaving tracks." He demonstrated this by walking back and forth. No impression was left by his shoes, and no vegetation was trampled down by his passage. "And, of course, I asked him to freeze Moriarty, as earlier he had frozen the Swiss lad, before he and I could become locked in mortal combat."

"Fascinating," said I.

"Indeed. Now, consider the spectacle before you. What do you see?"

"Just what I saw that horrid day on which I had thought you had died: two sets of tracks leading to the falls, and none returning."

Holmes's crow of "Precisely!" rivaled the roar of the falls. "One set of tracks you knew to be my own, and the other you took to be that of the black-clad Englishman—the very Napoleon of crime!"

"Yes."

"Having seen these two sets approaching the falls, and none returning, you then rushed to the very brink of the falls and found—what?"

"Signs of a struggle at the lip of the precipice leading to the great torrent itself."

"And what did you conclude from this?"

"That you and Moriarty had plunged to your deaths, locked in mortal combat."

"Exactly so, Watson! The very same conclusion I myself would have drawn based on those observations!"

"Thankfully, though, I turned out to be incorrect."

"Did you, now?"

"Why, yes. Your presence here attests to that."

"Perhaps," said Holmes. "But I think otherwise. Consider, Watson! You were on the scene, you saw what happened, and for three years—three years, man!—you believed me to be dead. We had been friends and colleagues for a decade at that point. Would the Holmes you knew have let you mourn him for so long without getting word to you? Surely you must know that I trust you at least as much as I do my brother Mycroft, whom I later told you was the only one I had made privy to the secret that I still lived."

"Well," I said, "since you bring it up, I *was* slightly hurt by that. But you explained your reasons to me when you returned."

"It is a comfort to me, Watson, that your ill-feelings were assuaged. But I wonder, perchance, if it was more you than I who assuaged them."

"Eh?"

"You had seen clear evidence of my death, and had faithfully if floridly recorded the same in the chronicle you so appropriately dubbed 'The Final Problem.'"

"Yes, indeed. Those were the hardest words I had ever written."

"And what was the reaction of your readers once this account was published in the *Strand*?"

I shook my head, recalling. "It was completely unexpected," said I. "I had anticipated a few polite notes from strangers mourning your passing, since the stories of your exploits had been so warmly received in the past. But what I got instead was mostly anger and outrage—people demanding to hear further adventures of yours."

"Which of course you believed to be impossible, seeing as

how I was dead."

"Exactly. The whole thing left a rather bad taste, I must say. Seemed very peculiar behavior."

"But doubtless it died down quickly," said Holmes.

"You know full well it did not. I have told you before that the onslaught of letters, as well as personal exhortations wherever I would travel, continued unabated for years. In fact, I was virtually at the point of going back and writing up one of your lesser cases I had previously ignored as being of no general interest simply to get the demands to cease, when, much to my surprise and delight—"

"Much to your surprise and delight, after an absence of three years less a month, I turned up in your consulting rooms, disguised, if I recall correctly, as a shabby book collector. And soon you had fresh adventures to chronicle, beginning with that case of the infamous Colonel Sebastian Moran and his victim, the Honorable Ronald Adair."

"Yes," said I. "Wondrous it was."

"But Watson, let us consider the facts surrounding my apparent death at the falls of Reichenbach on May 4th, 1891. You, the observer on the scene, saw the evidence, and, as you wrote in 'The Final Problem,' many experts scoured the lip of the falls and came to precisely the same conclusion you had—that Moriarty and I had plunged to our deaths."

"But that conclusion turned out to be wrong."

Holmes beamed intently. "No, my Good Watson, it turned out to be *unacceptable*—unacceptable to your faithful readers. And that is where all the problems stem from. Remember Schrödinger's cat in the sealed box? Moriarty and I at the falls present a very similar scenario: he and I went down the path into the cul-de-sac, our footprints leaving impressions in the soft earth. There were only two possible outcomes at that point: either I would exit alive, or I would not. There was no way out, except to take that same path back away from the falls. Until someone came and looked to see whether I had re-emerged from the path, the outcome was unresolved. I was both alive and dead—a collection of possibilities. But when you arrived, those possibilities had to collapse into a single reality. You saw that there were no footprints returning from the falls—meaning that Moriarty and I had struggled until at last we had both plunged over the edge into the icy torrent. It was your act of seeing the results that forced the possibilities to be resolved. In a very real sense, my good, dear friend, you killed me."

My heart was pounding in my chest. "I tell you, Holmes, nothing would have made me more happy than to have seen you alive!"

"I do not doubt that, Watson—but you had to see one thing or the other. You could not see both. And, having seen what you saw, you reported your findings: first to the Swiss police, and then to the reporter for the *Journal de Genève*, and lastly in your full account in the pages of the *Strand*."

I nodded.

"But here is the part that was not considered by Schrödinger when he devised the thought experiment of the cat in the box. Suppose you open the box and find the cat dead, and later you tell your neighbor about the dead cat—and your neighbor refuses to believe you when you say that the cat is dead. What happens if you go and look in the box a second time?"

"Well, the cat is surely still dead."

"Perhaps. But what if thousands—nay, millions!—refuse to believe the account of the original observer? What if they deny the evidence? What then, Watson?"

"I—I do not know."

"Through the sheer stubbornness of their will, they reshape reality, Watson! Truth is replaced with fiction! They will the cat back to life. More than that, they attempt to believe that the cat never died in the first place!"

"And so?"

"And so the world, which should have one concrete reality, is rendered unresolved, uncertain, adrift. As the first observer on the scene at Reichenbach, your interpretation should take precedence. But the stubbornness of the human race is legendary, Watson, and through that sheer cussedness, that refusal to believe what they have been plainly told, the world gets plunged back into being a wave front of unresolved possibilities. We exist in flux—to this day, the whole world exists in flux—because of the conflict between the observation you really made at Reichenbach, and the observation the world *wishes* you had made."

"But this is all too fantastic, Holmes!"

"Eliminate the impossible, Watson, and whatever remains, however improbable, must be the truth. Which brings me now to the question we were engaged by this avatar of Mycroft to solve: this paradox of Fermi. Where are the alien beings?"

"And you say you have solved that?"

"Indeed I have. Consider the method by which mankind has been searching for these aliens."

"By wireless, I gather—trying to overhear their chatter on the ether."

"Precisely! And when did I return from the dead, Watson?"

"April of 1894."

"And when did that gifted Italian, Guglielmo Marconi, invent the wireless?"

"I have no idea."

"In eighteen hundred and ninety-*five*, my good Watson. The following year! In all the time that mankind has used radio, our entire world has been an unresolved quandary! An uncollapsed wave front of possibilities!"

"Meaning?"

"Meaning the aliens are there, Watson—it is not they who are missing, it is us! Our world is out of synch with the rest of the universe. Through our failure to accept the unpleasant truth, we have rendered ourselves *potential* rather than *actual*."

I had always thought my companion a man with a generous regard for his own stature, but surely this was too much. "You are suggesting, Holmes, that the current unresolved state of the world hinges on the fate of you yourself?"

"Indeed! Your readers would not allow me to fall to my death, even if it meant attaining the very thing I desired most, namely the elimination of Moriarty. In this mad world, the observer has lost control of his observations! If there is one thing my life stood for—my life prior to that ridiculous resurrection of me you recounted in your chronicle of 'The Empty House'—it was reason! Logic! A devotion to observable fact! But humanity has abjured that. This whole world is out of whack, Watson—so out of whack that we are cut off from the civilizations that exist elsewhere. You tell me you were barraged with demands for my return, but if people had really understood me, understood what my life represented, they would have known that the only real tribute to me possible would have been to accept the facts! The only real answer would have been to leave me dead!"

Mycroft sent us back in time, but rather than returning us to 1899, whence he had plucked us, at Holmes's request he put us back eight years earlier in May of 1891. Of course, there were younger versions of ourselves already living then, but Mycroft swapped us for them, bringing the young ones to the future, where they could live out the rest of their lives in simulated scenarios taken from Holmes's and my minds. Granted, we were each eight years older than we had been when we had fled Moriarty the first time, but no one in Switzerland knew us and so the aging of our faces went unnoticed.

I found myself for a third time living that fateful day at the Falls of Reichenbach, but this time, like the first and unlike the second, it was real.

I saw the page boy coming, and my heart raced. I turned to Holmes, and said, "I can't possibly leave you."

"Yes, you can, Watson. And you will, for you have never failed to play the game. I am sure you will play it to the end." He paused for a moment, then said, perhaps just a wee bit sadly, "I can discover facts, Watson, but I cannot change them." And then, quite solemnly, he extended his hand. I clasped it firmly in both of mine. And then the boy, who was in Moriarty's employ, was upon us. I allowed myself to be duped, leaving Holmes alone at the Falls, fighting with all my might to keep from looking back as I hiked onward to treat the nonexistent patient at the Englischer Hof. On my way, I passed Moriarty going in the other direction. It was all I could do to keep from drawing my pistol and putting an end to the blackguard, but I knew Holmes would consider robbing him of his own chance at Moriarty an unforgivable betrayal.

It was an hour's hike down to the Englischer Hof. There I played out the scene in which I inquired about the ailing English-woman, and Steiler the Elder, the innkeeper, reacted, as I knew he must, with surprise. My performance was probably half-heart-ed, having played the role once before, but soon I was on my way back. The uphill hike took over two hours, and I confess plainly to being exhausted upon my arrival, although I could barely hear my own panting over the roar of the torrent.

Once again, I found two sets of footprints leading to the precipice, and none returning. I also found Holmes's alpenstock, and, just as I had the first time, a note from him to me that he had left with it. The note read just as the original had, explaining that he and Moriarty were about to have their final confronta-tion, but that Moriarty had allowed him to leave a few last words behind. But it ended with a postscript that had not been in the original:

> My dear Watson [it said], you will honour my passing most of all if you stick fast to the powers of observation. No matter what the world wants, leave me dead.

I returned to London, and was able to briefly counterbalance my loss of Holmes by reliving the joy and sorrow of the last few months of my wife Mary's life, explaining my somewhat older face to her and others as the result of shock at the death of Holmes. The next year, right on schedule, Marconi did indeed invent the wireless. Exhortations for more Holmes adventures continued to pour in, but I ignored them all, although the lack of him in my life was so profound that I was sorely tempted to relent, recanting my observations made at Reichenbach. Nothing would have pleased me more than to hear again the voice of the best and wisest man I had ever known.

In late June of 1907, I read in *The Times* about the detection of intelligent wireless signals coming from the direction of the star Altair. On that day, the rest of the world celebrated, but I do confess I shed a tear and drank a special toast to my good friend, the late Mr. Sherlock Holmes.

Fallen Angel

Finalist for the Bram Stoker Award
for Best Short Story of the Year

Author's Introduction

Since 1974, my parents have owned a vacation home on Canandaigua Lake in upstate New York. For the last several years, Carolyn and I have borrowed it from them, especially in the winter months, so that I can get away from all the distractions in Toronto and have some quiet to write. This story was written there in December 1998.

Lisa Snellings is a fabulous sculptor whose work has been featured at many recent science-fiction, fantasy, and horror conventions. Edward E. Kramer decided to commission stories for a horror anthology based on Lisa's art. It was the narrowest theme I'd ever been given to write to for an anthology—each author had to pick a character already sculpted by Lisa—but the result was one of my favorites of all my stories.

Fallen Angel

Angela Renaldo never knew if it was an act of homage or of defiance—whether it was the ultimate show of faith in God, or whether it was tantamount to flipping the bird at the Almighty.

Carlo, the eldest of her five brothers, doubtless had an opinion. From his position, planted firmly on the ground, near the bleachers, hands resting on the gray rubber rims of the twin wheels that propelled him along, there could be no doubt. God had enough to keep Himself busy looking after regular folk; He had no time for those who deliberately tempted fate.

Angela, the youngest Renaldo child, loved Carlo; she didn't love all her brothers, but her affection for Carlo was pure. He was the only one who had played catch with her, the only one who had listened to her, the only one who never seemed to mind her being around.

Now, of course, things were different. Now, Carlo didn't play catch with anyone. He just sat in his chair, almost never looking up.

There was nothing to fear, Poppa always said. We'll be so high up that we'll catch God's eye.

The high wire ran for ten meters, three stories above the crowd, below the peaked apex of the big top. Guys along the wire's length anchored it to the ground, preventing it from swaying, minimizing its sagging. A ladder at one end gave access to the high wire; atop the ladder were three platforms, one above another.

Poppa left the lower platform first, a twenty-kilogram balancing pole in his arms, a shoulder brace supporting an aluminum crossbar that stuck out a meter and a half behind him. The crossbar ended in another shoulder brace, and Franco, the youngest son, donned that, following his father out onto the wire, a wire no thicker than Franco's index finger, his own balancing pole held underhand in front of him.

And then Momma stepped from the middle platform, walking onto the crossbar that was supported by the shoulders of her husband and her son, her own balancing pole gripped in her hands. And on her shoulders rested *another* brace, with a second crossbar stretching behind her.

Poppa and Franco inched their way across, locked together, the length of their crossbar setting the distance between them. Neither man looked down at the ground, nor up at Momma, whose weight was distributed across their shoulders. Step, and step again. In unison. An incremental dance.

Once Franco was far enough from the lower platform, Dominic started across the high wire behind him, a third crossbar supported by his shoulders. Antonio donned the shoulder brace at the opposite end of that crossbar, and followed Dominic onto the wire.

Mario, on the middle platform, stepped off, making his way along the crossbar supported by Antonio and Dominic, just as his mother had done for the one supported by Poppa and Franco. When Mario was far enough out, he put the yoke from his mother's crossbar on his shoulders.

Below, the crowd was spellbound—ten thousand mouths agape, staring at the spectacle of six people balancing on the high wire, four on the bottom supporting two more above.

And then—

And then it was Angela's turn.

Angela, the only daughter, the youngest, stepped gingerly off the highest of the three platforms and inched her way across the upper crossbar, supported between her Momma and Mario.

Angela had her own twenty-kilo balancing beam, and—

The audience is amazed.

—and a metal chair.

She's holding a metal chair, its four legs joined by thin metal bars at the base in an open square, and she proceeds to balance this square perfectly on the crossbeam, and then—

The audience goes nuts. They've never seen anything like this.

They can't believe it's possible; it defies all reason, all physics—

And then Angela climbs *onto* the chair, still holding her balance beam, and suddenly, incredibly, fantastically, the seven-person pyramid is complete: four members of her family on the bottom, two more in the next layer, and her, little Angela, balancing on a chair supported by a crossbar no thicker around than her tiny wrist, above them all, the whole incredible thing a feat of engineering at least as great as its namesakes at Giza.

The cheering of the crowd is thunderous, tumultuous.

It's almost enough to drown out the pounding of Angela's heart.

Angela was fifteen years old, blond, thin—but not too thin. Poppa said the audience liked to see curves on a girl: give the divorced fathers something to look at while their kids enjoyed the spectacle. Sometimes, thought Angela, Poppa looked at her in that way, too.

He must have known it was wrong, she thought. She didn't get regular schooling—the circus tutor taught her, five hours a day if they were in a jurisdiction that required that much; less, if the show had traveled to places with laxer rules—but she heard tell from kids who visited the circus of the kinds of things they were learning in normal schools. Things about how to protect yourself; things about making choices for the future.

But Angela had no choice; her future was preordained. She was a Renaldo—one of the Amazing Aerial Renaldos, the star attraction of Delmonico's Razzle and Dazzle Circus. And the Renaldos were a family act; none of Poppa's children had ever left. Instead, they trained day after day, from as soon as they could walk, learning not to misstep (lest Poppa slam their ankles with a stick), learning not to fear heights, learning to move with grace, until they were ready to tackle the high wire, to do stunts far above the ground, with no net—never a net, except when they were in New York, where a state law required one; Poppa said he was never so ashamed in his life as when they performed in New York.

No, the Renaldo kids had to stay. Poppa needed them. Who else could he trust? Who else could any of them trust? A trick like this, it required family.

They did the pyramid every day—and every day it terrified Angela. She'd position the chair just so, balancing it perfectly on the brace—for the only alternative to perfection was death—and then clamber up. She could feel the chair sway back and forth as she stood up on it, but the pyramid always held, a pyramid of flesh and metal, fifteen meters above the cheering crowd.

She hated every moment of it—hated the way her heart pounded, like a jackhammer. Hated feeling as though bats were gyrating in her stomach. Hated the overwhelming fear that she would fall, that she would end up like Carlo, who was watching and not watching far, far below.

She couldn't leave; she couldn't run away. She had to stay, and not just because it was a family act. She had to stay to look after Carlo. Franco, Dominic, Mario, and Antonio made little time for Carlo; he was an unpleasant reminder of what could go wrong. And Momma and Poppa felt too much guilt to really love him. So Angela took care of him, loving him, and fearing that she might end up like him.

The being came to her in a dream, as all beings whose visits could never be proven must.

He wasn't as she'd expected. Oh, she knew who he was— who he must be; the Renaldos were Catholic, and Sunday mornings they always found a mass to attend. Each week a different city, a different church but, presumably, the same God.

Yes, she knew who this must be. But he looked unlike any drawing of him she'd ever seen. Indeed, he looked like a clown. But not Yuri or Pablo or Gunter or any of the other clowns who worked here at Delmonico's; it was no clown she had ever seen before. But his face was painted white, except for rims of red make-up—no, no, of naked red skin—around his dark, burning eyes.

Some children who came to the circus were frightened of clowns, their parents dragging them despite wailed protests to see the harlequins, as if the parents knew better, as if they were sure the fear their children felt was nonsensical. But children *knew*.

"Don't be frightened," said the figure. He moved around the room. Angela, lying in bed, wearing flannel pajamas, a sheet pulled up to her chin, couldn't see his feet, but she knew that they weren't encased in giant, floppy shoes; the *click* of his footfalls made that clear. "I've come to help you." The voice was smooth, and with an accent that didn't so much sound foreign as it sounded *ancient*.

"Help me how?" asked Angela.

"You live in fear, don't you?" He paused. "Fear of falling, no?"

"Yes."

"I fell once," said the clown. "It's not as bad as you might think."

"It was that bad for Carlo."

"That's because he refused me."

Angela felt her eyes go wide. "What?"

"I offered Carlo what I'm about to offer you; he turned me down."

Angela knew she should abjure the being, but . . . but . . . He'd said he wanted to help.

"Help me how?" she said again, her voice small, wavering, uncertain.

"I could make sure that you never fall," said the clown. "Make sure that you will never hit the ground, never end up like Carlo."

"You could do that?"

The clown cocked his head. "I can do anything, but . . ."

"But what?"

"There would be a small price, of course."

"I don't have any money," said Angela. Poppa said he was saving her money, her share of the circus take, until she turned eighteen.

"It's not money I want," said the clown.

For a horrible instant, he was looking at her the way Poppa sometimes did, as though he were hungry all over, eyes seeing beneath her clothes.

"Not that . . ." she said, softly. "I . . . I'm a virgin."

The clown roared with laughter, a torrent of molten metal. "I don't want your flesh," he said.

"Then—then what?"

"Only your soul."

Ah, thought Angela, if that was all—

"No tricks?" said Angela.

The clown looked sad; clowns often did. "If you are true to me, I promise, no tricks."

Two years passed. The Amazing Aerial Renaldos formed their pyramid another seven hundred times. Angela had come to enjoy doing it; now that the fear was gone—now that she knew she would never fall—she could relax and actually enjoy the applause.

And, yes, she realized, when you're not afraid, the applause was wonderful. Poppa had been no older than she was now when he had first heard it, back in the Old Country. She understood, finally, why it captivated him so, why he had to hear it every day of his life. When you had no fear, it was a wonderful, incredible thing.

And Angela really did have no fear of falling, and yet—

When she was younger, she had wedged herself against the wall whenever she slept; she had to, or else she would wake up in a cold sweat, arms flailing, certain she was plummeting to her doom.

Now, she no longer had that fear, but . . .

But, each night, as she lay awake, trying to get to sleep, she wondered if she had given up too much, if bargaining away her soul had been a mistake. She still went to mass every Sunday, the family finding a new wheelchair-accessible church in the Yellow Pages. She'd seen hundreds of Jesuses nailed to hundreds of crosses above hundreds of pulpits; she used to stare into the face—whatever visage the artist had given the Son of God this week—but now she couldn't meet his eyes.

She couldn't meet him, period. Her soul belonged to another.

She was seventeen, going on eighteen, and—

Going on eighteen . . .

Yes, she thought.

Yes, indeed. That was it.

But how to plead her case?

Another day; another performance. A crowd, like every crowd—thousands of excited children, thousands of parents who looked fatigued after hours of trying to win prizes for their kids on the midway, of lining up for the roller coaster and Ferris wheel. Angela paid no attention to the individual faces; the Renaldo family was a single entity, and it played to them all collectively.

She positioned the chair on the crossbeam supported by Mario and Momma, lead weights in the square base helping it to balance on the beam, and then she herself stood upon it—a girl, atop six other people, high above the ground. The crowd cheered, a myriad of voices raised in unison.

It was intoxicating, the cheers—enough to quell, at least for the time being, the unease that haunted her, enough to—

No!

God, no.

Angela felt the chair moving under her. Dominic, in the base of the pyramid, had lost his footing, just for an instant. He had shifted left; Mario, on his shoulders, had shifted right to try to compensate. Antonio, he moved right, too, but perhaps a centimeter too far. And Momma, feeling the pull on her yoke but unable to look behind her, she let out a small yelp—never a scream, not from one of the Renaldo family, the fearless, the brave. The metal chair leaned far back.

Giving the bird to the Almighty . . .

Angela's heart was pounding, just as it had before she'd made the deal, before she'd been protected. Adrenaline surged within her.

The chair teetered, and, for an instant, it seemed as though it might right itself.

But no.

No.

The chair resumed going backward. She felt it come free from the crossbar between Mario and Momma's shoulders, felt it come free from her own feet.

Angela fell backward, too, falling separately from the chair, which, she imagined, must be turning end over end.

Time was attenuated; seconds became eternities.

Angela was indeed falling, too, but—

The adrenaline continued to surge.

She felt something happening to her body, her face. Her features felt as though they were contorting, and—

No. No, that wasn't it. They weren't contorting.

They were *changing*.

Her face was drawing out, into a muzzle. She could feel it. Flat nosed, wide-nostrilled; an animal's face.

And her ears—

Her ears were *spreading*, growing larger. She couldn't see them, but she could feel them.

And her arms, her fingers—

Those she could see . . .

Her fingers were elongating. Each segment was growing, each phalanx extending. And, as they grew, something spread between them, gossamer thin at first then growing more substantial, a membrane of thick, rough skin, stretched between the bones of the hand.

Wings. Wings like those of a bat.

He'd promised her she'd never hit the ground, promised her that she'd be spared the same fate as Carlo.

If her hands had become bat hands, then her face must have become the face of a bat—the muzzle, the ears, doubtless even the shape of her eyes.

Air was flowing by her like transparent jelly; she could feel it pushing her enlarged ears back against her skull.

At last the wings were beginning to catch the air, beginning to break her fall. She looked down. She was still wearing her usual get-up, the tiny pink dress and the gold lamé top. More like a ballerina, really, and—

And now she was dancing on air.

She brought her arms forward, pushing against the air with the wings—*her* wings—gaining altitude instead of losing it.

Below, the chair hit the ground, metal legs twisting and breaking. The crash, with her attenuated time-sense, seemed low and warbling.

Surely her metamorphosis would be temporary. Surely once she was safely on the ground, she would regain her normal proportions; surely her youthful beauty would be restored. After all, he'd promised no tricks . . .

She beat her wings again, rising higher still. The rest of her family was now below her. They'd managed to keep from falling, thank God—

God.

The one she had prayed to in all those different churches.

The one she'd turned her back on.

Angela had never seen the pyramid from above before. The Great Wallendas had invented the seven-man pyramid in 1947; when their pyramid collapsed during a show in Detroit in 1962, two members of their troupe were killed and a third—like poor Carlo—had been paralyzed. But if the Wallendas had invented it, and the Guerreros had refined it, the Renaldos had perfected it. Even without its apex, it was still a sight to behold—a thin wire supporting four people, with two more on their shoulders, three stories above the crowd—

A crowd that was screaming, the sounds low and drawn out. And pointing, hands moving in slow motion.

She beat her wings once more, gaining even more height. Although she'd never done it before, flying to her was now like walking the wire—knowledge ingrained, no thought required, her body responding perfectly.

Up.

And up again.

She'd have preferred to become a bird—a lark, perhaps, or a jay. But *he* was a creature of the night; the gifts he bestowed were crepuscular, nocturnal.

A bat, then.

A bat who would fly to safety; a bat who would never fall. Who could fly to safety . . .

She had sold her soul to the devil, and yet—

And yet she was a minor. Delmonico's Circus traveled to many jurisdictions. In some, the age of majority was eighteen; in others, nineteen; in others still, it was twenty-one.

But nowhere was it seventeen, the age she was now.

Or fifteen, the age she had been then.

Surely, this deal she'd made—this bargain with Satan—surely it could not be legally binding. Surely she could get out of it. And when would she have a better chance to make her case? If she flew high enough, surely she would catch God's eye, just as Poppa had always said.

God *was* forgiving—whether mass was in English, Italian, or Latin, they all said that. God would forgive her, take her back, protect her. She had but to confess her sins within his hearing.

Another stroke of her wings.

And another.

Of course, she was still under the big top. She couldn't just go up to escape. Rather, she had to go down.

Just not *too* far down . . .

She folded her wings against her body, letting herself fall, confident that she could gain height again with another beat of the leathery membranes. It was an exhilarating fall, a thrilling fall, excitement rushing through her, a frisson passing over her. Her time sense contracted again, to let her enjoy the rush, experience the headlong, overwhelming pull of gravity, what she'd feared for so long now what she craved the most.

She had no doubt that she could stop her fall before she hit—he had promised, after all, and she wasn't the first to have made a bargain with him. Thousands—millions—before her must have made similar deals; even if she herself didn't intend to keep it, he would have to hold up his end as long as he thought he would eventually get her soul.

The screams from the crowd had risen in pitch as her time sense had returned to normal, but now they were growing deeper again as she neared the ground—close enough now to see the spiral galaxies of sawdust here and there, the circular pits of elephant footprints, the cloud-freckles caused by a spilled bag of popcorn.

She swooped now, heading out the great tent's entrance, out into the circus grounds proper, out into the stinging light of day.

And then, at once, she began to rise higher and higher and higher and higher, beating her wings furiously, gaining as much altitude as she could. Soon she was far above the big top. She longed to look down, to see the fairgrounds from this new perspective, see the trailers, the animal cages, the horizontal circle of the merry-go-round, the vertical circle of the Ferris wheel. But she couldn't. She had to concentrate, just like when she was on the high wire, allowing no distractions, no stray thoughts.

Another beat of the wings, flying higher and higher and—

Pain.

Incredible pain—as though she'd hit a sheet of glass, hit the ceiling of the world.

No farther, said a voice in her head, a voice with a strange accent, a voice like liquid metal.

But she had to go higher—she had to catch the eye of God. She beat her wings again, and felt her face flatten—but not back into its original, human form. No, it was pressing against a transparency; there was no way to fly higher.

It's too close to Him, said the same voice, answering her unasked question.

She wanted to beat her fists against the transparency, but she had no fists—only elongated fingers supporting membranous wings. If she could just get God's attention—

You're not trying to cheat me, are you? said the splashing metallic voice in her head.

Her breathing was ragged from fighting so hard to break through the transparency. "No," she gasped. "No, I'm not."

I have a confession, he said. *I lied when I said Carlo had turned me down; I lie a lot. He did take the deal, but he, too, tried to break it.*

"And so you let him fall?" The words were forced out; her lungs were raw.

He didn't fall, said the voice. *He jumped. He thought if he jumped, then the deal would be broken. Oh, yes, he would die, but his soul would go up, not down. A pause. The irony was too much for me to resist: for one who had come so close to touching the heavens to now not even be able to stand—a perfect living hell.*

"No," said Angela, the words a hoarse whisper. "No, please—not that. Don't make me fall."

Of course not, splashed the voice. *Of course not.*

Angela breathed a sigh of relief.

For you, something different.

She was hit by an explosion of hot air, like the exhalation of a blast furnace, air so hot that sweat evaporated from her skin as soon as it beaded up. The wind slapped her like an open-palmed hand, pushing her down, down, down. Its impact had slammed her wings against her body, had flattened her little pink skirt against her thighs, had, she was sure, plastered her bat-ears flat against her skull once more. She tried to unfurl the wings, spreading her arms, splaying her protracted fingers, fingers as long as her legs. But the wind continued to blow, hot as hell, and she found herself tumbling, head over heels. Instinct took over, and instead of trying to extend her arms, she drew them in now to protect her face, her torso. Soon she was only a few meters above the ground, a ball of tightly wound limbs being pushed laterally through the air.

No, no. She had to fight her instincts. It was like being on the high wire. Do what your eyes tell you to do, and you'll fall for sure; the human mind wasn't made for such heights, such perspectives. She forced her arms to unfurl, forced the wings to try once more to catch the air, and—

Such pain, pain so sharp it made her wish her spinal cord was severed.

The wings were burning now, sheets of flame attached to her elongated, bony fingers. She could feel the membranes crisping, reducing to ash. Her long digits raked the air, but there was nothing much spread between them now to catch it—just a few singed and tattered pieces of skin. Incredibly, her clothes remained intact—or, perhaps not so incredibly, for all circus clothing had to be flame retardant . . .

She curled her sticklike fingers, as if clawing for purchase—but there was nothing but air, blisteringly hot, a wind from Hades propelling her along past the freak show, haunted faces looking up, past the arcade, children agape, past the fortune teller's tent, the line of suckers somehow parting just in time to permit her passage barely above their heads, farther and farther still, toward—

—toward the Ferris wheel, it rotating in one plane, she tumbling head over heels in a perpendicular plane.

She'd thought for sure that she would slam into the spokes of the Ferris wheel, knocking herself unconscious, but that didn't happen. Instead, she found herself reaching out instinctively with her feet, and hanging like the bat she'd become from one of the spokes, and—

No.

No, he could not be that cruel, that wicked . . .

But, if he could not, who could be?

It was as though her ankles were pierced through, like Christ's, and yet not like Christ's, for hers were joined now by a small axle, a spindle upon which she hung, rotating along with the great wheel, always facing down, pointing head-first toward the ground. She thought briefly of a butterfly, pinned on a collector's sheet. He was a collector, too, of course . . .

The wheel rotated on, and she hung from it, a macabre bauble, with skeletal fingers that once had supported flight membranes now hanging limp, like the boughs of a dead willow.

He had won, of course. Angela imagined he always won— and, she supposed, always would win. And, as she hung upside down, a pendant, she thought of her Poppa, and her fear of falling, and of failing him. No, things hadn't turned out as she'd hoped, but, still, this wasn't so bad; the old fears were indeed dead.

The wheel continued to turn. She felt sure it would always turn; no fireman could cut her free, no ladder would ever reach her. She rather suspected that the devil did not leave fingerprints, that she—indeed, the whole damned wheel, and its other occupants, whom she caught only horrid glimpses of—could only be seen when the lighting was just so, when it was not quite dawn, or just past dusk, when you weren't really looking.

She was up high now, the wheel having rotated her to her topmost position, the zenith of the cycle, the pinnacle of her punishment. Here, facing down, looking at the ground, at the hard, unrelenting earth—the crust over the underworld, the veneer over the furnace from which the wind that had propelled her along had doubtless come—here, it was frightening, for if the spindle broke, if her ankles slipped off the axle, an axle greased with her own blood, she would plummet face first to the hard, hard ground.

But that wouldn't happen. It wouldn't ever happen.

The wheel continued its rotation, with Angela always pointing down. At the nadir of the cycle she was indeed rather close to the ground, the ground that had shattered Carlo's spine, the ground that she had feared for so long.

But then she started upward again.

Had Poppa seen any of it? Had Momma? Had Carlo looked up long enough to see her transformation, her fall, her flight, her capture? Or had it all happened somewhere outside of human perception; certainly, she, just nine when it had occurred, hadn't seen anything unusual when Carlo fell—*jumped*—from the high wire.

Poppa would now have to do what he'd always feared—bring an outsider into the act, take on someone new to be the pinnacle of the pyramid.

She hoped whoever it was would look after Carlo.

The wheel took her down once more, bringing her close again to the ground.

It really was a comfort knowing that she was never going to hit it.

The Shoulders of Giants

Author's Introduction

I love to get out into the country to write, and most of this story was written at a cottage my wife and I had rented near Parry Sound, Ontario; during the same cottage trip, I wrote the outline for my *Neanderthal Parallax* trilogy of novels. The germ for this story came from Marshall T. Savage's fascinating nonfiction book *The Millennial Project*, in which he said only a fool would set out for a long space voyage on a generation ship . . .

This story ended up being the lead piece in the anthology *Star Colonies*, edited by Martin H. Greenberg and John Helfers. Edo van Belkom and Robert Charles Wilson are two of my closest friends in the Toronto SF-writing community; *Star Colonies* marked the first time any of us had appeared together in the same anthology with new (rather than reprint) stories, making it rather a special book for the three of us.

The Shoulders of Giants

It seemed like only yesterday when I'd died, but, of course, it was almost certainly centuries ago. I wish the computer would just *tell* me, dammitall, but it was doubtless waiting until its sensors said I was sufficiently stable and alert. The irony was that my pulse was surely racing out of concern, forestalling it speaking to me. If this was an emergency, it should inform me, and if it wasn't, it should let me relax.

Finally, the machine did speak in its crisp, feminine voice. "Hello, Toby. Welcome back to the world of the living."

"Where—" I'd thought I'd spoken the word, but no sound had come out. I tried again. "Where are we?"

"Exactly where we should be: decelerating toward Soror."

I felt myself calming down. "How is Ling?"

"She's reviving, as well."

"The others?"

"All forty-eight cryogenics chambers are functioning properly," said the computer. "Everybody is apparently fine."

That was good to hear, but it wasn't surprising. We had four extra cryochambers; if one of the occupied ones had failed, Ling and I would have been awoken earlier to transfer the person within it into a spare. "What's the date?"

"16 June 3296."

I'd expected an answer like that, but it still took me back a bit. Twelve hundred years had elapsed since the blood had been siphoned out of my body and oxygenated antifreeze had been pumped in to replace it. We'd spent the first of those years accelerating, and presumably the last one decelerating, and the rest— —the rest was spent coasting at our maximum velocity, 3,000 km/s, one percent of the speed of light. My father had been from Glasgow; my mother, from Los Angeles. They had both enjoyed the quip that the difference between an American and a European was that to an American, a hundred years was a long time, and to a European, a hundred miles is a big journey.

But both would agree that twelve hundred years and 11.9 light-years were equally staggering values. And now, here we were, decelerating in toward Tau Ceti, the closest sunlike star to Earth that wasn't part of a multiple-star system. Of course, because of that, this star had been frequently examined by Earth's Search for Extraterrestrial Intelligence. But nothing had ever been detected; nary a peep.

I was feeling better minute by minute. My own blood, stored in bottles, had been returned to my body and was now coursing through my arteries, my veins, reanimating me.

We were going to make it.

Tau Ceti happened to be oriented with its north pole facing toward Sol; that meant that the technique developed late in the twentieth century to detect planetary systems based on subtle blueshifts and redshifts of a star tugged now closer, now farther away, was useless with it. Any wobble in Tau Ceti's movements would be perpendicular, as seen from Earth, producing no Doppler effect. But eventually Earth-orbiting telescopes had been developed that were sensitive enough to detect the wobble visually, and—

It had been front-page news around the world: the first solar system seen by telescopes. Not inferred from stellar wobbles or spectral shifts, but actually *seen*. At least four planets could be made out orbiting Tau Ceti, and one of them—

There had been formulas for decades, first popularized in the RAND Corporation's study *Habitable Planets for Man*. Every science-fiction writer and astrobiologist worth his or her salt had used them to determine the *life zones*—the distances from target stars at which planets with Earthlike surface temperatures might exist, a Goldilocks band, neither too hot nor too cold.

And the second of the four planets that could be seen around Tau Ceti was smack-dab in the middle of that star's life zone. The planet was watched carefully for an entire year—one of its years, that is, a period of 193 Earth days. Two wonderful facts became apparent. First, the planet's orbit was damn near circular—meaning it would likely have stable temperatures all the time; the gravitational influence of the fourth planet, a Jovian giant orbiting at a distance of half a billion kilometers from Tau Ceti, probably was responsible for that.

And, second, the planet varied in brightness substantially over the course of its twenty-nine-hour-and-seventeen-minute day. The reason was easy to deduce: most of one hemisphere was covered with land, which reflected back little of Tau Ceti's yellow light, while the other hemisphere, with a much higher albedo, was likely covered by a vast ocean, no doubt, given the planet's fortuitous orbital radius, of liquid water—an extraterrestrial Pacific.

Of course, at a distance of 11.9 light-years, it was quite possible that Tau Ceti had other planets, too small or too dark to be seen. And so referring to the Earthlike globe as Tau Ceti II would have been problematic; if an additional world or worlds were eventually found orbiting closer in, the system's planetary numbering would end up as confusing as the scheme used to designate Saturn's rings.

Clearly a name was called for, and Giancarlo DiMaio, the astronomer who had discovered the half-land, half-water world, gave it one: Soror, the Latin word for sister. And, indeed, Soror appeared, at least as far as could be told from Earth, to be a sister to humanity's home world.

Soon we would know for sure just how perfect a sister it was. And speaking of sisters, well—okay, Ling Woo wasn't my biological sister, but we'd worked together and trained together for four years before launch, and I'd come to think of her as a sister, despite the press constantly referring to us as the new Adam and Eve. Of course, we'd help to populate the new world, but not together; my wife, Helena, was one of the forty-eight others still frozen solid. Ling wasn't involved yet with any of the other colonists, but, well, she was gorgeous and brilliant, and of the two dozen men in cryosleep, twenty-one were unattached.

Ling and I were co-captains of the *Pioneer Spirit*. Her cryocoffin was like mine, and unlike all the others: it was designed for repeated use. She and I could be revived multiple times during the voyage, to deal with emergencies. The rest of the crew, in coffins that had cost only $700,000 a piece instead of the six million each of ours was worth, could only be revived once, when our ship reached its final destination.

"You're all set," said the computer. "You can get up now."

The thick glass cover over my coffin slid aside, and I used the padded handles to hoist myself out of its black porcelain frame. For most of the journey, the ship had been coasting in zero gravity, but now that it was decelerating, there was a gentle push downward. Still, it was nowhere near a full g, and I was grateful for that. It would be a day or two before I would be truly steady on my feet.

My module was shielded from the others by a partition, which I'd covered with photos of people I'd left behind: my parents, Helena's parents, my real sister, her two sons. My clothes had waited patiently for me for twelve hundred years; I rather suspected they were now hopelessly out of style. But I got dressed—I'd been naked in the cryochamber, of course— and at last I stepped out from behind the partition, just in time to see Ling emerging from behind the wall that shielded her cryocoffin.

"'Morning," I said, trying to sound blasé.

Ling, wearing a blue and gray jumpsuit, smiled broadly. "Good morning."

We moved into the center of the room, and hugged, friends delighted to have shared an adventure together. Then we immediately headed out toward the bridge, half-walking, half-floating, in the reduced gravity.

"How'd you sleep?" asked Ling.

It wasn't a frivolous question. Prior to our mission, the longest anyone had spent in cryofreeze was five years, on a voyage to Saturn; the *Pioneer Spirit* was Earth's first starship.

"Fine," I said. "You?"

"Okay," replied Ling. But then she stopped moving, and briefly touched my forearm. "Did you—did you dream?"

Brain activity slowed to a virtual halt in cryofreeze, but several members of the crew of *Cronus*—the Saturn mission—had claimed to have had brief dreams, lasting perhaps two or three subjective minutes, spread over five years. Over the span that the *Pioneer Spirit* had been traveling, there would have been time for many hours of dreaming.

I shook my head. "No. What about you?"

Ling nodded. "Yes. I dreamt about the Strait of Gibraltar. Ever been there?"

"No."

"It's Spain's southernmost boundary, of course. You can see across the strait from Europe to northern Africa, and there were Neandertal settlements on the Spanish side." Ling's Ph.D. was in anthropology. "But they never made it across the strait. They could clearly see that there was more land—another continent!—only thirteen kilometers away. A strong swimmer can make it, and with any sort of raft or boat, it was eminently doable. But Neandertals never journeyed to the other side; as far as we can tell, they never even tried."

"And you dreamt—?"

"I dreamt I was part of a Neandertal community there, a teenage girl, I guess. And I was trying to convince the others that we should go across the strait, go see the new land. But I couldn't; they weren't interested. There was plenty of food and shelter where we were. Finally, I headed out on my own, trying to swim it. The water was cold and the waves were high, and half the time I couldn't get any air to breathe, but I swam and I swam, and then . . ."

"Yes?"

She shrugged a little. "And then I woke up."

I smiled at her. "Well, this time we're going to make it. We're going to make it for sure."

We came to the bridge door, which opened automatically to admit us, although it squeaked something fierce while doing so; its lubricants must have dried up over the last twelve centuries. The room was rectangular with a double row of angled consoles facing a large screen, which currently was off.

"Distance to Soror?" I asked into the air.

The computer's voice replied. "1.2 million kilometers."

I nodded. About three times the distance between Earth and its moon. "Screen on, view ahead."

"Overrides are in place," said the computer.

Ling smiled at me. "You're jumping the gun, partner."

I was embarrassed. The *Pioneer Spirit* was decelerating toward Soror; the ship's fusion exhaust was facing in the direction of travel. The optical scanners would be burned out by the glare if their shutters were opened. "Computer, turn off the fusion motors."

"Powering down," said the artificial voice.

"Visual as soon as you're able," I said.

The gravity bled away as the ship's engines stopped firing. Ling held on to one of the handles attached to the top of the console nearest her; I was still a little groggy from the suspended animation, and just floated freely in the room. After about two minutes, the screen came on. Tau Ceti was in the exact center, a baseball-sized yellow disk. And the four planets were clearly visible, ranging from pea-sized to as big as grape.

"Magnify on Soror," I said.

One of the peas became a billiard ball, although Tau Ceti grew hardly at all.

"More," said Ling.

The planet grew to softball size. It was showing as a wide crescent, perhaps a third of the disk illuminated from this angle. And—thankfully, fantastically—Soror was everything we'd dreamed it would be: a giant polished marble, with swirls of white cloud, and a vast, blue ocean, and—

Part of a continent was visible, emerging out of the darkness. And it was green, apparently covered with vegetation.

We hugged again, squeezing each other tightly. No one had been sure when we'd left Earth; Soror could have been barren. The *Pioneer Spirit* was ready regardless: in its cargo holds was everything we needed to survive even on an airless world. But we'd hoped and prayed that Soror would be, well—just like this: a true sister, another Earth, another home.

"It's beautiful, isn't it?" said Ling.

I felt my eyes tearing. It *was* beautiful, breathtaking, stunning. The vast ocean, the cottony clouds, the verdant land, and—

"Oh, my God," I said, softly. "Oh, my God."

"What?" said Ling.

"Don't you see?" I asked. "Look!"

Ling narrowed her eyes and moved closer to the screen. "What?"

"On the dark side," I said.

She looked again. "Oh . . ." she said. There were faint lights sprinkled across the darkness; hard to see, but definitely there. "Could it be volcanism?" asked Ling. Maybe Soror wasn't so perfect after all.

"Computer," I said, "spectral analysis of the light sources on the planet's dark side."

"Predominantly incandescent lighting, color temperature 5600 kelvin."

I exhaled and looked at Ling. They weren't volcanoes. They were cities.

Soror, the world we'd spent twelve centuries traveling to, the world we'd intended to colonize, the world that had been dead silent when examined by radio telescopes, was already inhabited.

The *Pioneer Spirit* was a colonization ship; it wasn't intended as a diplomatic vessel. When it had left Earth, it had seemed important to get at least some humans off the mother world. Two small-scale nuclear wars—Nuke I and Nuke II, as the media had dubbed them—had already been fought, one in southern Asia, the other in South America. It appeared to be only a matter of time before Nuke III, and that one might be the big one.

SETI had detected nothing from Tau Ceti, at least not by 2051. But Earth itself had only been broadcasting for a century and a half at that point; Tau Ceti might have had a thriving civilization then that hadn't yet started using radio. But now it was twelve hundred years later. Who knew how advanced the Tau Cetians might be?

I looked at Ling, then back at the screen. "What should we do?"

Ling tilted her head to one side. "I'm not sure. On the one hand, I'd love to meet them, whoever they are. But . . ."

"But they might not want to meet us," I said. "They might think we're invaders, and—"

"And we've got forty-eight other colonists to think about," said Ling. "For all we know, we're the last surviving humans."

I frowned. "Well, that's easy enough to determine. Computer, swing the radio telescope toward Sol system. See if you can pick anything up that might be artificial."

"Just a sec," said the female voice. A few moments later, a cacophony filled the room: static and snatches of voices and bits of music and sequences of tones, overlapping and jumbled, fading in and out. I heard what sounded like English—although strangely inflected—and maybe Arabic and Mandarin and . . .

"We're not the last survivors," I said, smiling. "There's still life on Earth—or, at least, there was 11.9 years ago, when those signals started out."

Ling exhaled. "I'm glad we didn't blow ourselves up," she said. "Now, I guess we should find out what we're dealing with at Tau Ceti. Computer, swing the dish to face Soror, and again scan for artificial signals."

"Doing so." There was silence for most of a minute, then a blast of static, and a few bars of music, and clicks and bleeps, and voices, speaking in Mandarin and English and—

"No," said Ling. "I said face the dish the *other* way. I want to hear what's coming from Soror."

The computer actually sounded miffed. "The dish *is* facing toward Soror," it said.

I looked at Ling, realization dawning. At the time we'd left Earth, we'd been so worried that humanity was about to snuff itself out, we hadn't really stopped to consider what would happen if that didn't occur. But with twelve hundred years, faster spaceships would doubtless have been developed. While the colonists aboard the *Pioneer Spirit* had slept, some dreaming at an indolent pace, other ships had zipped past them, arriving at Tau Ceti decades, if not centuries, earlier—long enough ago that they'd already built human cities on Soror.

"Damn it," I said. "God damn it." I shook my head, staring at the screen. The tortoise was supposed to win, not the hare.

"What do we do now?" asked Ling.

I sighed. "I suppose we should contact them."

"We—ah, we might be from the wrong side."

I grinned. "Well, we can't *both* be from the wrong side. Besides, you heard the radio: Mandarin *and* English. Anyway, I can't imagine that anyone cares about a war more than a thousand years in the past, and—"

"Excuse me," said the ship's computer. "Incoming audio message."

I looked at Ling. She frowned, surprised. "Put it on," I said.

"*Pioneer Spirit*, welcome! This is Jod Bokket, manager of the Derluntin space station, in orbit around Soror. Is there anyone awake on board?" It was a man's voice, with an accent unlike anything I'd ever heard before.

Ling looked at me, to see if I was going to object, then she spoke up. "Computer, send a reply." The computer bleeped to signal that the channel was open. "This is Dr. Ling Woo, co-captain of the *Pioneer Spirit*. Two of us have revived; there are forty-eight more still in cryofreeze."

"Well, look," said Bokket's voice, "it'll be days at the rate you're going before you get here. How about if we send a ship to bring you two to Derluntin? We can have someone there to pick you up in about an hour."

"They really like to rub it in, don't they?" I grumbled.

"What was that?" said Bokket. "We couldn't quite make it out."

Ling and I consulted with facial expressions, then agreed. "Sure," said Ling. "We'll be waiting."

"Not for long," said Bokket, and the speaker went dead.

Bokket himself came to collect us. His spherical ship was tiny compared with ours, but it seemed to have about the same amount of habitable interior space; would the ignominies ever cease? Docking adapters had changed a lot in a thousand years, and he wasn't able to get an airtight seal, so we had to transfer over to his ship in space suits. Once aboard, I was pleased to see we were still floating freely; it would have been *too* much if they'd had artificial gravity.

Bokket seemed a nice fellow—about my age, early thirties. Of course, maybe people looked youthful forever now; who knew how old he might actually be? I couldn't really identify his ethnicity, either; he seemed to be rather a blend of traits. But he certainly was taken with Ling—his eyes popped out when she took off her helmet, revealing her heart-shaped face and long, black hair.

"Hello," he said, smiling broadly.

Ling smiled back. "Hello. I'm Ling Woo, and this is Toby MacGregor, my co-captain."

"Greetings," I said, sticking out my hand.

Bokket looked at it, clearly not knowing precisely what to do. He extended his hand in a mirroring of my gesture, but didn't touch me. I closed the gap and clasped his hand. He seemed surprised, but pleased.

"We'll take you back to the station first," he said. "Forgive us, but, well—you can't go down to the planet's surface yet; you'll have to be quarantined. We've eliminated a lot of diseases, of course, since your time, and so we don't vaccinate for them anymore. I'm willing to take the risk, but . . ."

I nodded. "That's fine."

He tipped his head slightly, as if he were preoccupied for a moment, then: "I've told the ship to take us back to Derluntin station. It's in a polar orbit, about 200 kilometers above Soror; you'll get some beautiful views of the planet, anyway." He was grinning from ear to ear. "It's wonderful to meet you people," he said. "Like a page out of history."

"If you knew about us," I asked, after we'd settled in for the journey to the station, "why didn't you pick us up earlier?"

Bokket cleared his throat. "We didn't know about you."

"But you called us by name: *Pioneer Spirit.*"

"Well, it *is* painted in letters three meters high across your hull. Our asteroid-watch system detected you. A lot of information from your time has been lost—I guess there was a lot of political upheaval then, no?—but we knew Earth had experimented with sleeper ships in the twenty-first century."

We were getting close to the space station; it was a giant ring, spinning to simulate gravity. It might have taken us over a thousand years to do it, but humanity was finally building space stations the way God had always intended them to be.

And floating next to the space station was a beautiful spaceship, with a spindle-shaped silver hull and two sets of mutually perpendicular emerald-green delta wings. "It's gorgeous," I said.

Bokket nodded.

"How does it land, though? Tail-down?"

"It doesn't land; it's a starship."

"Yes, but—"

"We use shuttles to go between it and the ground."

"But if it can't land," asked Ling, "why is it streamlined? Just for esthetics?"

Bokket laughed, but it was a polite laugh. "It's streamlined because it needs to be. There's substantial length-contraction when flying at just below the speed of light; that means that the interstellar medium seems much denser. Although there's only one baryon per cubic centimeter, they form what seems to be an appreciable atmosphere if you're going fast enough."

"And your ships are *that* fast?" asked Ling.

Bokket smiled. "Yes. They're that fast."

Ling shook her head. "We were crazy," she said. "Crazy to undertake our journey." She looked briefly at Bokket, but couldn't meet his eyes. She turned her gaze down toward the floor. "You must think we're incredibly foolish."

Bokket's eyes widened. He seemed at a loss for what to say. He looked at me, spreading his arms, as if appealing to me for support. But I just exhaled, letting air—and disappointment—vent from my body.

"You're wrong," said Bokket, at last. "You couldn't be more wrong. We *honor* you." He paused, waiting for Ling to look up again. She did, her eyebrows lifted questioningly. "If we have come farther than you," said Bokket, "or have gone faster than you, it's because we had your work to build on. Humans are here now because it's *easy* for us to be here, because you and others blazed the trails." He looked at me, then at Ling. "If we see farther," he said, "it's because we stand on the shoulders of giants."

Later that day, Ling, Bokket, and I were walking along the gently curving floor of Derluntin station. We were confined to a limited part of one section; they'd let us down to the planet's surface in another ten days, Bokket had said.

"There's nothing for us here," said Ling, hands in her pockets. "We're freaks, anachronisms. Like somebody from the T'ang Dynasty showing up in our world."

"Soror is wealthy," said Bokket. "We can certainly support you and your passengers."

"They are *not* passengers," I snapped. "They are colonists. They are explorers."

Bokket nodded. "I'm sorry. You're right, of course. But look—we really are delighted that you're here. I've been keeping the media away; the quarantine lets me do that. But they will go absolutely dingo when you come down to the planet. It's like having Neil Armstrong or Tamiko Hiroshige show up at your door."

"Tamiko who?" asked Ling.

"Sorry. After your time. She was the first person to disembark at Alpha Centauri."

"The first," I repeated; I guess I wasn't doing a good job of hiding my bitterness. "That's the honor—that's the achievement. Being the first. Nobody remembers the name of the second person on the moon."

"Edwin Eugene Aldrin, Jr.," said Bokket. "Known as 'Buzz.' "

"Fine, okay," I said. "*You* remember, but most people don't."

"I didn't remember it; I accessed it." He tapped his temple. "Direct link to the planetary web; everybody has one."

Ling exhaled; the gulf was vast. "Regardless," she said, "we are not pioneers; we're just also-rans. We may have set out before you did, but you got here before us."

"Well, my ancestors did," said Bokket. "I'm sixth-generation Sororian."

"*Sixth* generation?" I said. "How long has the colony been here?"

"We're not a colony anymore; we're an independent world. But the ship that got here first left Earth in 2107. Of course, my ancestors didn't immigrate until much later."

"Twenty-one-oh-seven," I repeated. That was only fifty-six years after the launch of the *Pioneer Spirit*. I'd been thirty-one when our ship had started its journey; if I'd stayed behind, I might very well have lived to see the real pioneers depart. What had we been thinking, leaving Earth? Had we been running, escaping, getting out, fleeing before the bombs fell? Were we pioneers, or cowards?

No. No, those were crazy thoughts. We'd left for the same reason that *Homo sapiens sapiens* had crossed the Strait of Gibraltar. It was what we did as a species. It was why we'd triumphed, and the Neandertals had failed. We *needed* to see what was on the other side, what was over the next hill, what was orbiting other stars. It was what had given us dominion over the home planet; it was what was going to make us kings of infinite space.

I turned to Ling. "We can't stay here," I said.

She seemed to mull this over for a bit, then nodded. She looked at Bokket. "We don't want parades," she said. "We don't want statues." She lifted her eyebrows, as if acknowledging the magnitude of what she was asking for. "We want a new ship, a faster ship." She looked at me, and I bobbed my head in agreement. She pointed out the window. "A *streamlined* ship."

"What would you do with it?" asked Bokket. "Where would you go?"

She glanced at me, then looked back at Bokket. "Andromeda."

"Andromeda? You mean the Andromeda *galaxy*? But that's —" a fractional pause, no doubt while his web link provided the data "— 2.2 *million* light-years away."

"Exactly."

"But . . . but it would take over two million years to get there."

"Only from Earth's—excuse me, from Soror's—point of view," said Ling. "We could do it in less subjective time than we've already been traveling, and, of course, we'd spend all that time in cryogenic freeze."

"None of our ships have cryogenic chambers," Bokket said. "There's no need for them."

"We could transfer the chambers from the *Pioneer Spirit.*"

Bokket shook his head. "It would be a one-way trip; you'd never come back."

"That's not true," I said. "Unlike most galaxies, Andromeda is actually moving toward the Milky Way, not away from it. Eventually, the two galaxies will merge, bringing us home."

"That's billions of years in the future."

"Thinking small hasn't done us any good so far," said Ling.

Bokket frowned. "I said before that we can afford to support you and your shipmates here on Soror, and that's true. But starships are expensive. We can't just give you one."

"It's got to be cheaper than supporting all of us."

"No, it's not."

"You said you honored us. You said you stand on our shoulders. If that's true, then repay the favor. Give us an opportunity to stand on *your* shoulders. Let us have a new ship."

Bokket sighed; it was clear he felt we really didn't understand how difficult Ling's request would be to fulfill. "I'll do what I can," he said.

Ling and I spent that evening talking, while blue-and-green Soror spun majestically beneath us. It was our job to jointly make the right decision, not just for ourselves but for the four dozen other members of the *Pioneer Spirit*'s complement that had entrusted their fate to us. Would they have wanted to be revived here?

No. No, of course not. They'd left Earth to found a colony; there was no reason to think they would have changed their minds, whatever they might be dreaming. Nobody had an emotional attachment to the idea of Tau Ceti; it just had seemed a logical target star.

"We could ask for passage back to Earth," I said.

"You don't want that," said Ling. "And neither, I'm sure, would any of the others."

"No, you're right," I said. "They'd want us to go on."

Ling nodded. "I think so."

"Andromeda?" I said, smiling. "Where did that come from?"

She shrugged. "First thing that popped into my head."

"Andromeda," I repeated, tasting the word some more. I remembered how thrilled I was, at sixteen, out in the California desert, to see that little oval smudge below Cassiopeia for the first time. Another galaxy, another island universe—and half again as big as our own. "Why not?" I fell silent but, after a while, said, "Bokket seems to like you."

Ling smiled. "I like him."

"Go for it," I said.

"What?" She sounded surprised.

"Go for it, if you like him. I may have to be alone until Helena is revived at our final destination, but you don't have to be. Even if they do give us a new ship, it'll surely be a few weeks before they can transfer the cryochambers."

Ling rolled her eyes. *"Men,"* she said, but I knew the idea appealed to her.

Bokket was right: the Sororian media seemed quite enamored with Ling and me, and not just because of our exotic appearance—my white skin and blue eyes; her dark skin and epicanthic folds; our two strange accents, both so different from the way people of the thirty-third century spoke. They also seemed to be fascinated by, well, by the pioneer spirit.

When the quarantine was over, we did go down to the planet. The temperature was perhaps a little cooler than I'd have liked, and the air a bit moister—but humans adapt, of course. The architecture in Soror's capital city of Pax was surprisingly ornate, with lots of domed roofs and intricate carvings. The term "capital city" was an anachronism, though; government was completely decentralized, with all major decisions done by plebiscite—including the decision about whether or not to give us another ship.

Bokket, Ling, and I were in the central square of Pax, along with Kari Deetal, Soror's president, waiting for the results of the vote to be announced. Media representatives from all over the Tau Ceti system were present, as well as one from Earth, whose stories were always read 11.9 years after he filed them. Also on hand were perhaps a thousand spectators.

"My friends," said Deetal, to the crowd, spreading her arms, "you have all voted, and now let us share in the results." She tipped her head slightly, and a moment later people in the crowd started clapping and cheering.

Ling and I turned to Bokket, who was beaming. "What is it?" said Ling. "What decision did they make?"

Bokket looked surprised. "Oh, sorry. I forgot you don't have web implants. You're going to get your ship."

Ling closed her eyes and breathed a sigh of relief. My heart was pounding.

President Deetal gestured toward us. "Dr. MacGregor, Dr. Woo—would you say a few words?"

We glanced at each other then stood up. "Thank you," I said looking out at everyone.

Ling nodded in agreement. "Thank you very much."

A reporter called out a question. "What are you going to call your new ship?"

Ling frowned; I pursed my lips. And then I said, "What else? The *Pioneer Spirit II*."

The crowd erupted again.

Finally, the fateful day came. Our official boarding of our new starship—the one that would be covered by all the media—wouldn't happen for another four hours, but Ling and I were nonetheless heading toward the airlock that joined the ship to the station's outer rim. She wanted to look things over once more, and I wanted to spend a little time just sitting next to Helena's cryochamber, communing with her.

And, as we walked, Bokket came running along the curving floor toward us.

"Ling," he said, catching his breath. "Toby."

I nodded a greeting. Ling looked slightly uncomfortable; she and Bokket had grown close during the last few weeks, but they'd also had their time alone last night to say their goodbyes. I don't think she'd expected to see him again before we left.

"I'm sorry to bother you two," he said. "I know you're both busy, but . . ." He seemed quite nervous.

"Yes?" I said.

He looked at me, then at Ling. "Do you have room for another passenger?"

Ling smiled. "We don't have passengers. We're colonists."

"Sorry," said Bokket, smiling back at her. "Do you have room for another colonist?"

"Well, there *are* four spare cryochambers, but. . ." She looked at me.

"Why not?" I said, shrugging.

"It's going to be hard work, you know," said Ling, turning back to Bokket. "Wherever we end up, it's going to be rough."

Bokket nodded. "I know. And I want to be part of it."

Ling knew she didn't have to be coy around me. "That would be wonderful," she said. "But—but why?"

Bokket reached out tentatively, and found Ling's hand. He squeezed it gently, and she squeezed back. "You're one reason," he said.

"Got a thing for older women, eh?" said Ling. I smiled at that.

Bokket laughed. "I guess."

"You said I was one reason," said Ling.

He nodded. "The other reason is—well, it's this: I don't want to stand on the shoulders of giants." He paused, then lifted his own shoulders a little, as if acknowledging that he was giving voice to the sort of thought rarely spoken aloud. "I want to *be* a giant."

They continued to hold hands as we walked down the space station's long corridor, heading toward the sleek and graceful ship that would take us to our new home.

Publication History

"The Hand You're Dealt" copyright 1997 by Robert J. Sawyer. First published in *Free Space*, edited by Brad Linaweaver and Edward E. Kramer, Tor Books, New York, July 1997.

"Peking Man" copyright 1996 by Robert J. Sawyer. First published as the lead story in *Dark Destiny III: Children of Dracula*, edited by Edward E. Kramer, White Wolf, Atlanta, October 1996.

"Iterations" copyright 2000 by Robert J. Sawyer. First published as the lead story in *TransVersions: An Anthology of New Fantastic Literature*, Paper Orchid Press, November 2000.

"Gator" copyright 1997 by Robert J. Sawyer. First published as the lead story in *Urban Nightmares*, edited by Josepha Sherman and Keith R. A. DeCandido, Baen Books, New York, November 1997.

"The Blue Planet" copyright 1999 by Robert J. Sawyer. First published as "Mars Reacts!" in *The Globe and Mail: Canada's National Newspaper*, Saturday, December 11, 1999.

"Wiping Out" copyright 2000 by Robert J. Sawyer. First published in *Guardsmen of Tomorrow*, edited by Martin H. Greenberg and Larry Segriff, DAW Books, New York, November 2000.

"Uphill Climb" copyright 1987 by Robert J. Sawyer. First published in *Amazing Stories*, March 1987.

"Last But Not Least" copyright 2000 by Robert J. Sawyer. First published in *Be Afraid!: Tales of Horror*, edited by Edo van Belkom, Tundra Books, Toronto, September 2000.

About the Author

Robert J. Sawyer is the author of the bestselling "Neanderthal Parallax" and "Quintaglio Ascension" trilogies plus ten stand-alone science-fiction novels. His *Hominids* won the Hugo Award for Best Novel of 2003, and his *The Terminal Experiment* won the Science Fiction and Fantasy Writers of America's Nebula Award for Best Novel of 1995.

Rob has also won eight Canadian Science Fiction and Fantasy Awards ("Auroras")—four for year's best novel, and four for year's best short story. He's also won three Japanese Seiun Awards for Best Foreign Novel of the Year (for *End of an Era, Frameshift,* and *Illegal Alien),* as well as the Collectors Award for Most Collectable Author of 2003, presented by Barry R. Levin Science Fiction & Fantasy Literature, the world's leading SF rare-book dealer.

Rob edits the Robert J. Sawyer Books imprint for Red Deer Press; is profiled in *Canadian Who's Who;* has been interviewed over 200 times on TV; and has given talks and readings at countless venues, including the Library of Congress and the Canadian embassy in Tokyo. Born in Ottawa in 1960, he now lives just west of Toronto, with poet Carolyn Clink, his wife of twenty years.

For more information about Rob and his work, visit his World Wide Web site—which was the first SF author site ever and now contains more than one million words of material—at www.sfwriter.com.